FIRST IMPRESSIONS

A Selection of Recent Titles by Margaret Thornton

ABOVE THE BRIGHT BLUE SKY
DOWN AN ENGLISH LANE
A TRUE LOVE OF MINE
REMEMBER ME
UNTIL WE MEET AGAIN
TIME GOES BY
CAST THE FIRST STONE *
FAMILIES AND FRIENDSHIPS *
OLD FRIENDS, NEW FRIENDS *
FIRST IMPRESSIONS *

* *available from Severn House*

FIRST IMPRESSIONS

Margaret Thornton

This first world edition published 2014
in Great Britain and 2015 in the USA by
SEVERN HOUSE PUBLISHERS LTD of
19 Cedar Road, Sutton, Surrey, England, SM2 5DA.
Trade paperback edition first published
in Great Britain and the USA 2015 by
SEVERN HOUSE PUBLISHERS LTD.

British Library Cataloguing in Publication Data

Thornton, Margaret, 1934- author.
  First Impressions.
  1. Widows–Fiction. 2. Vacations–Germany–Black
  Forest–Fiction. 3. Bus travel–Fiction. 4. Love stories.
  I. Title
  823.9'14-dc23

ISBN-13: 978-0-7278-8472-5 (cased)
ISBN-13: 978-1-84751-575-9 (trade paper)
ISBN-13: 978-1-78010-621-2 (e-book)

Typeset by Palimpsest Book Production Ltd.,
Falkirk, Stirlingshire, Scotland.

One

Jane Redfern leaned back in her seat as the coach pulled away from the depot just outside Preston. The seat next to her was empty at the moment, and she couldn't help hoping that it would remain so. She knew, however, that that was not very likely. Most probably every seat would be booked for this popular coach tour to the Black Forest in Germany.

Don't be so faint-hearted! Jane rebuked herself. She had come on this holiday for a change of scenery and a well-earned rest, and, so her friends had assured her, for a chance to meet interesting people. As they headed south along the motorway the driver broke into her wandering thoughts.

'Good morning, everyone. My name is Mike, and I'm your driver for the next ten days. So let's start by saying hello, shall we? Good morning, everyone . . .'

There was a feeble reply from the passengers. 'Good morning . . .'

Some added, '. . . Mike.'

'Now, that won't do at all, will it?' the driver rejoined. 'Let's sound as though we mean it. Good morning, everyone . . .' His voice was louder this time.

The reply from the passengers was louder too, and Jane made herself join in the greeting. She was hoping, though, that Mike wouldn't turn out to be one of those larger than life chaps, forcing everyone to join in and have a jolly good time. It wasn't that she was averse to mixing with people, but she liked it to be on her own terms.

'That's much better!' said Mike. 'Now, I'll leave you alone for a while to catch up on your sleep if you like, or to have a natter. We'll be picking up the rest of our passengers at our depot in the Midlands, that'll be in a couple of hours, so I'll leave you in peace till then.'

Jane tried to relax. She opened her copy of *Woman's Own* but her mind would not settle to reading a romantic story or details of people's problems. She had problems of her own, but nothing like the lurid tales that were to be found here; stories of infidelity and double-dealing and wayward children. And some even more personal than those, if you could believe the half of it!

She turned to the fashion page. For the summer of 2005 skirts were still short, but if you had worn a miniskirt back in the nineteen seventies maybe you were too old to wear one again. Jane had been a teenager then and had worn miniskirts when she was not in school uniform. Now, at the age of forty-five, she felt she was unable to wear very short skirts, but she had bought a couple of new dresses for her holiday, with hemlines that were rather more modest, just above the knee. Most of the time, though, she wore trousers and jumpers, or what they now called 'tops', which covered a wide variety of garments: blouses, sweaters, T-shirts, tunics – they were all known as tops. Colours were vibrant again this year: raspberry pink, acid yellow, lime green . . . Jane favoured bright colours as a rule as her complexion was pale, and her dark hair and brown eyes were enhanced by more glowing shades, or so her friends had told her. Left to herself she was not inclined to be an avid follower of fashion. Not any more . . .

She closed her magazine. Her thoughts kept straying to her mother whom she had left behind the previous day in a retirement home on the outskirts of the town. It had taken a great deal of persuasion for her mother to agree to this measure. Indeed, Jane herself had been loath to take such a step, but her friends had insisted that she was badly in need of a break, and surely her mother would not object, 'just for a week or ten days?'

Jane had agreed that she did need a rest and a break from routine. She had suffered from a nasty attack of flu during the winter and had never really regained her strength. She was working almost full time as well as running her home and caring for her mother. When she had first broached the subject of the rest home her mother had been adamant that she would not go into what she called 'one of those old folks' homes'.

'Not on your life!' Alice Rigby had retorted. 'I'm not going to one of those places where they sit around like zombies all day, staring at the telly. I may be getting on a bit, Jane, but I've still got all my marbles.'

'But it isn't like that at the place I've found, Mother.' Jane had visited the few homes that had been recommended to her and had found one that she considered very suitable. 'It's called 'Evergreen', and it's more like a hotel than a rest home. You'd have your own private room – en suite – and your own TV, although there's a large one in the lounge as well that the residents like to watch together. They all seemed very nice and friendly.'

'And why are they there, eh? Tell me that. Because their children can't be bothered to look after them, that's why.'

'I don't know, Mother! I don't know their life histories, do I?'

Jane couldn't help feeling a little exasperated. Her mother was enough to try the patience of a saint at times. And Jane knew that she wasn't a saint although she did do her best. She and her mother had never got along all that well. Even as a child Jane had felt that her mother was overcritical of her, unwilling to give her too much praise for her achievements. She always felt that Mother would have preferred to have had a son, but her parents had been blessed with just the one child.

Jane's father, Joe Rigby, had adored his little girl and had done his best to ease the tension that often built up between his two womenfolk. When Joe had died, some eight years ago, Jane had felt as though she had lost a friend and ally as well as a father. Fortunately, though, she was happily married by that time to Tom Redfern. They had both been in their early thirties when they married and they had had no children. They would have liked to have had a family, but no children had come along. Rather than having tests to discover why, they had decided they were very happy as they were. And adoption had never been considered. When Alice had started to suffer with osteoarthritis a year after her husband's death, Jane had persuaded her, eventually, to sell her home and go to live with them.

It was lucky that Tom was easy-going and bore with the often difficult elderly lady. But it was a devastating blow to Jane when, two years ago, Tom died after an attack of bronchitis that had turned to pneumonia. The two women were left alone together and had to get along as well as they could. It was far from easy at times, and Jane knew that her mother would benefit from a change of company just as much as she would.

'It would only be for ten days, Mother,' Jane had told her, 'while I have a holiday, and I'm sure you'd enjoy it. It's a big old house that's been modernized, and there's a lovely garden at the back where you can sit and relax. And a games room . . .'

'I can't see myself playing ping-pong!' retorted Alice.

'Not those sort of games, Mother! They were playing cards, and dominoes, and some of them were doing a big jigsaw puzzle.'

'Huh! Jigsaws! Those are for kids.'

Jane sighed. 'Well, I've done my best. You said yourself that I needed a break, didn't you? And it would be a nice change for you as well.'

Alice didn't answer for a moment. Then, 'Well, I suppose I might give it a try,' she admitted. 'And where are you thinking of gadding off to on this holiday?'

Jane had already made a provisional booking with the travel company, crossing her fingers that her mother would eventually see reason. 'It's a little trip abroad, Mother, with the Galaxy Travel company; to France and then on to Germany.'

'Germany!' Alice stared at her in amazement. 'Why in heaven's name do you want to go to Germany? They were our enemies not so long ago. Don't you remember?'

'That was years ago, Mother. And of course I don't remember. How could I? I wasn't even born then. And people don't think like that any more. We're all in the EU now, aren't we?'

'And the least said about that the better,' Alice muttered.

Jane went on as though she hadn't heard her. 'Well, that's where I intend to go. From what I've heard Germany is a beautiful country. The hotel is in a village in the Black Forest, and we'll be travelling through the Rhine valley as well.'

But Alice was still way back in the past. 'Your father did his best for King and Country in the war. He was in the D-Day landings. I didn't know him then, of course, but he told me enough about it. He never had any time for the Germans. I'm sure I don't know what he would have thought about it, you going hobnobbing with the folks he was fighting against.'

Jane felt that her father would have told her to go and enjoy herself. Like many of the men who had served in the Second World War, Joe Rigby had not wished to relive his experiences. There were many who did so, looking back with pride and nostalgia to their glory days, and going off each year to reunions. But Joe had taken up a new career on leaving the army, looking to the future and not back to the past. Jane believed his policy had been to live and let live, despite what his widow was saying.

'It's all history, Mother,' Jane had told her. 'So . . . are you willing to give it a try in this place I've found? I want you to be very sure about it,' she added.

'I'm as sure as I'll ever be,' said Alice, with an exaggerated sigh. 'You go ahead and do as you please. I know I'll have no peace if I don't agree.'

'Thank you, Mother,' Jane said quietly. She had confirmed the reservation the next day, and for the last two months had been looking forward to her trip abroad.

She had been abroad before, but only twice. The first time had been on a school trip to France when she was fifteen years old. The group of twelve fifth-formers had stayed at the homes of their penfriends in the town of Rouen. It had been Jane's father who had persuaded her mother that it would be good for Jane to go, and because her dad had been keen she had gone along with the idea. She had been homesick, though, for some of the time and had found everything very strange. She and her penfriend, Adele, had got on reasonably well, though, and Jane had learnt to speak French quite fluently after furthering her study of the language when she got back to school.

She and her husband, Tom, had spent their honeymoon in Paris; a wonderful five days that she looked back on with poignant nostalgia. Since that one time they had holidayed in the UK, touring Scotland, the Yorkshire Dales or the Cotswolds in their own car. They had both been drivers, and Jane still used the car for work and for ferrying her mother around. She had never wanted to go touring alone, and although she had several friends, some of them close ones, they were all happily married.

After a couple of hours the coach pulled up at the depot in the Midlands.

'We'll stop here for forty minutes,' said Mike. 'It's a comfort stop, so make use of the facilities, and have a quick cup of tea or coffee, if you wish. We'll be picking up the rest of our passengers here. Then we have one more stop for lunch in another two hours or so, and after that it's full steam ahead for Dover. OK, ladies and gents, see you in a little while . . .'

Jane made use of the facilities, as suggested. There was a toilet at the back of the coach, which seemed to be obligatory now, but the majority of passengers preferred not to use it. Jane had a fear of opening the wrong door and ending up on the motorway! She paid an exorbitant price for a polystyrene beaker of coffee, had a look round WH Smith's, then it was time to return to the coach.

She noticed as soon as she stepped aboard that there was now someone sitting in the seat next to hers, halfway down the coach. And it was a man! She felt her heart plummet to the soles of her new summer shoes. She had been hoping that it might be a woman of around her own age, with whom she could form a friendship, if only for the duration of the holiday.

It wasn't that she disliked men. She had been happily married, and she got along well enough with the men she met in the course of her work and with her friends' husbands. But she found herself ill at ease and a little tongue-tied when she was with men she didn't know. For the past year, by which time her friends had thought she might be glad of some male company, she had been subjected to various attempts at match-making. Several times she had been asked to go to supper parties, and had found herself sitting next to a man who, also, was without a current partner. To her friends' disappointment, nothing had come of these attempts. They did not seem to realize that she was content on her own, for the time being at least. She still missed Tom very much and had never felt the need for exclusive male friendship. She could never feel for anyone else what she had felt for Tom.

At first glance she saw a man whom she guessed to be around her own age, very spruce and efficient-looking with sleek dark hair. She could not judge his height as he was sitting down, but he stood as he saw her approaching, rather diffidently, although she was trying to summon up her courage. He was of medium height, as she was, and of a slim athletic build.

She smiled, unsurely, and he nodded at her, his lips curving just a little. He stood to one side to allow her to pass. 'Yours is the window seat, I believe,' he said.

'Er . . . yes; I think so,' she faltered. 'That's where I was sitting, but I don't mind. You can sit by the window if you like.'

He smiled then, as though he was amused. 'Well, we're not going to fall out about it, are we? I only booked a couple of weeks ago, so I'm sure the seat is yours. I thought I was lucky to get a place at all as I'd left it so late.'

They both sat down, then Jane decided she would take off her jacket. The weather was improving now, it had been cloudy in the early morning when she had left home and it had looked as though it might rain. It had been an unsettled month so far, but now, by mid-June, everyone was hoping that the summer would eventually arrive. The clouds had dispersed and the sun was shining now.

'Shall I put that up on the rack for you?' her travelling companion asked as she shuffled out of her jacket.

'Oh, thank you, that's very kind,' she replied. It was more of a cupboard than a rack over each seat where smaller belongings could be stored.

They had not yet introduced themselves, and Jane was wondering whether to make the first move when the driver came down the coach counting heads.

'All present and correct,' Mike said as he sat down behind the wheel. 'Thanks for getting back on time. If you continue to do that it will make life much easier for us drivers. I've got my mate with me now to assist with the driving. This is Bill . . .'

A cheerful-looking man of a somewhat corpulent build stood

up and said, 'How do, everyone,' to the passengers. It would be easy to remember which was which driver as they were dissimilar in looks. Bill was ginger-haired, whereas Mike was dark and slimmer than his colleague.

'How do, Bill,' most of them replied, not quite so timidly now.

'We won't be travelling enormous distances,' said Mike. 'It's a pretty easy tour, lots of time for looking around, not a whistle-stop tour like some of them are. But Galaxy Travel have been surprisingly generous in allowing us two drivers, and I'm sure we're all going to have a very pleasant time together. So, ladies and gents, off we go again . . .'

It was Bill who addressed them as Mike drove away. He stood facing them at the front of the coach. 'I'm obliged to draw your attention to the emergency exits,' he said, pointing to the windows at the front and rear. 'And there's a first aid box above the driver's seat. So now that's out of the way it's time to get to know one another. I dare say most of you know the person sitting next to you, your hubby or the wife, or your best friend or partner, eh? But if you don't know them, then say hello to them now. Or else say 'how do' to the people sitting across from you. It's good to make new friends, isn't it?'

Jane and her travelling companion turned to look at one another, then, to her relief, he laughed and held out his hand. 'Hello, or should I say how do? I'm David Falconer, usually known as Dave.'

He held her hand in a firm grasp, and as he smiled at her in a friendly way she noticed that his eyes were a luminous grey, candid and clear. She began to feel more at ease. Perhaps it was going to turn out all right.

'How do you do?' she said politely. She had been told it was not correct to say 'Pleased to meet you', although lots of people did. 'I'm Jane Redfern, always known as Jane! That's the only name I've got,' she added. 'I've often wished my parents had given me a second one.'

He smiled. 'Not always a good thing, believe me! My second name is Archibald – after my father, but I hate it! He was always called Archie – I guess he didn't like it either – so I can't imagine what possessed my parents to saddle me with it.

But there's nothing wrong with Jane; a good old English name, isn't it?'

'Yes, I suppose so . . .'

'So . . . what brings you here, Jane, travelling to Germany with Galaxy? And on your own? I assume you're on your own?'

'Yes, I am,' she replied. 'It took quite a lot of courage for me to make the booking. But my friends tried to assure me that I'd nothing to worry about, and Galaxy Travel was highly recommended. I would have preferred to come with a friend, but it just wasn't possible. They're all married, you see . . . and my husband died two years ago.'

'Oh . . . I see; I'm sorry,' Dave said quietly. 'I'm in the same position myself, as a matter of fact. I lost my wife four years ago and I've never been able to find anyone to come away with me. Actually, I'm not bothered, I suppose I'm a bit of a loner. I don't mind my own company, but it's usually a friendly crowd on these Galaxy tours.'

'You've been with them before, then?'

'Yes, this is my third time. The first time I did a five-day tour to the bulb fields in Holland, and last year I went to Belgium – to Brussels and Bruges. So I thought I'd go a little further afield this time. What about you? Why did you choose Germany?'

'I liked the sound of it in the brochure, and it's a leisurely tour – a night in Calais, then a night in the Rhine valley, then six nights in the Black Forest. I like to see nice scenery and interesting places, rather than sea and sand. My mother threw up her hands in horror, though, at the idea of me going to Germany.'

Dave smiled. 'Yes, elderly folk have long memories. But we're never likely to forget, are we, while they're still showing war films on the TV? My father loved to watch them even though he'd served in the war. He came through it unscathed, though, he was one of the lucky ones.'

'Yes, so was my father,' said Jane. 'He never talked about it, though. It's Mother who still thinks of the Germans as our enemies.'

'You still have both your parents, have you, Jane?'

She told him briefly of her circumstances; about her father's death and how, as she was the only child, she now lived with and cared for her mother. 'I hope she's settled down in the home,' she said, 'and isn't finding fault with everything.'

'Try not to worry,' said Dave. 'It's not for very long and the majority of homes are very comfortable. I do know how you feel, though. My mother is in a retirement home, permanently, I'm afraid. But she loves it and she's made lots of new friends. It was a hard decision for me and my sister to make, but in the end it was Mother who decided for us. She chose the place she wanted to go to and she's very happy there. She would have felt isolated living with me – out in the wilds, she said – and my sister lives down in the south of England.'

'Do you live in the country, then, Dave?' asked Jane. To her surprise she found it quite easy to use his Christian name.

'Yes, I have a farm in Shropshire, a few miles from Shrewsbury, on the way to Welshpool. It's not all that far from the Welsh border. Mother finds it lonely after living in Shrewsbury all her life.'

'You mean . . . you're a farmer?' Jane looked at him in some surprise. Dressed, as he was, in a smart sports jacket, with a modern striped shirt and a toning tie he looked the picture of elegance. The last thing she would have expected him to be was a farmer. He looked more like a bank manager.

He laughed. 'Yes, that's what I am. What did you expect? A pork pie hat and corduroy breeches, and a straw between my teeth?'

'No, of course not,' said Jane hurriedly, fearful that she might have offended him. 'I was just . . . rather surprised, that's all.'

'Yes, I know I don't look much like a farmer when I'm not working. I seldom get a chance to dress smartly, so I make the most of it when I can. I'm not able to get away from the farm all that often.'

'You've left someone in charge this week?'

'My son. He works there along with me. I expect he'll take it over . . . one of these days. And we have a couple of farm hands, and casual labour when we need it.'

'So it's a family business, is it, passed from one generation to the next?'

'Sort of . . . It belonged to my grandfather, then my uncle

took it over. My father wasn't interested in farming – just the opposite, he became a solicitor – but the love of the land was passed on to me. I started working with my uncle when I left school. Then I did a college course to learn more about it, and so . . . there I am. A real live farmer, though I may not fit the image!'

Jane couldn't help thinking that he looked more like a gentleman farmer, but she didn't say so. Maybe, despite his immaculate appearance now, he would not be afraid of mucking in with the rest of his fellow workers.

'What sort of a farm is it?' she asked. 'Arable, sheep, cows . . .?' She laughed. 'I'm afraid I'm very ignorant when it comes to farming.'

'Mainly arable,' he replied. 'It's good fertile soil in Shropshire. But we have a small herd of cows as well, and pigs and poultry. No sheep. We're quite near to Wales but the land is fairly flat where we are; ideal for growing crops . . . And I think that's quite enough about me. What about you, Jane? I should imagine you have a job, as well as running a home? I know most women do nowadays.'

'Yes, I have a job,' she replied. 'I work for the GPO. I've been with them ever since I left school.'

'You work on the counter?'

'Yes, I trained as a counter clerk. I was sent all over the place when I was training – to Yorkshire and Manchester and Liverpool. Then I was fortunate in getting a post at the main office in Preston, which is where I live. That's where I met my husband, when he was transferred there from the office in Coventry. It was his first job as a supervisor after being a postman.' She stopped, aware that she might be rambling on about things that were irrelevant. 'Anyway, I'm in charge of a sub post office now, near to where I live. It's convenient because it means I'm able to get home at lunchtime to see to Mother.'

'A lot of sub post offices have closed down, haven't they?' said Dave.

'Yes, I'm afraid so. More and more are disappearing, even some of the larger ones. Fingers crossed, though, we're still open. It's a thriving little business, part of a newsagent's and general store so we think it might be safe for a while.'

The couple of hours to the lunch stop had flown by, and Jane was surprised when Bill announced that they would be stopping in five minutes' time. 'I know some of you will have brought your own sandwiches,' he said, and you can stop on the coach to eat them if you wish. Or there are some tables and wooden benches outside the service place. OK, ladies and gents, see you in forty-five minutes.'

'I expect you've brought your own lunch, haven't you?' asked Dave. Jane agreed that she had done so.

'I'm afraid I'm not so well organized,' he told her. 'I'll go and stretch my legs and have a spot of lunch. I know it'll cost me an arm and a leg!' He grinned. 'But never mind, eh? We're on holiday, aren't we? See you later, Jane . . .'

She was relieved that he had gone. She was enjoying his company, but she would have felt embarrassed if they had left the coach together, as though they were a couple. She wouldn't have known what to do. Stay with him? Or wander off on her own? Luckily the decision had been made for her. She stayed where she was for a few moments, then she decided that as it was a pleasant day she would eat her ham sandwiches outside, and perhaps buy a carton of orange juice at the shop.

Then she would phone her mother, as she had promised to do. It might be the last chance she had before leaving the shores of England.

Two

'Phone call for you, Alice . . .' Nancy, one of the care assistants popped her head round the door of the lounge where several of the residents were watching the television. 'I expect it'll be your daughter.'

'Yes, no doubt it will.' Alice Rigby eased herself out of the armchair, then, with the aid of her stick she made her way slowly to the hallway where the telephone was situated. She took her time about it. She was unable to walk quickly anyway, but it wouldn't do any harm to keep her daughter waiting a moment or two. She'd be on that mobile phone, of course, a newfangled idea that Alice had no time for.

She sat down on the chair by the telephone table and picked up the receiver. 'Hello . . .' she said.

'Hello, Mother; it's me.' Jane sounded bright and cheerful, as well she might, setting off on a Continental holiday.

'Well, of course it's you!' answered Alice. 'Who else would be ringing me? Hardly anyone knows I'm here, and if they do they're not likely to ring.'

'No . . . well, I just wanted to make sure that you've settled in and that everything's as it should be. You're all right, are you, Mother?'

'As right as I'll ever be, I suppose,' Alice replied grudgingly. 'I was just watching that antique programme, *Bargain Hunt* or whatever it's called, where they go round flea markets and car boot sales, so I won't talk for long or I'll miss it. Anyway, it'll be running up your bill on that mobile phone.'

'That's all right, I told you I got a good deal for the mobile . . . I'm glad you're enjoying your TV. It's a good set in your room, is it?'

'It's OK, but I was in the lounge, watching on the big set. Nearly as big as the Odeon screen it is! There's a few of them like to watch the antiques, like I do.'

'Well, that's great, isn't it? I told you that you'd meet some nice people and make new friends, didn't I?'

'Yes, I suppose so. They're not so bad, some of them seem nice enough. I don't know about friends, mind, but I dare say I can put up with 'em for ten days.'

'What's the food like? Have you had a good dinner . . . or lunch, whatever they call it?'

'Can't grumble. It was lamb casserole today, quite tasty, and apple crumble for afters. They have the main meal at midday, lunch, they call it, but it's a substantial meal. I've no complaints there, not so far. Then they have what they call high tea at half past five. It was ham salad last night, then there's a supper time drink if you want one.'

'Sounds like a four-star hotel, Mother! I'm pleased you're enjoying it.'

'I didn't say that, did I? I'm putting up with it 'cause I know it won't be for long.' Alice knew, though, that she was enjoying it far more than she had thought she would, but she was determined not to let Jane get away with it so easily. She was aware, however, that she might have sounded a little abrupt. It had become second nature to her now to appear so. She relented a little.

'Anyway, you go and have a good holiday, Jane. Don't worry about me; I'll be OK. I'll still be here when you get back, God willing.'

'Of course you will, Mother. I'll try to phone you from France or Germany, but I don't know what the signal will be like for the mobile. There'll be phones at the hotels, of course.'

'Don't bother. I've said I'll be all right. Just . . . just have a good time, and take care of yourself in those foreign lands. Bye for now . . .'

Bye, Mother. You take care as well . . .'

Alice was surprised to find that her eyes were a little moist as she put down the phone. She blinked hastily. She really had no time for that sort of sentimental nonsense. Jane was a good girl, though, and Alice knew that she deserved a holiday. She really didn't know how she would manage without Jane to look after her nowadays, but it worked both ways, of course. Jane was glad of the financial help that Alice was able to provide for bills and the upkeep of their home.

It was, in truth, Jane's house. It had been Jane's and Tom's until he had died two years ago. Alice had fought against the idea of giving up her own home, but after Joe had died it had become increasingly difficult for her to manage alone. She had arthritis in her knees and hips but, so far, had refused to undergo an operation despite the advice of the doctors. She was very stubborn, always insisting that she could manage well enough. She had been very grateful, though, to Jane and Tom for sharing their home with her. Then Tom had died, unexpectedly, two years ago, and she and her daughter had been left alone together.

That was the trouble. They saw too much of one another and tended to get on one another's nerves. Alice loved her daughter far more than she let on. She had been forty when Jane was born, and her husband five years older. She had always been very much a 'daddy's girl', and Alice had never been a maternal sort of person. She had found it hard to show her feelings although she loved their little girl just as much as Joe did. The child was a great blessing to them. Alice had been thirty-six when she and Joe married, and they had given up hope of having children. Then when Jane had been born four years after their marriage it had seemed like a miracle. She had loved her then, and she loved her now. The sad thing was that Jane did not know how much.

Alice limped back into the lounge where the antiques programme was just finishing.

'The red team won,' said Flora, the woman with whom she had struck up a sort of friendship. 'They got a lot for that Doulton jug, but the blue team came a cropper with that figurine – it wasn't Chelsea, just a reproduction.'

'Sorry I missed it,' said Alice, 'but I had to chat to my daughter, seeing that she'd taken the trouble to ring me.'

'You told her you were settling in nicely, did you?'

'I told her I was OK.' Alice grinned. 'I must admit I'm pleasantly surprised, but it wouldn't do to sound too keen.'

'You're a crafty one, Alice,' said Flora with a chuckle. 'Never give too much away, do you? I thought as soon as I met you, there's more to this one than meets the eye!'

'Yes, maybe so. But you don't start telling people your life story till you get to know them, do you?' Alice felt, though, that she would like to get to know Flora better as the week went on.

'As far as my daughter's concerned, I'm not going to tell her that everything's fine and dandy, not so soon. She knows I've always had an aversion to these places. It took a good deal of persuasion, I can tell you, to get me to agree to come here. So I'm not going to tell her that I'm . . . well, that I might be changing my mind about old folks' homes.'

'Come on now,' said Flora. 'You can't really call this an old folks' home, can you? I must admit that I wasn't too keen on the idea myself, not at first. I'd seen some dreadful programmes on the TV about the neglect – even ill treatment – in some homes, and I wondered how anyone could let their loved ones live in such places.'

'Yes, I know what you mean,' said Alice. 'But even the places where the staff are kind and caring – like they are here, of course – I didn't fancy the idea of that either. I'm not keen on jolly sing-songs, or playing Bingo, or acting daft, all that sort of thing. And some of the folk that they show on the telly! Honestly! Dribbling and snuffling, or else just staring into space. They look about a hundred years old, some of them. I know I'm no spring chicken myself, but God forbid that I should ever get like that. "No thanks," I said to Jane. "You'll not get me into one of those places, not even for a week."'

'But you changed your mind?' Flora's beady brown eyes twinkled behind her spectacles.

'Well . . . I had to, didn't I? The lass deserves a holiday. I gave the place a once over, though, before I committed myself, and I decided it didn't seem so bad. Of course, it's not for folk who are seriously ill, is it, or those that are . . . well, past it, if you know what I mean?'

'No, it's more for rest and recuperation. They get a lot of people who are recovering from an operation – that's why I came here the first time – or staying for a short time, like you are. There are several, though, who are here on a more permanent basis, like I am now. We don't know how permanent, though, do we?' Flora gave a wry grin. 'But it's best not to think about that, eh?'

'Definitely not!' said Alice. 'I intend to keep going for many more years . . . God willing. This arthritis is a blessed nuisance, but it's not going to kill me. It's your heart that keeps you going, isn't it? And I've never had any problems there, thank the Lord.'

Flora nodded. 'It's the same with me.' She, too, suffered from arthritis. 'I should imagine we're about the same age, Alice, you and me, aren't we?'

Alice did not readily admit to being eighty-five. She knew she didn't look her age, so she tried to keep it a secret from 'nosy parkers'. However, she didn't put Flora into that category. She had only known the woman for a day, but she had decided that she liked her. She would be here for the next ten days – well, only nine days now – so she might as well find someone with whom she was compatible, and Flora seemed to fit the bill. Alice guessed that, like herself, the woman was intelligent and quite well educated. She preferred to mix with people with whom she could hold an interesting conversation, not just idle chit-chat about the weather, or about their wonderful grandchildren. Alice had to admit, however, that that might be a question of sour grapes. She hadn't any grandchildren of her own, nor was she likely to have now.

She smiled at Flora. 'Go on then. I don't often tell folk how old I am, but I might just make an exception. You go first.'

Flora beamed. 'Well, I may not look it . . . but I'll be seventy-six next birthday! Now, what about you?'

Alice was taken aback. Good grief! She was Flora's senior by almost ten years! She was flattered, she supposed, that Flora had assumed they were the same age. And Flora was confident that she looked even younger. The idea was encouraging.

Alice had always tried to make the most of the face and figure that God had given her. She knew that she was not beautiful, not at all, but neither was she too plain. She had strong features. Possibly her nose was a little too long and her mouth too wide, but her blue eyes had kept their brightness. (She wore glasses, though, but who didn't at her age?) And her dark hair had kept its colour, with only an occasional visit to the hairdresser. Alice was above average height, but she had learnt to 'walk tall' and not feel awkward because she was taller than her friends and acquaintances, that was until the arthritis had made her stoop a little.

'Well, you may not believe it either,' she answered now, 'but I'm eighty-five. How about that then? I can give you ten years!'

Flora gasped. 'No, you're right, I would never have believed it. I thought I was doing well. But you . . . that's just incredible!'

'If you two are going to talk at the top of your voices, would you please go and sit somewhere else. You're like a couple of cackling hens. Jack and me, we're trying to watch the snooker.' The speaker was Henry, whom Alice had met at lunchtime along with his pal, Jack. She did not take offence as she might have done, were she not feeling in quite such a good mood. She had already gathered that Henry was an outspoken Yorkshireman – typical of his breed – but that his bark was worse than his bite, as the saying went. He was laughing as he spoke so she knew there was no malice in his words.

'Oh . . . sorry,' said Flora. 'We didn't realize. Come on, Alice, let's go and sit on the settee.'

'Reckon you must be going deaf,' added Henry with a sly grin. 'Ne'er mind, it comes to all of us.' He was, in fact, wearing a small hearing aid.

'That I'm not!' said Alice, rising stiffly to her feet. 'I've still got all my faculties. Sorry if we disturbed you, though . . .'

She followed Flora to a settee in the corner of the room. Some of the residents had gone to their own rooms after the midday meal, maybe for a rest on the bed, or to watch TV or read in peace. Alice was finding that this was one of the good things at Evergreen. You were left to your own devices. You could join in with the activities and with other people, only if you wished to do so. If you were a 'loner' then they were content to leave you alone.

Alice had decided before she came that she would keep herself to herself. She had brought several books to read, and a puzzle and crossword book, but, to her surprise, she was enjoying the change of company.

She looked across at her new friend. Yes, she supposed she could regard Flora as a friend. The woman was the opposite of herself as far as looks were concerned. She was what might be termed 'petite', about five foot two, but just a tiny bit plump. She had a pretty round face that was enhanced by discreet make-up and pale pink lipstick, fairish hair with golden highlights – artifice rather than nature, Alice guessed – and brown, rather inquisitive eyes.

'Yes,' said Flora, as the two of them settled themselves against the plump cushions. 'You've certainly surprised me. I hope I look as good as you do when I'm eighty-five . . . if I live that long!'

'That's something we mustn't dwell on,' replied Alice. 'We've to make the most of every year – every day – that's left to us.'

She thought, a shade guiltily, as she made the remark that she, in point of fact, had not been doing that, certainly not of late. She had allowed herself to get into a rut, never venturing far from home. When Jane was available she had taken her in the car to various places: to church on Sunday, if she felt like going; to the library; to Sainsbury's or Tesco; and occasionally into Preston to visit the market or the shops. Jane had been a willing horse, and she, Alice, had been guilty of driving her too hard.

She wasn't sure what had brought it on, but the realization of how she had been behaving was coming home to her. No wonder the girl had been tired and ready for a holiday. She decided she would have to make it up to her, somehow. Maybe the first way to make amends was to settle down here at Evergreen and try to enjoy her stay.

'So, Flora . . .' She looked enquiringly at her new friend. 'Why are you living here when you're still quite young? Young as elderly people go, I mean. I hope you don't mind me asking, I've always been forthright.'

'I don't mind,' said Flora cheerfully. 'I'm on my own, you see; no husband, no children, just one brother in Australia. I moved in here a year ago. I felt it was the right thing to do, and I've never regretted it.'

'You've had a husband, though, haven't you?' said Alice, looking at Flora's left hand. She wore a plain gold wedding ring, and her engagement ring was a large solitaire diamond, which must have cost a pretty penny!

'Yes, I've had a husband – two, in fact.' Alice grinned. 'My first husband turned out to be a gambler. I didn't know that, of course, when I married him. He was charming and plausible, and I was young and gullible. That didn't last long. Then I met Clive. I'd been on my own for quite a while. I'd had one or two boyfriends – well, men friends. I was into my thirties by then – but I didn't feel like risking it again. But Clive . . . I couldn't resist him. I went to work for him as a secretary and sort of aide. He was a successful business man, finger in all sorts of pies, something of a wheeler dealer, but an honest one. My job didn't last long because we got married and I gave up work. I must admit I lived a life of luxury. It was a magic world to me. I'd been brought up in a humble semi with parents who had been hard-working ordinary folk. They made sure I had a reasonable education. I went to a grammar school, but I left when I was sixteen to get an office job. I travelled all over the world with Clive; a cruise every year, holidays in the States, the Far East, the Caribbean . . . then he died suddenly of a heart attack, five years ago.'

'So the good life came to an end?' observed Alice, but not unkindly. Her new friend's life, though, had been vastly different from her own.

'Yes . . . I was devastated at first. I'd become so dependent on him. We had a lot of friends, but they were his friends rather than mine. When he'd gone they still kept in touch with me, but it wasn't the same. I was on my own. He'd left me very well provided for, of course: big house, more money than I'd ever need . . .' She didn't sound boastful, just regretful.

'Anyway, after I'd stopped feeling sorry for myself I decided I was too young to sit around and stagnate. I joined the local branch of the Townswomen's Guild, and a book club, and a ladies' choir.'

'And do you still keep up with all these things now that you're living here?' asked Alice.

'Of course, why not?' answered Flora. She laughed. 'We're not prisoners, you know. We come and go as we please. They run a bus to take us into Preston a couple of times a week, for those who want to go. And we have theatre trips and outings to places like Southport or Blackpool. But I take a taxi when I want to go somewhere on my own. A lot of us do that.'

Alice was beginning to realize that living in a retirement home was not like being in a sort of prison – albeit a lenient one – as she had supposed. 'But it must have been a big step for you to give up your home, wasn't it?' she asked.

'Oh, the house was far too big for me, it had been too big for the two of us to be honest. I had someone to help with the cleaning even when Clive was alive, and I'd got out of the habit of housework. I used to cook for the two of us, I quite enjoyed that, but I never got used to cooking just for myself. And then my arthritis got worse – you'll know all about that – so I decided to look around for a nice retirement home. I visited a few, but this was by far the best. It's more like a hotel really, but there's medical help there if you need it. There's a nurse on the staff, and several of the assistants have had training in first aid. I've had no regrets, Alice, about coming here, I can assure you.'

'Yes, I suppose I can understand it in your case,' said Alice, a little doubtfully, 'with you being on your own. But a lot of the people who end up in homes – nice ones like this, or others that are . . . not so nice – they have sons and daughters, don't they? It never used to be like this. I remember going to friends' houses when I was a little girl, and more often than not there was a grandma or grandad living there with the family. We had my old grandma living with us. She died when I was eight. I say old, but she wasn't nearly as old as I am now. But they seemed much older in those days, somehow.'

'Things are much different now, Alice, in all sorts of ways,' said Flora. 'Old people know how to keep themselves young, that is if they want to. There are some folk, of course, who were born old, if you know what I mean.'

'Yes, I do.' Alice smiled. 'You can be old at forty, or young at eighty. It's a state of mind, isn't it?' It was coming home to her, though, that although she looked younger than her age she had, in truth, perhaps allowed herself to become somewhat old in outlook. Maybe it was time for her to start looking at things differently . . .

'You were saying, Alice, about grandparents living with the

family,' Flora went on. 'I remember that as well, but sometimes it isn't possible nowadays. Most women go out to work as well as the men; a lot of them need to, to make ends meet. I was fortunate, but I can't imagine how some of them manage to pay the mortgage and the bills and put food on the table. And maybe it's impossible to look after an ageing parent as well. I know there are some that could do it, and don't want to, but it must be a dreadful problem for a lot of people to know what to do.'

Alice was thoughtful. She remembered the times she had remarked to Jane that old folk were put into homes because their children couldn't be bothered with them. It was dawning on her now that it was the sort of remark that a cynical embittered person might make. Was that what she was turning into? Was that how others saw her? Alice knew that she was outspoken, and she had prided herself on it, she had believed in being honest and saying what she thought. As they said in Yorkshire, she called a spade a spade. Her husband, Joe, had been born in Bradford and he was proud of it, but he had teased her by saying that his fellow Yorkshiremen had nothing on her.

Joe had been more tolerant, far less abrasive than Alice. Despite this they had lived together amicably and had had a good marriage. His tendency to live and let live had had a calming effect on her . . . most of the time at least. But since he had died the old Alice had come to the fore again, probably more than she had realized.

'Alice . . . what's up? You're miles away, aren't you?' Her new friend was looking at her curiously. 'I was just saying that it must be a hard decision for some sons and daughters to make, with regard to their parents.'

'Yes, I heard you,' replied Alice. 'It was making me think of my own situation, mine and Joe's, because we never had that problem. We were both working, and there was no way that I could have given up my job. But my parents, and Joe's, stayed in their own homes right till the end. Goodness knows what we'd have done if they hadn't been able to cope because neither of us had brothers or sisters; only children, both of us. But they all lived to a ripe old age, scarcely ailing anything.

And then both my parents, and Joe's as well, died within a few months of one another. We were fortunate, I suppose. We never needed to make any difficult decisions. Maybe that's why I've . . . well . . . perhaps I've never understood what a problem it might be.'

'It's something I never had to face with my parents, either,' said Flora. 'What did you do when you were working, Alice, if you don't mind me asking?'

'I was a teacher,' replied Alice promptly. 'We both were, Joe and I. That's how I met him, of course.'

Flora smiled. 'Now why doesn't that surprise me? I might have guessed you'd been a teacher.'

'Oh dear! Is it so obvious?' Alice grimaced. 'I don't know whether to be pleased or offended.'

'I meant it as a compliment,' said Flora. 'You have that way with you – an air of authority.'

'Bossy, you mean?'

'No . . . Not standing for any nonsense, that's what I meant. You don't suffer fools gladly, as they say. That's a daft expression, though, I've always thought.'

'No.' Alice sighed. 'I dare say I've become a bit intolerant in my old age. It's since Joe died, of course.' She smiled reminiscently, and a little sadly.

'You had a good marriage, then?' asked Flora, quietly, 'I can tell that you did.'

'Yes, so we did,' said Alice. 'It was more of a marriage of minds, though, than . . . anything else. We only had the one daughter, Jane.'

'And is she a teacher as well?'

'Good gracious, no!' said Alice. 'She'd seen enough of it with the two of us. She attended the school that we taught at because it was near our home. So she never had any aspiration to follow in our footsteps. No. Jane works for the GPO. She was a clever girl – well, she still is – and she did very well as a counter clerk. She's in charge of a sub post office now, near to our home.'

'So there are just you and Jane living together?'

'Yes, that's right. Her husband, Tom, died two years ago. He was a grand fellow . . .' And very tolerant of me, she thought to herself, but didn't say. 'His death was a terrible blow to Jane, but she seems to be getting over it now.'

'So this holiday she's on will be a nice change for her, won't it? I don't know her, but I hope she has a lovely time.'

'Yes, so do I,' answered Alice briefly. 'She missed her father just as much as I did,' she added, 'but she was married to Tom by that time, so it softened the blow somewhat. Neither Jane nor I were young when we married, I was thirty-six. I didn't think I'd get married at all. Not that I was all that bothered. I was doing the job I enjoyed. I'd always wanted to be a teacher.'

'And then you met Joe,' said Flora encouragingly.

'Yes. He came to our school in 1955 as our new headmaster. He'd only trained as a teacher when he came out of the army, but he had what it takes and he soon worked his way up the promotion ladder. They were crying out for men teachers at that time. The war had taken its toll, and the fifties were the years of the 'baby boom'; the post-war children all starting school. I was deputy head by that time, so we had to work closely together.'

'That was at a school in Preston, was it? A junior school?'

'Yes. juniors and infants, quite near to where lived with my parents. I did my training in Manchester during the first two years of the war. Most of the men teachers had been called up for war service, so there was no shortage of jobs for women. I was lucky, though, to get a post so near to my home. I didn't see it as a disadvantage, living at home with my parents. It was convenient. Girls weren't so anxious to fly the nest then and get a place of their own. So I stopped where I was, then I was promoted to deputy head.'

'And then Joe came along.' Flora prompted again.

'That's right. We got on well together right from the start. We didn't fall madly in love or anything like that, but we knew we were . . . compatible. We were right together. Then he asked me to go out with him, and we started courting – to the amusement of the rest of the staff, of course! We both knew that. No doubt we were the subject of a few ribald jokes! They were all pleased for us, though, when we got married the following year. They bought us a lovely Royal Doulton dinner service. I've still got it, at Jane's house. She was born in 1960, so I gave up teaching for a while. Then when she was five and ready to start school, there was a vacancy there, at the same place. So I went back, as an ordinary teacher, of course.

'I've only ever taught at the one school. Not like today's young teachers, seeking promotion before they've hardly got started, and wanting more money all the time. Joe retired when he was sixty, I was a few years younger, but I went at the same time. Yes, we enjoyed our retirement.'

She reflected that her retirement – in fact the whole of her married life – had been vastly different from that of Flora. She and Joe had never had any yearning to visit exotic places. They had toured around the British Isles in their family car. Jane had accompanied them until she was well into her teens, after which she had her own circle of friends. They had never been abroad, only once had they crossed the sea when they had gone on a coaching holiday touring southern Ireland. But Alice felt sure that they had been as happy, in their own way, as Flora and her Clive had been, jetting all over the world.

'You're miles away again,' remarked Flora, bringing her out of her reverie. 'Thinking about old times, eh?'

'Yes, maybe I was,' replied Alice, a little brusquely. 'But we've to think about the present and the future, haven't we? Now, if you don't mind, I'm going to my room to read for a little while. I'll see you at teatime.' Then, aware that she might have sounded rather dismissive, she turned back. 'We've had a good chat, Flora. Thank you for listening to me. I'm pleased to have met you. I'll see you later . . .'

Three

Jane was more at ease with herself when she had phoned her mother. She had felt guiltier than she needed to do when she had said goodbye to her at the home. Jane knew that Evergreen was a very satisfactory place. The staff seemed kind and helpful and, from what she had seen of the residents, they were not the bunch of decrepit old fogies that her mother had imagined. Mother was being difficult, determined to show Jane that although she had agreed to give the home a try she was there against her will.

Jane knew her mother only too well, her unwillingness to admit that she might possibly have been wrong or made a mistake. She could tell now that she was, in fact, settling down there very nicely. She had admitted that the food was good, she appeared to have made some friends, or at least, fellow residents with whom she was compatible, and she was enjoying her favourite programmes on a much larger television set than she was used to. Jane smiled to herself. She felt she could relax now and really start to enjoy her holiday.

Dave, her travelling companion, was already seated when she rejoined the coach and he stood up to allow her to occupy the window seat again.

'Have you had a good meal?' she asked him.

'Passable,' he replied. 'Fish and chips; you can't go far wrong with that. The prices though! You'd think you were paying for smoked salmon and caviar. But we're a captive audience, I suppose. I've found the motorway cafes on the continent are far more reasonable. How about you? You enjoyed your packed lunch?'

'Yes, I'm OK for now. It'll be a while before our first proper meal though, won't it?'

'Yes, at the hotel in Calais. Sometimes they ask you to dine on the ship, but it's only a short crossing to Calais. We should be there by early evening.'

Mike came down the coach, counting heads. 'All present and correct,' he said again. 'You're very good timekeepers. Now, off we go to Dover.'

'I rang my mother at the home,' said Jane, as they rejoined the motorway. Dave turned to smile at her.

'Oh, that's good. Is she settling in all right?'

'I do believe she is, but she won't admit it outright. She can be a stubborn old devil, my mother. She won't want to admit that she was wrong, or that I might have been right, of course!' She laughed. 'She's always been the same. It's because of the job she had, career, I should say. She can't bear to admit that she might have made a mistake.'

'Oh? And what did she do before she retired?' asked Dave.

'She was a teacher. Both my parents were teachers. But my father was much more easy-going even though he was a head-master. I thought the world of my dad.'

Dave cast a surreptitious glance at his companion. She was smiling reminiscently, not sadly, though. Her words implied that she had got along with her father much better than with her mother. That did not surprise him. From what he had gathered so far the woman seemed to be a right old harridan!

'Didn't they want you to go into the same profession?' he asked her.

'No, surprisingly enough, they didn't. Fortunately for me, because teaching was the last thing I wanted to do. I'd seen enough of it at home, and to make matters worse, I attended the school where they both taught, a primary school – juniors and infants.'

'Oh dear! That sounds rather claustrophobic.'

'It was mainly because it was convenient, near to our home, you see. I know some people travel miles to their workplace nowadays, but it was more usual to have a job nearer home forty or so years ago.'

'Didn't it affect your friendships with the other children, you having both your parents teaching there?'

'No, not at all,' Jane replied. 'I had some very good friends at school and I still see a few of them. It wasn't as bad as it might have been because I was never in my mother's class, thank the Lord! My father had a rule about it, because there were one or two others whose mothers taught there. My mother was a good teacher but I know she put the fear of God into some of those children! They seemed to like her, though, despite her strictness, and they certainly respected her.'

'And your father? I should imagine he was a popular headmaster, from the way you speak about him?'

'Yes, he was very popular, both with the children and their parents. He didn't believe in corporal punishment, which was unusual in those days. It's forbidden now, of course, but there used to be a lot of heads who were handy with the cane. Dad believed in other ways of maintaining discipline; taking away privileges for miscreants – like removing them from the football team – and it seemed to work very well.

'Yes, my dad was a remarkable man in all sorts of ways. I missed him very much when he died. I must admit that I still do . . . that's not to say that I don't love my mother,' she added, almost apologetically. 'I do, but she's not all that easy to love. And since Dad died it's been just the two of us, and I suppose we tend to get on one another's nerves. My husband, Tom, was great with her. He was a sort of buffer between us, and he didn't seem to mind her nowtiness.' She smiled. 'A good old Lancashire word, that! Tom was able make her laugh, whereas all I seemed to do was to make her irritable.'

'I'm sure these ten days away from each other will do you both a world of good,' Dave commented. 'You're both badly in need of a change, aren't you? A change of scene and a change of company.'

'That's true. It's not so bad for me, of course. I go out to work each day, and I have a lot of friends, mostly married, though, and I get rather tired of their attempts at matchmaking.' Jane smiled and Dave smiled back at her. She was an attractive woman, but she obviously still missed her husband very much.

'It's different for Mother. She isn't able to get about as much now, but she seems as though she doesn't want to make the effort any longer. There's been such a change in her since Dad died. They had a good retirement together; they didn't seem to want anyone else's company, and since he died she's been so reclusive. She was such a determined, go-ahead sort of woman – well, she's still just as determined, of course! – but she's lost interest in so many things. I suppose teaching was her whole life, until she met my father. I know it was what she'd always wanted to do, and she was jolly good at it, too. She made it her hobby as well as her career. She didn't mind how much extra work she did at home, planning projects, writing Nativity plays, – she was always doing something. So now there's a big gap in her life, made worse since Dad died . . . and then Tom.'

'But you've always been there for her, Jane,' said Dave. 'She'll miss you this week, believe me. 'It will make her appreciate you all the more.'

Jane nodded thoughtfully. She was quiet for a few moments, and Dave reflected on what she had said. It seemed to him that the old lady needed a short sharp shock to bring her to her senses. Good for Jane that she had found the courage to make a break, be it only for a short time.

She was sitting with her hands folded in her lap, deep in thought after all she had said about her mother. He was finding her a restful sort of person, although he hardly knew her yet. She was easy to talk to, although he guessed that she didn't open up so readily to everyone she met. Maybe she found him compatible? He hoped so because they would be spending most of the next nine days together.

The thought did not displease him. He found her attractive, in a quiet way. Demure . . . he thought that was the word for her. She was neatly dressed in navy blue trousers and a shirt style top of pale blue and white stripes. Her short dark hair waved gently over her forehead and ears, in which she wore a pair of tiny diamond studs. Her eyes were her most outstanding feature, dark brown, glowing with warmth and what he guessed was a genuine wish to be friendly, though perhaps not with everyone she met? Her mouth was rather small and her chin was not exactly weak, but indeterminate. It prevented her from being beautiful or even pretty, but she had a quiet charm and dignity that, maybe, was not always apparent. Her remark about matchmaking suggested that she was possibly a little shy with men. Her father, then her husband, had clearly been all in all to her.

He could have done much worse with regard to a travelling companion. He considered, moreover, that he had done very well when he compared Jane with some of the folk who had sat next to him on previous holidays. There had been a garrulous middle-aged woman, then, by contrast, a very silent introspective young man who had scarcely wanted to talk at all. This was always the problem when you were travelling alone. Away from the coach you could do as you pleased, but the longish periods on the coach could become difficult if you were not at ease with your neighbour.

Dave decided that he had been lucky this time. He was not wanting anything other than a holiday friendship; neither, he guessed, was Jane. It was sufficient that they had formed a bond, in that they were both on their own, and that both their mothers were staying in retirement homes. Their circumstances, however, were very different. Dave's mother was the gentlest person you could wish to meet, so accommodating and never wanting to cause any bother. Not like Jane's mother who sounded a real old battleaxe! Dave's marital situation had been very different, too, from that of Jane. But he had loved his wife once, and had tried to think about the times when they had been happy together. It was not something he talked about to those who had not known her. The one good thing to come out of his marriage was his son, Peter, who would be managing the farm very competently in his absence.

Dave had been more than content with his work – exhausting at times but always rewarding – and the happiness he enjoyed with his son and his many friends. He had not wished for anything else, but perhaps it was now time for him to broaden his horizons, to look to the future? After all he was still young, not yet fifty.

'I'm sorry, I've talked you to death, haven't I?' said Jane after a few moments had passed. 'I'm not surprised you've gone quiet. I didn't mean to offload my problems on to you.'

'You didn't, not at all,' he answered. 'It's good to talk, as they say. I wasn't quiet because I didn't want to talk any more. To be honest I was thinking about the folk I've been forced to sit next to on other Galaxy tours. A talkative woman who hardly stopped to take breath, then there was a silent young man who hardly spoke two words. But this time, I've struck lucky, haven't I?' He smiled at Jane, and she blushed a little as she smiled back at him.

'Thank you. Yes, I hope so,' she replied. 'I'll read my magazine for a while, then you can have a bit of peace. You could read your book.' There was a paperback book in the rack in front of his seat; one of the Sharpe novels by Bernard Cornwell. 'My husband used to read those,' she commented.

'He is a good storyteller. I've read them all before, but I like a bit of escapism.' He took out the book and put on a pair of dark-framed glasses which gave him a studious air. 'I'm not tired of talking. Don't think that, Jane. But we've all week to chat and get to know one another, haven't we?'

'Yes; I'm pleased about that . . . and I think I've been lucky too,' she added shyly.

It didn't seem long before they were on the approach road to Dover. Very soon the sea came into view between the roofs of the dock buildings, and in the distance a large ship at anchor. Jane began to feel excited. Was that the ship they would travel on? She knew it was a Stena Line vessel, built to carry cars and coaches and hundreds of passengers. She found it amazing, almost terrifying, that a ship could stay afloat with such a weight inside it. But there were scarcely any accidents. There had been one several years ago due to carelessness, but she was determined to put all her fears behind her and enjoy the new experience.

When they arrived at the dock area they joined a queue of scores of other vehicles waiting to go through passport control. Then they drove up a ramp right into the bowels of the huge ship. There were several decks for the vehicles, and Mike warned them to remember that their coach was on the red deck.

'Get that fixed in your minds, ladies and gents,' he told them. 'We don't want anyone getting lost. And please remember the position of the coach on the deck. Fortunately we're near the steps, so you shouldn't have any problems. If you've travelled on one of these ships before you'll know what I mean. If you haven't, then please take care. It can all be very confusing.'

Jane cast an anxious glance at Dave.

'Don't worry,' he said. 'We'll stay together then I can make sure you don't go astray.' He grinned. 'Not that I'm suggesting you need looking after, but it can get rather fraught with people pushing and scrambling around trying to find their coach.'

'Thank you,' she replied. She hoped that he really did want to be with her and was not suggesting it because he thought she was a silly helpless woman.

'Ready now?' he asked. 'You won't need your travel bag, just your handbag. And take your jacket. It'll be warm on the ship, but it might feel cold if we go out on to the deck.'

They alighted from the coach on to the iron floor of the deck, then made their way through part of a tightly packed crowd of people, up the iron steps. There were three steep flights to negotiate before they reached the top, finding themselves in a comfortable lounge area, luxuriously carpeted, with armchairs grouped around little tables and a bar, not yet open, at one end. There were signs showing the way to the restaurants, toilets, shops and the enquiries and the foreign exchange desks. Jane already had a supply of euros tucked away safely in her shoulder bag which she was wearing slung around her body for safety.

'Be careful with your money,' her mother had warned her. 'Keep it close to you, and watch out when you're in a crowd. Especially when you get to Germany. I wouldn't trust any of them as far as I could throw them!'

'Yes, Mother,' she had replied dutifully. She felt, though, that she would sooner trust the Germans rather than the French these days. She had heard that the Germans were a very meticulous, law-abiding race of people, and that the younger generation knew very little about the last war. 'Don't mention the war!' had become a catchphrase, thanks to *Fawlty Towers*. But some of the older folk had long memories.

'Shall we go out on to the deck and say goodbye to England?' said Dave. 'The white cliffs are an impressive sight. Then we could come back and have a drink. What do you say to that?'

'Yes . . . thank you,' replied Jane. 'But I'd better pay a visit to the . . . er . . . to the ladies' room first,' she said, a trifle embarrassedly.

'Good idea. So will I,' agreed Dave. 'To the gents, I mean, of course. See you in a few minutes then.'

The ladies was busy already, as such places always seemed to be. Jane washed her hands, straightened her hair, and applied a dusting of powder and a smear of pink lipstick. She could scarcely stop herself from smiling at her reflection in the mirror. Butterflies were fluttering inside her, partly due to excitement at the start of a holiday, and partly at the thought of being in the company of a man, one that she hardly knew but already felt she liked and trusted. It was the first time since Tom died that she had looked forward to such an occasion with pleasure. She had been asked out a time or two with men who had been introduced to her by well-meaning friends, but had gone only from a sense of duty.

They made their way past the shops then another similar lounge and bar area on to the deck at the stern of the ship. There were a few people there leaning against the railings. They stood there, too, in a companionable silence, and after several moments the ship slipped away from its moorings. It was not the first time that Jane had seen the white cliffs of Dover, it was, as she remembered, a truly impressive sight. She felt a lump in her throat as she thought about the significance of this place, of the centuries that had gone by whilst the cliffs had stood there, the first sight of England to both friends and foes, to English folk and to foreigners.

On top of the cliff stood Dover castle, a bastion against the enemies who had tried in vain to conquer our tiny island. This was the shortest route across the channel, from Dover to the port of Calais; such a short distance away that the sounds of warfare in successive conflicts – the Napoleonic wars and the two more recent world wars – had been heard in the villages and farmlands of Kent. Jane reflected that the country was now at peace, or comparatively so, but it seemed that there was always news of strife and discord in various parts of the world.

She was deep in thought as the ship gathered speed and the foam-topped waves beat against the side of the vessel. She became aware of Dave looking at her.

'Are you OK, Jane?' he asked. 'You're very quiet. It's a

thrilling sight, isn't it, watching the shores of England slip away from us? I never tire of it.'

'Yes, I'm OK,' she replied. 'Just . . . thoughtful, you know? The white cliffs of Dover evoke so many stories. I was thinking that I'm proud to be British, or English, to be more specific.'

'So am I,' Dave agreed. 'I like to go abroad but it's always good to return to our own shores. Anyway, we don't need to think about that for quite a while. We can concentrate on enjoying ourselves.'

A sudden gust of wind tugged at the light scarf around Jane's neck. She gave an involuntary shiver.

'Let's go and have a drink, shall we?' said Dave. 'It's turning chilly now.'

'Yes, why not?' she answered cheerfully. She was starting to believe, now, that Dave really did want to be with her and was not keeping her company just out of politeness.

The lounge was quite crowded. They found a seat near, but not too near, to the grand piano where a man in evening dress was playing a selection of nostalgic melodies.

'Now, what would you like to drink?' asked Dave. 'Lager, shandy? Or are you more of a sherry or Martini lady?'

'I usually like a sweet sherry,' Jane replied, 'but would you think I was awfully silly if I say I would like a coffee?'

Dave agreed at once. 'Good idea,' he said. 'They're serving tea and coffee as well, and snacks. What about a bite to eat? It's a long time since we had our lunch, and goodness knows what time we'll get our evening meal in Calais.'

'That's just what I was thinking.' Jane realized that she was quite hungry, but with all the excitement of the journey she had scarcely noticed.

'Right. How about a ham sandwich or a buttered scone?'

'Just a scone, please. That will be enough. And a cappuccino . . . is that all right?'

'Of course it is.' Dave laughed. 'I'll have the same.'

He went across to the bar, and Jane sat contentedly humming along to the tune of 'Moon River'. She felt like pinching herself to make sure she was really there, that she would not suddenly wake up from a delightful dream. Could she be here, travelling to the Continent in the company of an attractive man who actually seemed to enjoy being with her? She looked around at her fellow passengers. A mixed crowd of people: a lot of elderly and middle-aged couples, families with children, ladies sitting quietly on their own, a group of lads laughing and making a heck of a din in the far corner. It seems that anything goes here, she thought to herself. The surroundings were elegant, but there were no restrictions, no first- or second-class lounges. Only the smokers, it seemed, were frowned upon. 'No smoking' notices were on all the tables. If you wished to indulge you had to go out into a draughty area near to the deck.

She remarked on it to Dave when he returned with a laden tray.

'Do you smoke, Dave?' she asked.

'Not any more,' he replied. There was a time when I did smoke quite a lot. When I . . . lost my wife, I found it helped to settle me down, to relieve the tension, you know? But I managed to kick the habit. Just as well in the present climate. But I must admit that I don't approve of all the paranoia about smokers. We're all lectured to far too much, in my opinion.

'Now, here's your coffee and scone. They're a bit stingy with the butter, so I pinched an extra portion or two. I don't think they noticed. And there's a little pot of jam . . .'

'Lovely,' said Jane. She reached for her bag. 'Let me settle up with you.'

'What? For a cup of coffee?' He laughed. 'Don't be silly! My treat.'

'But you mustn't. Not all the time . . .' She felt embarrassed and confused. It looked as though they might be together for a lot of the time. Or was she wrong in assuming that they might be? 'Thank you, anyway,' she added. 'It's very kind of you. But the next time . . .'

'Forget it, Jane.' He grinned at her. 'I do know what you mean, but don't worry. We'll sort it out.'

They chatted easily for a while. Dave told her about the farm, at her request. She was interested to hear about something so remote from her everyday experience. She was definitely a town girl, although she loved the beauty of the countryside when she was able to escape, occasionally, from her urban

surroundings. Dave looked pleased at her absorption in what
he was telling her.

Far sooner than she expected – the time had flown by –
there was an announcement on the loud speaker, first in French,
then in English, that they were approaching Calais. Would
passengers please assemble at the various exits.

'Oh dear! Have I time to go to . . . to the ladies' room?'
asked Jane in a fluster.

'Yes, of course. There's no immediate rush,' said Dave. 'It
takes ages for everyone to embark. I'll pay a visit myself, then
we'll make our way to our exit. Don't worry. I know exactly
which stairs we're heading for . . .'

Jane was relieved to hear that. She was finding the ship very
confusing, exits at every corner, people dashing hither and
thither, and she did not know whether she was fore or aft.
Goodness knows how she would have managed to get back
to the coach on her own. It was pandemonium at the exit,
crowds of folk jostling one another, anxious to get down the
stairs to locate their vehicles.

'Hang on to me if you like,' Dave told her. 'I'll go first. Just
be careful on the stairs, they're rather steep.'

They negotiated their way down the three flights – Jane did
not cling on to Dave, but made sure she was right behind his
tweed jacket all the way – and then they were back on the
red deck.

'There's our coach,' said Dave. 'We're not the first back, but
we certainly won't be the last.'

Mike and Bill were already there, Mike on the driving seat.

'Take your time,' said Bill. 'They're not all back yet, but it'll be
about ten minutes or so, I reckon, before we're ready to drive off.'

The passengers climbed aboard, mostly couples, husbands
and wives, or friends, travelling together. Bill went down the
coach, counting heads. 'Two missing,' he muttered. 'Now, who
are they? I don't know everyone's name yet.'

'It's the couple who sit there,' Dave said to Jane, pointing
to the seat across the aisle from them. An elderly couple,
possibly in their late seventies. Dave had noticed them and had
thought to himself that it was an adventurous trip for them,
but the lady had seemed to be very much in charge.

Mike and Bill were consulting their list. 'Mr and Mrs Johnson,' said Mike. 'Bloody hell! They're cutting it fine. That's the trouble,' he grumbled. 'You can't stop folk from travelling, even if they're getting on a bit. I bet they're turned eighty, the pair of 'em. This blasted job is getting too much for me, I can tell you, Bill.'

'Calm down, mate,' said Bill. 'Here they are, see . . .' The missing couple arrived back, just in the nick of time.

'Sorry, sorry . . .' said the woman. 'We got lost. Arthur insisted it was the other staircase. Go on, up you go.' She shoved her husband, none too gently, up the coach steps.

'Never mind, love,' said Bill. 'You're here now. No harm done. Just settle yourselves down. We'll be off in a minute or two.'

Mike breathed a sigh of relief. It wasn't the first time that this had happened, and he vowed every time that he would pack the job in. He put a smile on his face.

'Right, ladies and gents, off we go. Welcome to France,' he said as the coach drove off the gangway and Bill put on a tape which played 'La Marseillaise'.

Four

It was only a short distance across the channel from Dover to Calais, twenty-one miles – just a bit further than it was from Preston to Blackpool, Jane thought to herself – but how different it all seemed now that they were on the Continent. The styles of the houses, many of them three-storied with shutters at the windows, the names of streets and the signs on the shops – which Jane was able to read and understand having enjoyed her French lessons at school and learnt a lot from them – and, above all, the traffic driving on the right-hand side of the road.

Their hotel was situated on a side street off the main boulevard. It was an unprepossessing sort of building from the outside, opening straight on to the street. They would be allowed to park there just long enough to unload the luggage.

'Go inside and collect your keys,' Mike told them. 'Your cases will be brought up to your rooms. And dinner will be at eight o'clock this evening, so that should give you nice time to sort yourselves out. See you later, ladies and gents.'

They all trooped through the revolving door into the foyer, making an orderly queue at the reception desk. The hotel presented a more pleasing aspect inside. It was an old building, partly modernized, with a boldly striped carpet and the walls adorned with large format posters of paintings by Monet and Degas. There were two display cabinets filled with souvenirs for sale and a revolving rack with postcards of Calais on the desk. A pretty dark-haired girl handed them their keys – ones that might well belong to the outer door of a castle, suspended from a brass ball and chain – repeating their names in a quaintly accented English.

They queued at the lift, an old-fashioned one with a gate as well as a door. It would hold only four at a time, so there was a wait of several minutes before everyone was taken up to their rooms. The single rooms were on the third floor – most of the passengers had been allocated double rooms on the lower floors – and Jane found that her room was next to Dave's.

'See you in a little while,' he said, fitting his gigantic key into the lock and opening the door.

'Yes . . . see you,' she replied. She, too, opened her door, finding herself in a fair-sized room with a single bed, and a wardrobe and chest of drawers in a plain, functional design such as was found in thousands of hotels; adequate but by no means luxurious, but at least it was clean and it was only a stopping place for the night. She opened the shutters and found that the room was at the front of the hotel, overlooking the street. On the other side of the road there was a pharmacy, a *boulangerie*, and what seemed to be a shop selling ladies' wear, judging by the sign above the window which read 'Madame Yvette'. The shutters were closed on all the shops as it was now almost seven thirty. (They had been told to put their watches forward an hour on arriving in France.)

Jane flopped down on the bed feeling strangely disorientated. She was slightly dizzy and felt as though she might have a headache coming on. That was not surprising after such an unusually hectic day, but by no means an unpleasant one. She would take a couple of tablets in a minute when she had become acclimatized to her surroundings. She sat very still, gathering her thoughts together, a myriad of new scenes and experiences following one upon the other in a bewildering manner. And it was only the first day of the holiday!

She opened her bag and took out a couple of soluble headache tablets. They would need to dissolve in water. Now, hadn't she heard that one shouldn't drink the water from the tap when on the Continent? Just too bad, she decided. She had no choice and it wasn't likely that it would kill her!

She opened the door leading off the bedroom. It was not a bathroom as she had hoped it might be, just a small cubicle with a toilet, washbasin and shower. Not a handheld shower like the one she had had installed at home, but one that came straight down from the ceiling, drenching your hair as well as the rest of your person if you were not wearing a shower cap. Fortunately Jane had brought one, although there was one on the shelf above the washbasin, in a tiny plastic bag.

She dissolved her tablets in water from the cold tap – she was able to read the words '*chaud*' and '*froid*' on the taps – in the glass that was provided. Just as she had finished using the other facility there was a tap at the bedroom door. She hurried to answer it and found the hotel porter standing there with her overnight case.

'Oh . . . come in,' she said, smiling at him.

He carried her case into the room, then he stood there, his head on one side smiling pleasantly – expectantly? – at her. Oh crikey! she thought. Is he waiting for a tip? That was the trouble of travelling alone, especially without a husband; she was not sure of the protocol.

'Wait a minute . . . *un moment*,' she said, reaching for her bag on the bed. She took out her purse and found a one euro piece. She had asked for some at the travel agency as well as the notes. She handed it to him and he bowed his head, smiling more broadly.

'*Merci, madame, merci beaucoup* . . .' He backed out of the room as though he were leaving a royal bedchamber.

Breathing a sigh of relief she glanced at her little travelling clock. Only about half an hour left in which to get ready for the evening meal. Her sponge bag was at the top of her case and she took out the requisites for overnight – toothbrush and toothpaste, deodorant, soap, flannel and spray cologne. It would have to be a quick wash, there was no time for a shower even though she felt rather grubby after the long journey.

She filled the washbasin and swilled her hands and face and underneath her arms. Now, where was the 'thingy' to let the water out? The stopper was a modern design and it wouldn't budge. At last she found a little lever at the back of the taps; there was nothing to beat a plug on a chain in Jane's opinion!

She put on a silky polyester top, pale green with embroidery at the lowish neckline – recently purchased from Marks and Spencer – as it was rather more dressy than the one she had worn earlier, but she decided to wear the same trousers. A quick comb of her hair which, luckily, was easy to manage, a touch of moisturizer, pressed powder and a smear of lipstick, then she slipped on a pair of sandals with a higher heel, and she was ready.

She picked up her bag and her giant-sized key and went out into the corridor. You couldn't lock yourself out as you might do in some hotels as the door had to be locked from the outside. This she did, then she stood there unsurely. What should she do? Knock on Dave's door, or would that seem presumptuous? As she stood there pondering, but only for a moment or two, his door opened.

'Ah, there you are,' he said. 'I was going to knock and see if you were ready.' Jane was relieved to hear that. 'Let's go and see what pleasures are in store for us at the evening meal . . .'

There was no one else in the lift when it finally arrived at the third floor. Dave pressed the button for the lower ground floor where the restaurant was situated but it stopped at the first floor and two more people joined them. It was the elderly couple who had sat opposite them in the coach, the ones who had been late back on the ferry. They all smiled at one another in recognition.

'You were sitting across from us in the coach, weren't you?' said the woman. 'Do you mind if we share a table with you in the dining room? I said to Arthur that you're a nice young couple.'

'Certainly,' said Dave, looking at Jane who nodded her agreement. After all, what else could you say? You could hardly refuse and they seemed pleasant enough.

'It all depends on the seating arrangements, though, doesn't it?' Dave remarked. 'Sometimes they put a coach party all together on a long table, or two tables.'

'Aye, like a Sunday school outing,' said the older man. 'I don't care for that meself. Anyway, we'll wait and see, won't we?'

When they entered the dining room they saw that it was laid with tables for four, or for six; the ones reserved for the coach party had a notice on them saying 'Galaxy Tours'. The woman led the way to a table in the corner. They sat down, smiling at one another again.

'We'd better introduce ourselves, hadn't we?' said the woman. 'I'm Mavis, and this is my hubby, Arthur. Arthur and Mavis Johnson.'

'How do you do?' The four of them nodded and smiled but did not shake hands.

'I'm Dave, and this is Jane.' He turned to her, raising his eyebrows in an unspoken question, then he went on to say, 'We're not actually a couple, as you probably thought we might be. What I mean is . . . we only met today because we were given seats together. But we seem to be getting along very well, don't we, Jane?'

She nodded and smiled, feeling a little embarrassed. 'Yes, so we do.'

'Well, fancy that!' exclaimed Mavis. 'I thought you'd been married for ages. Of course, you can never tell these days, can you? So many folk come away with what they call partners, even a partner of the same sex. Anything goes now, doesn't it? Not that I'm bothered. Each to his own, that's what I say. Anyway, I hope you have a happy time together, the pair of you.' She beamed at them.

Jane and Dave exchanged amused glances. Jane decided to forget her embarrassment. This was bound to happen, the two of them being mistaken for a 'couple'. She would just have to go with the flow.

The room was low-ceilinged and rather stuffy. There was a faint aroma – by no means an unpleasant one – coming from the direction of the kitchen at the far end. Arthur sniffed once or twice before remarking, 'It'll be chicken tonight; it always is on t'first night. I'd've guessed that even if we couldn't smell it. It's what they always give to coach parties on t'first night.'

'I'm sure it will be very nice, Arthur,' said his wife. 'Anyway, there's your starter before that.'

'A plate of lettuce, or else watery soup, that's what it'll be,' rejoined Arthur.

His wife tutted good-humouredly, shaking her head at him in mock exasperation. No doubt she was used to all his funny little ways. He seemed like a bit of a know-all, and a grumbler, although not a cantankerous one. It was probably second nature to him to have his say about everything, rather like her own mother, thought Jane. Anyway, it was all part of the holiday, meeting different folk.

Jane guessed that Mavis and Arthur might be in their late seventies, possibly older than that, Arthur at any rate. He was a corpulent man and he seemed to have a little difficulty with his breathing. He was bald on top with a fringe of white hair at either side, and he wore dark-rimmed glasses. He was smartly dressed with a collar and tie and had his jacket on, whereas several of the men were in shirtsleeves.

His wife, Mavis, was smartly dressed as well, possibly a little overdressed in a purple satin blouse with a pattern of sequinned flowers. She obviously liked to 'dress for dinner' when on holiday. She was plumpish but by no means fat. Like her husband, she wore glasses; hers were designer ones with diamanté frames. She was grey-haired and the discreet mauve tint on her perfectly waved and styled coiffure complemented the top she was wearing. She had a lovely friendly smile which made up for her possibly too outspoken remarks. Neither of them, in fact, were afraid of saying what they thought. Jane guessed, however, that Mavis must have 'a lot to put up with' regarding her husband – as Jane's mother might say – but that they were a very contented couple.

Arthur was proved right as far as the starter was concerned, the soup was, indeed, watery, though piping hot with noodles and onion rings, served with chunks of rather dry brown bread. The chicken – another accurate guess – was a large breast portion for each of them, served with the inevitable French fries. It was very tasty and Jane realized how hungry she was. She emptied the plate, which was unusual for her, apart from a few over-crisp chips.

There had been a bit of a friendly argument when the wine waiter appeared, Jane insisting that she really must pay for her own glass of wine, and Dave saying that he wouldn't hear of it.

'Stop yer quibbling, the pair of you,' Arthur had intervened. 'We'll have a bottle of wine for the four of us. I'm paying, and that's that! White wine alright for you? That's what Mavis likes.'

They settled on a medium-sweet French wine of Arthur's choice. He seemed to consider himself something of a connoisseur. Conversation was flowing easily by the time they had almost emptied their glasses.

'We were so embarrassed when we were late back at the coach,' Mavis told them. 'I was afraid Arthur might have one of his turns with us dashing about all over the place.'

'Give over, Mavis, I've not had a funny turn for ages. It was you that was getting in a tizzy. I knew we'd get back in time. And I've admitted I was wrong, haven't I? But I was sure it was t'other staircase. Aye, I should've listened to you, I know.'

'Never mind, you got back safely and no harm done,' said Dave. 'You're not the first couple to be late back, nor will you be the last. I should imagine it's a nightmare for the drivers, especially on the Continent, waiting for people who are late.'

Conversation drifted, inevitably, to tales of the various tours they had been on before. Jane admitted it was all new to her and how much she was looking forward to the new experience. Mavis and Arthur, it turned out, were seasoned travellers on the Continent.

'We're not much for the seaside,' said Mavis, 'at least not over here. What's the point of going abroad if all you do is lie on the beach and get sunstroke? If you want to do that you might as well go to Blackpool or Scarborough.'

'Except that you're more likely to get blown off the beach than to get heat stroke,' said Dave with a laugh. 'I know what you mean though. I must admit I've never been to Spain. Sun and sand and sangria has never appealed to me, though I'd like to see the interior of Spain, cities like Madrid and Barcelona. One day, perhaps . . .' He caught Jane's eye, and she smiled and looked away.

'Arthur's not keen on flying either,' said Mavis. 'That's why we come on these coach tours. I tell him it's as safe as houses up in the air. You're far more likely to have a car crash . . . or a coach crash. God forbid!' she added hastily. 'Galaxy has an excellent record, though. We've been travelling with them for years now.'

'Aye, one trip up in an aeroplane was quite enough for me,' said Arthur. 'She managed to persuade me to go to America, about ten year ago, wasn't it, Mavis?'

'Yes, that's right,' replied his wife. 'Well, eleven years to be exact. We went to New England, in the fall, as they call it over there.' She smiled reminiscently. 'The maple trees in Vermont . . . I've never seen anything quite so lovely, before or since. You must admit it was a grand sight, Arthur.'

'Aye, it was; I'll not deny it. But you'll not get me there again. Besides, I don't know as aeroplane travel would do for me now, not with my blood pressure and what have you. I'd be happy enough to stay in Britain – or the UK as it's now called. There's some lovely places back home: Scotland and t'Cotswolds, and t'Yorkshire Dales; but Mavis likes to go further afield once a year, don't you, love?'

'Yes. Austria, Switzerland, the Loire Valley; we've even been to Czechoslovakia – the Czech Republic, that is. But it's the first time I've managed to persuade him to visit Germany, isn't it, Arthur?'

Arthur nodded. 'Aye, so it is,' he said meaningfully. 'I'd vowed I'd never set eyes on another German, not as long as I lived. I saw more than enough of 'em sixty year ago, an' I can't see as how they'll have changed all that much. Leopards don't change their spots, you know.'

'You served in the last war then, Arthur?' asked Dave.

'Aye, so I did. I joined up in 1940, when I was eighteen. I didn't wait to be called up. Of course by that time – it was after Dunkirk – most of the troops were back in England, except for the Desert Rats. So we had to bide our time. I was at a camp in the south of England. We made up for it in the end though, damned sure we did. I went over for the D-Day landings. Came through it all in one piece, thank God, at least as far as my body was concerned. But it's what it does to your mind . . . I've never talked about it, not to anyone, certainly not to Mavis, nor to my parents. I was one of them that went to Dachau, you see, to release the prisoners.' He gave a shudder. 'Enough said. It's still with me, though I try to forget what I saw. And I never go to any of their damned reunions.'

Dave did a quick calculation. He had guessed that Arthur might be eighty. By his reckoning now the man must be eighty-three, his wife possibly a few years younger.

'I've managed to persuade him that it's all a long time ago,' said Mavis, gently touching his hand as it rested on the table. 'It was a couple of years after the war ended that I met Arthur. He was a sales rep – commercial travellers, they used to call them then – and he came into the hardware shop where I worked.'

'Aye, we met over the pots and pans and kettles, didn't we, love?' Arthur looked at his wife fondly. 'It didn't take me long to realize that she was the one for me. And we've been married for fifty-five years, haven't we, Mavis?'

'That's right,' she replied, smiling. 'And never a cross word, eh, Arthur?' Her lively blue-grey eyes twinkled at him.

'I wouldn't go so far as to say that,' he replied. 'She's had summat to put up with, looking after me, I can tell you. But we've made a go of it, haven't we, love?'

Their new friends learned that Mavis would be eighty later that year. They still lived in Blackburn, where they had met, and they had two children, one of each, and six grandchildren.

After they had eaten their pudding – a slice of Neapolitan ice cream with a serving of diced fruit at the side – they went into the adjoining lounge where coffee was being served. Jane found herself sitting next to Arthur. She confided to him that her mother held exactly the same views about the Germans.

'She's the same age as you, well, a couple of years older, actually, and she still tends to think of them as the enemy. My father served in the war, like you did. He was in the D-Day landings, but I never heard him talk about it either. He didn't give the impression that he hated the Germans . . .' Jane mused that her father had been a much more placid person than Arthur appeared to be, more ready to let bygones be bygones. '. . . but of course he might not have seen the same horrors that you did.'

'No, p'raps not,' agreed Arthur. 'But my good lady says I've to put it all behind me and enjoy the trip to Germany. And that's what I've made up my mind to do, though I haven't actually told her that,' he added with a quiet chuckle. 'I've heard that the Rhine valley is worth seeing, and the Black Forest. And I believe they have some pretty good wines, don't they?'

'So I've heard,' said Jane, smiling at him. She had thought at first that Arthur might be a bit of a 'clever clogs', and one who found fault with everything, but the elderly gentleman was growing on her. On the chairs on the other side of the small table Mavis and Dave were chatting comfortably together. Arthur and Mavis were a pleasant couple with whom they would, no doubt, spend quite a lot of their holiday time. There was a coach full of people, though, some of them younger than herself and Dave, and many of them considerably older. All of them, however, judging by the lively chatter in the room, looking forward to an enjoyable holiday.

Five

Mavis Johnson awoke with a start and looked round the unfamiliar room. A faint light was filtering through the shutters against the window. She could make out the shape of a wardrobe and dressing table, and another bed a few feet away from her where Arthur was still fast asleep. For a brief moment she couldn't think where she was. Then, as a fleeting, scarcely remembered dream vanished from her mind she awoke to reality. Of course! She was not at home, she was in France, in Calais, where they had just spent the first night of their holiday, and today they would be travelling on through France and into Germany.

She reached for her glasses – she was needing them more and more these days – then glanced at her little bedside clock that she always took away with her. It was just turned six o'clock. She had set the alarm for six thirty. They had been told that breakfast was at half past seven, then they would be on their way as soon as everyone was ready, hopefully at half past eight.

Mavis heard a sound coming from the street, a sort of clanging noise. She realized now that it was the same sound that had awakened her. And now Arthur was awake as well. He made a grunt, then sat bolt upright in bed.

'What the dickens is that? What time is it, Mavis?'

'It's five past six,' she told him.

'For crying out loud! Can't a chap have any peace? We're supposed to be on holiday, aren't we? I reckon nothing to be woken up at six o'clock in the morning.'

He was always irritable when he awoke, but the mood would soon pass and Mavis had learnt to take no notice. She smiled to herself. He was a comical sight sitting up in bed, what little hair he had standing on end, his boldly striped pyjamas ruckled around his middle, and his eyes peering short-sightedly around the room. He, too, reached for his glasses.

'Can't see a damned thing without these,' he muttered. 'Six o'clock! What a time to be waking up!'

'We'd be getting up at half past anyway, Arthur,' Mavis told him, 'or we won't be ready in time. Come along now; stop being so grumpy, and I'll make us a nice cup of tea.'

A small travelling kettle and two beakers, plus tea bags, powdered milk and sugar lumps were essential items in Mavis's luggage whenever they went abroad. And the Continental plug and adaptor, of course, so that the kettle would work. Most, if not all, the hotels in the UK now provided tea-making facilities in all their bedrooms, but very few of the Continental hotels had, so far, cottoned on to the idea.

'Good idea; thanks, love.' Arthur was coming round a bit now. 'That'll be grand, there's nothing like a cup of tea first thing in a morning.'

Mavis had by now donned her dressing gown and fluffy bedroom slippers and was busy seeing to the tea-making; there was a handy plug socket over the dressing table.

'Let's get these shutters back, then we can see what we're doing,' she said, going to the window and fastening back the wooden blinds. Then, 'Oh look, Arthur,' she cried. 'Look at those young people in the street, outside the bread shop; it's called a *boulangerie*. I remember that from French lessons at school.'

As Arthur joined her at the window they saw a man in a voluminous white apron, with a baker's cap on his head, pushing up the shutter on the shop window. It made a loud clattering sound, and Mavis realized that must have been what she had heard earlier. It was a double-fronted shop. There was a small crowd, seven or eight teenage boys and girls standing by the shop all carrying long loaves. Some of them were nibbling at the end of the loaf, others tearing off chunks and devouring them as though they were starving. Then the man who had put up the shutter could be seen inside the shop, filling the window with loaves of all shapes and sizes. The youngsters were laughing and shouting and having a whale of a time.

'I expect they've had a night on the town,' said Mavis, 'and now they're having their breakfast. And look, he's got some other customers already.' A couple of middle-aged women, clad in dark coats and headscarves and carrying wicker shopping baskets were going into the shop. 'They'll be buying bread for their breakfast. I can just imagine how nice and fresh it will taste.'

'Shopping, at six o'clock in the morning!' exclaimed Arthur. 'I couldn't see you doing that, Mavis.'

'Well . . . no, I agree that I wouldn't, but it's different here, Arthur. They like to buy fresh bread each day. Those long loaves don't keep fresh like our bread does, but they taste delicious; baguettes, they're called. We might be having some ourselves for breakfast.'

'Can't see what's wrong with sliced bread meself,' replied Arthur. 'Bloomin' Froggies! They have to be different, of course.'

'We're in a different country, Arthur,' said Mavis, patiently. 'Different food, different ways of doing things. You should know that by now, we've been abroad often enough.'

It all added to the enjoyment of her holiday, how they did things in other lands. Mavis felt herself smiling at the young people, remembering a time when she, too, had been young and giddy. And she knew that Arthur didn't mean half of what he said. He always had to have his little grumble about 'damned foreigners', but she knew that, secretly, he enjoyed these holidays abroad as much as she did.

'Come on, Arthur,' she said now. 'Your tea's ready.'

'Thanks, love,' he said. 'The cup that cheers. Sorry I'm such a trial to you, Mavis love.' He grinned at her. 'I don't know how you put up with me sometimes.'

'No, neither do I.' She smiled back at him. 'But it's a bit late now to be thinking of swapping you for someone else. I reckon I'll have to make the best of it.'

'I don't know what I'd do without you, Mavis,' he said now, putting an arm around her in an unusual show of affection.

'Nor I without you, Arthur,' she answered quietly.

It was true. He drove her mad at times, but she couldn't imagine how she would manage without him . . . if anything were to happen to him. That was the expression everyone used, 'if anything happened', when what they really meant was if the loved one was to die. Something one didn't want to think about or talk about. And yet it would happen, sometime. Mavis knew that. It happened to everyone, eventually.

She worried about Arthur, more than he realized. He took tablets for his blood pressure, which was sometimes rather higher than normal, and for a rapid heartbeat that troubled him from time to time. Arthur, though, to give him credit where it was due, was not a hypochondriac. He made light of his ailments, insisting that he was fighting fit. Indeed, their doctor had given him the all-clear. Mavis had insisted that he should pay a visit to the surgery before they embarked on the holiday. It might have been different had they been flying, but neither of them really liked that form of travel.

Arthur had a little grumble again because it was a shower and not a bath. Mavis, also, preferred a bath, but was happy enough to put up with a shower for one night. There might be a proper bathroom at the main hotel, with a bit of luck. She remembered the time – twenty, thirty years ago, maybe? – when all you had was a washbasin in your room and you had to go down the corridor to the bathroom, and to the loo. Facilities had improved, both at home and abroad.

They were ready in good time for breakfast at seven thirty, leaving their suitcase outside the bedroom door, as instructed, for the porter or one of the drivers to collect. Their companions of the previous night, Dave and Jane, were already seated at the same table, so they went to join them. Mavis thought how happy Jane looked, and how attractive in a pale green shirt and neat navy trousers. There was a quiet radiance about her. Mavis guessed – and hoped – that a romance might blossom between her and that nice man Dave before the holiday was over.

There was the usual conversation about how well they had slept, or otherwise. Arthur complained that the sound of the plumbing had kept him awake half the night. Mavis bit her tongue. It would not be tactful to say that she had been kept awake by the sound of his snoring! At home they sometimes slept in separate rooms, but when they were abroad the extra cost of single rooms would have been prohibitive.

Continental breakfasts had improved as well. Mavis remembered the time when all you got was a roll with butter and jam. Now there was quite a feast laid out on a side table for you to help yourself. A choice of cereal and of fruit; brown and white bread rolls and croissants (no baguettes, but the rolls looked just as fresh and crisp); small jars of jam, honey or marmalade; there were even hard-boiled eggs, cold ham and thin slices of cheese. Coffee and tea as well, in large Thermos jugs, for the guests to help themselves. Mavis had learnt that it was as well to stick to coffee when abroad. Their Continental friends had no idea how to make tea, but the coffee, although strong and rather bitter was sure to wake you up.

After breakfast, and when the travellers had got together all their bits and pieces, and had made sure they had left nothing behind, they assembled outside the hotel whilst Mike and Bill loaded the cases on to the coach.

'A lovely day for our onward journey,' Mavis remarked to Jane. Although it was still early the sun was shining in a cloudless sky and there was no nip in the air as there often was at home in early summer.

'I've been very daring and put trousers on this morning,' Mavis whispered confidentially. 'I don't often wear them but I thought why not? I'm on holiday. You don't think they make me look fat, do you?'

'No, of course not,' replied Jane. 'You look fine.' She smiled to herself. What else could she say? She could hardly tell her new friend that she did look fat if, indeed, it were so. As it happened she was telling the truth. The older woman looked very smart in well-fitting navy trousers – very similar to the ones that Jane herself was wearing – and a crisp pink and white striped blouse. Admittedly she was a little on the plump side, but she carried herself well. Jane guessed that she always paid great attention to her appearance.

There were some women who really should not wear trousers. Jane noticed a few middle-aged ladies amongst their number whose nether regions were bulging alarmingly in crimplene trousers. But they didn't seem to be aware of how they looked, or else they didn't care. After all, as Mavis said, they were on holiday.

Jane noticed two ladies standing nearby. She had seen them

the night before in the lounge. She guessed that before the holiday was over they would all have got to know one another, at least by sight, but you were sure to know some better than others. One of the ladies caught her eye and smiled in a friendly way. Jane moved across to speak to her.

'Hello,' she said. 'Are you enjoying the trip so far?'

'Oh, very much so,' replied the woman, who looked to be the elder of the two. Jane had taken them, from a distance, to be mother and daughter. Now she could see that they were much closer in age, but this one appeared older than her friend – or sister or whoever it was – because of the way she was dressed. 'We're enjoying it, aren't we, Shirley?' She addressed the woman who was standing next to her, and she turned to join in the conversation.

'Yes we are; this is the third trip we've been on with Galaxy,' she said. 'I'm Shirley, by the way, and this is my friend, Ellen.'

They all nodded and said 'How do you do?' Jane introduced herself. 'I came on my own,' she told them. 'I was really quite nervous about it, but I've made some friends already. That's Dave, who I'm sitting with on the coach, and the older couple are Mavis and Arthur.' Those three were chatting and laughing together. 'We all sat together for dinner last night, and we got on really well. It's nice to make new friends, isn't it?'

'Oh, those are the two who were late back on the ship, aren't they?' remarked Shirley.

Her friend, Ellen, glanced at her reprovingly. 'You've no room to talk, Shirley!'

'Oh, come on, Ellen. We've never been late back,' Shirley replied with a little laugh.

'Well, we've cut it fine a time or two,' said Ellen. She turned to Jane. 'She will insist on waiting till the very last minute before we go back to the coach. "He said half past, and that's the time we're going back," she'll say. And there's me panicking and thinking they'll go without us. It's a wonder I've not had a heart attack with her goings-on!' She was smiling though, so Jane knew there was no malice in her words.

'Now you know they have to wait till everyone's back,' said Shirley. 'They're not allowed to go and leave you. Anyway, I promise to do better this time. But I like making the most of every minute, you see.'

'It's a thankless job for the drivers, isn't it?' remarked Jane. 'I bet they feel like driving away when people keep them waiting. And it's such a big responsibility, looking after a coach load of people. How do they manage to know them all? I'm sure I could never do it.'

'Maybe it gets easier with practice,' said Ellen. 'Oh . . . they're getting on now, see. Come along, Shirley. Nice talking to you, Jane. Maybe we'll chat again later.'

Jane watched them as they stood there waiting to board the coach. Chalk and cheese, one might say, but she had the impression that they were good friends. It would be interesting to find out how they knew one another. The younger one – or so she took her to be – called Shirley, was the height of fashion. She was wearing cream trousers and a smart red and white striped top with a bright blue cotton scarf tied at a jaunty angle. She was carrying a jacket that matched her trousers, and her feet – with bright red toenails – were shod in a pair of strappy red sandals.

Ellen, in complete contrast, wore a summer skirt in a floral design and a cotton blouse with a Peter Pan collar. She carried a woollen cardigan and wore sensible Clarks' sandals. She looked very neat and tidy but . . . so old-fashioned!

Jane noticed when she and Dave boarded the coach that the two women were sitting on one of the front two seats. People often booked early to get these prime positions.

'Good morning all,' said Mike, in his usual jovial manner. 'Slept well, have you? And enjoyed your first evening? Good, good . . . Now, have you all handed in your keys?'

There were one or two audible gasps, then two ladies, looking rather sheepish, handed the giant-sized keys to Mike. He laughed. 'Never mind, there's always somebody, believe me! I'll just nip back with them.'

When everyone was finally settled Mike counted heads, then, with Bill at the wheel, they set off on what would be a long journey to the Rhine valley.

Leaving Calais they headed east on the motorway that linked northern France with Belgium. It was an attractive tree-lined road, and seemed quiet compared with the M1 and M6 back home. Jane remarked on the fact to Dave.

'They have to pay tolls to use the motorways over here,' he reminded her, 'so drivers often prefer to use an alternative route. Coach drivers have to take the shortest route from A to B, unless there's something of particular interest to see.'

'Yes, of course,' said Jane. 'It's all so interesting, though. I get bored travelling on our motorways, or if I'm driving myself I get worried by all the traffic. It's so nice to be able to relax.' She gave a contended sigh, and was aware of Dave smiling at her. The place names they read as they bypassed the towns – Mons, Ypres, Armentieres – were familiar because they evoked such poignant memories. No one on board would have lived through the First World War, but they all knew of the carnage and the sorrow it had caused. There was a song that the soldiers used to sing. How did it go?

> Mademoiselle from Armentieres,
> Never been kissed for forty years . . .

At least that was the polite version. Jane smiled to herself. There would no doubt have been a bawdier one, but women in those days weren't supposed to know about such things. Times had certainly changed.

Now and again through the trees they caught a glimpse of war graves, row upon row of white crosses. The countryside they were passing through was where so many British soldiers – and German ones too – had died in the trenches. It was a peaceful scene now, the fields bright with golden dandelions, but here and there by the roadside were clumps of blood-red poppies, a stark reminder of what had taken place almost a hundred years ago.

Mike, who was doing a commentary on matters of interest, pointed out that some of the fields still contained tank traps – triangular concrete blocks like miniature pyramids – because they were travelling along what had once been the Siegfried Line, a German line of demarcation, but to most people, including Jane, the place where the British soldiers vowed to hang out the washing.

Now and again they passed an idyllic scene: tall poplar trees evenly spaced along a cart track and a red-tiled farmhouse in the distance, just like a painting Jane remembered having seen called 'The Avenue at Middelharnis'.

The coach sped along, eating up the miles, or kilometres as it was over here. Jane noticed that Arthur, in the seat across the aisle, had dozed off, his head nodding and his glasses slipping forward. He gave a snort, and his wife nudged him. He awoke with a start.

'Come along, Arthur,' Jane heard Mavis say to him. 'We're getting off soon, for a coffee stop.' Mike had just informed them that they would be stopping for half an hour, no more, at the next service station.

It turned out to be a pleasant place with cosy little alcoves interspersed with flowering plants and small palm trees. It seemed very attractive and welcoming compared with the hustle and bustle of the service areas on the M6; they were so huge and impersonal. Or maybe it was just because it was different and 'foreign'. Jane was still almost pinching herself at the idea of being abroad and, what was more, being in such congenial company when she had thought she might be on her own. But there was no time to linger. They scarcely had time to drink their hot fragrant coffee and pay a visit to the facilities before they were back on the coach.

Mike told them that their lunch stop, in another couple of hours, would also be in Belgium, near to the German border. It was a similar place to the former one – as in England, they seemed to follow a pattern – where Jane and Dave dined on vegetable soup with crusty bread. Jane was tempted by the apple pie and cream, but Dave reminded her that they might be having *apfelstrudel* that evening at their overnight stop on Rüdesheim; so she chose a slice of gateau instead.

She no longer felt embarrassed at being with Dave. He seemed to take it for granted that they would stay together. And he no longer insisted on paying, which was as it should be. So that was another little problem that had been solved.

Soon after the lunch stop they crossed the German border, and by early afternoon they were approaching the Rhine. Ahead of them they could see on the horizon the twin towers of the huge Gothic cathedral at Cologne, but they bypassed the city, taking the road towards Bonn.

'The birthplace of Beethoven,' Bill reminded them, putting on a tape of the composer's Fifth Symphony. The drivers had changed places now, with Mike at the wheel and Bill doing the commentary. Not that any comments were necessary to help them appreciate the lovely riverside towns and villages through which they were passing. Königswinter, Bad Godesburg, Oberwinter, with houses painted in pastel shades of cream and pink. High on the hillsides were turreted castles, and steeply sloping vineyards ran down to the river. The Rhine was the lifeline of the area, a broad silver-grey ribbon of river with parallel roads and railway tracks running alongside each bank.

They were approaching Remagen, famous for the capture of the bridgehead by the Americans at the end of the war. Jane noticed that Arthur was now wide awake and appeared to be listening intently, though with a stern expression on his face, as Bill told them the story of the bridge at Remagen. It was the only bridge that had not been destroyed by the retreating German army. The Americans had established a bridgehead there, and Hitler, consumed with rage, had ordered that all those in charge of the bridge defences must be shot. Ten days later the bridge collapsed except for two massive towers, like castles, one on each bank. One of them was now a museum of peace.

Jane knew the story. She had watched the film, *A Bridge Too Far*, on the television with her husband, Tom, although he had been far more engrossed in it than she had been. As far as she was concerned it was all a long time ago. We were all part of the European community – be it for better or worse – so what good did it do to keep looking back on it all?

They stopped at Boppard, a lively, more modern-looking town with a mile-long promenade.

'This is where you will be boarding the pleasure steamer for a sail up to Rüdesheim,' Mike told them. He glanced at his watch. 'You can go and stretch your legs for quarter of an hour, but make sure you are back here by ten minutes to three. The boat leaves at three o'clock, and you mustn't miss it; it's a lovely trip. Bill and I won't be coming with you. We're taking the coach along, and we'll meet you at the other end at Rüdesheim, that's where you leave the boat, then it's not very far to our hotel. So . . . enjoy yourselves, ladies and gents, and we'll see you later.'

Boppard was a popular tourist resort. There was a good number of holidaymakers strolling along the promenade and around the narrow streets behind the hotels and shops that faced the river

All the passengers heeded the instructions and were back in time to board the steamer. The day had kept its earlier promise of fine weather, and the sun was shining brightly, albeit with a gentle breeze, as Jane and Dave sat on the open-air top deck enjoying the passing scenery, and the commentary, given first in German then in English, with a guttural accent.

It was reputed to be the most picturesque part of the Rhine. Pastel-coloured houses and steepled churches on both riverbanks, and on every craggy hilltop another castle. Here was a village church you could enter only through the pub, as the vicar was both the publican and the priest! Here was Maus – Mouse – castle, then Katz – Cat – castle, and here was the village of St Gaur which took its name from the patron saint of innkeepers, Jane doubted that she would remember all these facts when she arrived home, but she was busy with her camera, snapping away at each interesting scene.

They rounded a bend in the river, and the guide told them that they were approaching the Lorelei rock. He stopped talking, then the boat was filled with the sound of German voices singing the song that told the story of the famous legend. Jane couldn't understand the German words, but she remembered the song that they had learned long ago at school.

I know not what comes o'er me, or why my spirits fail;
Strange visions arise before me, I think of an ancient tale . . .

There on a promontory running out from the cliff was the bronze statue of the Lorelei maiden. The legend told of sailors at twilight being lured to a watery grave by the maiden singing her song as she combed her golden hair. Just a story – a sad story – but there was an element of truth in that there were dangerous rocks in that part of the river, and boats had been known to come to grief there.

'Rüdesheim,' called the guide a few moments later, and the Galaxy passengers all alighted from the boat to find their coach waiting for them at the side of the road.

Mike counted heads. 'Thank goodness for that! You're all here. No one has been swept away by the Lorelei maiden. Good trip, isn't it?'

They all agreed that they had enjoyed it very much. Their hotel was no more than half a mile along the river. Bill pulled up outside a white painted hotel with a brightly coloured awning, and little tables where guests were enjoying coffee or ice cream.

'Here we are,' he called. 'Hotel Niederwald. Collect your keys at the desk, and your luggage will be taken care of. See you later, everyone . . .'

Six

Compared with its light and sunny aspect on the outside, the hotel appeared somewhat forbidding and gloomy inside, until one became accustomed to the dark wooden doors and balustrades, the deep red carpet and the subdued lighting from the wrought-iron chandeliers. First impressions, however, could be deceptive, and guests soon learnt that it was a friendly, welcoming hotel. The receptionist at the huge oaken desk, which resembled a dock in a court of law, received them all with a cheery smile and good wishes for a pleasant stay, along with – once again – a key with a giant-sized brass plate with the room number on it.

The lift, like the one in the previous hotel, was antiquated with room for only four, at a tight squeeze, as they made their way up to the second floor where the single rooms were situated. Dave and Jane were sharing the lift with Shirley and Ellen, the ladies whom Jane had met that morning. She was surprised that they were not sharing a room – it was a good deal cheaper to do so – but maybe they each liked their privacy. It could well be that having spent the day together they preferred just their own company at night.

And so it was that when they had had a wash and change of clothes – their cases arrived promptly outside the doors – the four of them found themselves sharing the lift down to the dining room on the ground floor. As was customary on coach tours, the tables were set for six or eight; there rarely tables for two as it was supposed that the travellers would have become acquainted and would wish to dine with new friends.

Mavis and Arthur were already there, waiting for the dining-room doors to open at seven o'clock. By mutual agreement, it seemed, the six of them sat down at the same table, one with a notice saying 'Galaxy Travel'. There was another coach party staying there as well; their tables had different coloured napkins – green rather than the red for the Galaxy people – and their notices said 'Richmond Travel', suggesting that they were from Yorkshire. Or it might be the Richmond near to London. The accents soon indicated that they were Yorkshire folk. The dining room was busy, but the service was surprisingly prompt, the coach parties being served first, to be followed later by the private guests.

The watery minestrone soup with chunks of – not very fresh – bread did not bode well; but the following courses made up for it.

'There! What did I tell you?' proclaimed Arthur when the main course arrived. 'Wiener Schnitzel; they always serve that the first night.'

'How do you know, Arthur?' said his wife. 'We've not stayed in Germany before.'

'No, but that's what we got in Austria, and they speak the same language. And I reckon we'll have it tomorrow in the Black Forest.'

'Well, we'll have to wait and see, won't we?' said Mavis. 'I must say this is delicious.'

And so it was; tender fillets of veal in breadcrumbs, served with slices of lemon, fluffy mashed potatoes and green beans. The dessert was no surprise either. *Apfelstrudel*, as they had anticipated, apples and raisins, flavoured with cinnamon, encased in mouth-watering puffed pastry, with lashings of cream. Five of them, all except Ellen, shared a bottle of the Rhine wine recommended by the waiter, whilst Ellen chose to drink *Apfelsaft*.

Conversation flowed easily around the dining tables as they all talked about how much they had enjoyed the day, and became better acquainted with one another. Jane was sitting between Dave and Shirley, with Ellen, Mavis and Arthur at the other side of the table.

Many of the guests had made an effort to 'dress for dinner', especially the ladies, although it was not obligatory. Only a few of the men, the older ones, were wearing jackets and ties, the majority had opted for open-necked shirts. The ladies, though, had all tried to look their best. Jane had chosen to wear an ankle-length black skirt rather than her usual trousers, with a floral top. Shirley was dressed 'to the nines' in a long skirt and a top of heavy cream-coloured lace with a diamond (well, probably diamanté) necklace and earrings. She was carefully made up: mascara and eyeliner, delicate blue eyeshadow and shimmering pale pink lipstick. Her dark brown hair was highlighted with blonde streaks. A lady who liked to look glamorous and liked people to notice her appearance. As Jane talked with her she discovered that she was a friendly, likeable person, but possibly the teeniest bit vain?

Her friend, Ellen, was wearing a 'two-piece', a maroon dress and matching jacket made of what Jane thought was called Moygashel? Well, something like that, more the sort of suit her mother might wear. Her hair was grey and newly permed, and she wore a light dusting of powder and the tiniest smear of lipstick. It was clear, though, that she had made an effort to look nice, according to her way of thinking. She looked happy as she talked animatedly to Mavis who was sitting next to her.

'Ellen never touches alcohol,' Shirley told Jane in a quiet voice as they sipped their golden wine, but her words were not critical or derisory. 'She had very strict parents, you see – dyed-in-the-wool Methodists – and it's had quite an effect of her, poor Ellen. Although I don't know why I say "poor Ellen". She's a very contented person, she tries to find good in everything and everyone. She's a good friend to me; we've known one another for ages . . . haven't we, Ellen?' she said as her friend looked across at them and smiled.

'Yes. Would you believe we started infant school together?' said Ellen. 'We lived in the same street and our parents knew one another.'

Jane learnt that this was in the mid-fifties. She estimated their age as fifty-five or so, ten years older than herself. They had progressed to the same secondary school and had both left at sixteen, Ellen to work in a bank, and Shirley to follow her bent for fashion and design, training as a window dresser at a store in Manchester where they both lived; not in Manchester itself but in nearby Salford. Shirley had moved on to a more prestigious store in the city, where she was the chief window dresser, and Ellen still worked in the same bank.

'It's only recently, though, about four years ago,' said Ellen, 'that we started going on holiday together, although we'd always kept in touch. I was looking after my elderly parents, you see.

They died five years ago, both of them in the same year, God
bless them . . .'

'And that was the time when my marriage came to grief,'
said Shirley. She gave a rueful smile. 'The least said about that
the better! I've decided I'm quite happy on my own. I've lots
of friends, though; women friends, I mean. I wouldn't get
married again. Once bitten twice shy.'

'I'm a widow, too,' said Jane quietly. She smiled. 'We were
very happy. I never thought I would—' she stopped suddenly
– 'what I mean to say is . . . it's the first time I've been away
on my own. But I'm very glad I came.'

Shirley smiled at her in a confidential way. 'You're enjoying
it then . . . more than you thought you would?'

Jane nodded. 'Yes, indeed I am,' she answered. 'I'm having
a lovely time.'

Coffee was served in the adjoining lounge before they all
went their separate ways.

'Shall we take a walk along the riverside?' Dave said to Jane.
'Then we could have a drink on the Drosselgasse later on. I
know it will probably be heaving with tourists, but you can't
come to Rüdesheim without seeing its famous street. You've
heard of it, have you?'

'Yes, I have,' said Jane. 'Anyway, what are we but tourists like
all the rest? I'll just change my skirt for a pair of trousers.'

They walked away from the town up to the part of the river
where the cruise ships that travelled along the Rhine and Moselle
were berthed for the night. They crossed the railway line that
ran alongside the river to take a closer look at them. They were
nowhere near the size of the QE2 and other ocean-going liners,
but they were handsome-looking vessels, streamlined and
gleaming white, some cabins having windows and others with
portholes.

'I should imagine that's a nice leisurely way to see the sights,'
observed Jane. 'Like the cruise we had this afternoon, but every
day. And a different stopping place each night.'

'And not so rushed as a coach tour,' said Dave. 'Not that
I'm complaining. But it's a thought for the future, maybe . . .'
His words lingered on the air as they smiled at one another,
crossing the railway line back to the main promenade.

'Hello there,' called a cheery voice. 'Seeing what Rüdesheim has to offer, are you?' Mike and Bill were walking towards them, smartly dressed in their regulation bright blue blazers with the Galaxy motif on the pocket and blue and red striped ties. They were both smoking as they were not on duty. This was forbidden on the coaches, of course, for passengers as well as drivers, as it had been for many years. But they often indulged in the weed when they stopped for coffee and lunch breaks, as did some of the travellers.

'Yes, it's a lovely little town,' replied Jane. 'It's the first time I've been to these parts, and it's all so new and interesting.'

'Glad you're enjoying it,' said Bill. 'See you later . . .'

'A nice couple,' he remarked to Mike, as they strolled back towards the town. 'They've only just met, at least that's how I see it. They seem to be getting on very well. What do you bet there's a romance in the air? It won't be the first one I've seen.'

'Nor me,' replied Mike. 'You're probably right. Jolly good luck to them . . . What about your love life, eh? Is it still on with the lovely Lise?'

Lise was a waitress at the hotel where they were staying that night, with whom Bill had been having a casual relationship. He visited the place every few weeks, sometimes with Mike, sometimes not, according to the schedules. Mike knew that they always had a drink together; only a half or a shandy, though, because there was a strict rule that Galaxy drivers must not drink when on duty, and they knew it was foolish not to obey. The drivers shared a room, and Mike knew that his colleague would be missing for part of the night, so he drew his own conclusions.

'No,' Bill answered curtly, in answer to Mike's question. 'I'm afraid not. It seems I've got my marching orders. She told me when we arrived that she's friendly with one of the porters now, so that's that! But I'm not bothered . . . You'll have noticed the girl – the young woman, I should say – on the front seat? She's called Christine Harper.'

'I did, and I saw you talking to her while I was driving. She's with her mother, isn't she?'

'Actually, it's her elder sister, quite a bit older I imagine.

She lost her husband last year – the older one, I mean – and reading between the lines, I think that Christine is recovering from a broken relationship. So they decided to come on holiday together, the first time they've done so.'

'So you're on first name terms. Christine, eh? You fancy your chances there, do you?' Mike was laughing, but Bill answered more seriously.

'I've between thinking it's time I settled down. I know what you think of me – a girl in every port, so to speak. I've played the field, but I'm getting older now, and it's time I looked to the future. I'm forty now, time to think about a more stable relationship; a home and marriage, kids maybe, though I might have left it a bit late for that.'

'I don't see why, if you're really serious about settling down,' said Mike. 'But our job isn't exactly conducive to a settled life, is it? My wife's been getting on to me about it. She'd like me to give up these Continental tours and do the ones in the UK. I'd see more of the family that way. They're mostly five-day tours, so you get home every weekend.'

'And how do you feel about that?' asked Bill.

Mike shrugged. 'There's for and against. I must admit I enjoy coming over here. We're not always on the same tour, and you see a bit of the world. And I try to make it interesting for the clients, you and me both, of course. I know some of the blokes just do their job, drive from A to B with hardly a word about the sights and all that. But the folk do like to know about the places they're visiting. I know they've got guide books, and maps, too, some of 'em, following the route. God knows why! They're not doing the driving.'

'Yes, I think we do our best for them,' said Bill. 'They seem a good crowd this time, a mixed age group. No problems so far, touch wood.' He tapped his forehead. 'So . . . what are you going to do? Will you ask if you can go on the UK jobs, to please Sally?'

'I can see what she means,' said Mike. 'The kids are getting to a difficult age. Tracey's fifteen now, studying for her GCSEs next year. At least she's supposed to be studying, but she's got in with a daft crowd at school. Staying out late, and Sally thinks she might be going into pubs. And she's wanting to go to late-night discos. Sally's said no to that, and it's caused friction between them. Tracey can be a right little madam.'

'So Sally wants you to be at home and lay the law down, does she?'

'I've never been much good at playing the heavy-handed father. I was a bit of a tearaway myself, till I met Sal, so I suppose I can remember what it's like. Our Gary's only twelve; he's a good kid, no problems there so far. Anyway, we'll see. I've told her I'll think about it this week.'

'I'd miss you if you were based at home,' said Bill. 'I know we're not always on the same tour. But I'm glad when we are. They're not all as easy as you are to work with.'

'Nice of you to say so.' Mike grinned at him. 'The same goes for you, of course. So . . . what about you and Christine? Have you tested the water there?'

'As a matter of fact, I've asked her to have a drink with me in the hotel bar, later tonight. I said ten o'clock. I know they'll all want to see the town first.'

'What about her sister?'

'Oh, I think I've made it clear. They were sitting with two other ladies at dinner time, and they all seemed to be getting on well. I dare say Norah – that's her sister – will take the hint.'

'Unless she's the overprotective sort?'

'Well, we'll see won't we? I tell you what, though; I must try and get some of this off if I want to make a good impression.' He patted his rather corpulent stomach. 'The trouble is I can't resist these strudels and dumplings and the Black Forest gateaux at the next place. It's too tempting, and they do feed us up, don't they, because we're doing the driving?'

Mike laughed. 'You can always say no. It's our lifestyle as well, all this sitting at the wheel every day, and lack of exercise, except for a stroll in the evening. What about your other lady friend, Olga? Isn't that a bit more serious?'

Olga was a receptionist at the hotel in the Black Forest. It was common knowledge that she and Bill were 'an item', at least whilst he was staying there. They had been friendly for a couple of years.

'I really ought to make a clean break there,' said Bill. 'We both agreed the last time we met that it was going nowhere.

I don't see how it can really. I'll see how it goes this week with Christine. She might decide she doesn't like me. But it struck me as soon as I met her that she's a nice homely sort of girl, the sort I should be looking for.'

'Pretty as well, though,' said Mike. 'I couldn't see you being interested if she wasn't. Anyway, the best of luck, mate.'

They had turned aside to look in one of the shop windows on the promenade. 'D'you think anyone buys this junk?' said Bill. 'Just look at it!'

A lot of it was junk, as Bill had said. Small statuettes of the Lorelei maiden; plates, mugs, ashtrays, tea towels, all emblazoned with pictures of Rüdesheim and the River Rhine; beer steins with pewter lids; dolls dressed in national costume; cheap jewellery, perfume bottles, souvenir pens and pencils. Amidst the dross, though, there was some merchandise for the more discerning. Hummel figurines of cute rosy-cheeked children; a boy sitting on the branch of an apple tree; a girl driving home the geese; another holding a bouquet of flowers.

There was a rack of postcards in the doorway – the shop was still open to catch the passing trade – depicting the high-lights of the area. The famous Drosselgasse with its half-timbered houses and numerous Wienstuben; the Lorelei maiden on her rock; the vineyards sloping steeply down to the river; the Brömserburg Castle, the oldest one on the Rhine; and the Niederwald Monument after which the hotel was named. It could be viewed from the road, a thirty-seven-metre-high statue known as Germania, built as an expression of power following the Franco-Prussian war in the nineteenth century. A cable lift took visitors up to view the sword-brandishing Valkyrie, but there was rarely time for tourists staying for only one night to take the trip.

'Who knows what you might buy if you were on holiday?' said Mike. 'Some of it is tat, I agree, but it might well bring back happy memories. Come on, let's get back to the hotel, then you can get ready for your date with the lovely Christine. I hope it turns out well.'

Dave and Jane set off together for a stroll around the town. They ended up, as tourists did at least once, in the Drosselgasse.

As was to be expected it was crowded and noisy, but a scene not to be missed. Dusk was falling, and lights streamed out from the myriad of shop windows; many of the souvenir shops were still open along with the hamburger stalls. The sound of merry laughter and singing drifted from the many Wienstuben where tourists, and locals as well, sat at long tables drinking lager and joining in the German drinking songs, many of them familiar back home in the UK.

'Might this be too noisy for you, too raucous?' asked Dave with a grin as they stopped outside one of the wine bars.

'No, why should it be?' replied Jane. 'It's not something I would normally do, but we're on holiday, aren't we? And you can't come here without joining in the fun, just once.'

'That's all it will be,' replied Dave. 'Just once. Tomorrow night we'll be in the Black Forest, although there'll be ample opportunity for a 'knees up' there as well. Come on, let's see if we can find a seat.' He took her hand and guided her to a space on a long bench, not too far from the doorway. From there they could watch the passing crowds as well as the activity in the room.

Everyone seated at the bare wooden table was friendly and in a holiday mood.

'How do?' A man with a Yorkshire accent greeted them as they sat down opposite him. 'Enjoying yerselves?'

'Yes, very much,' answered Jane politely. 'Are you?'

'Yes, we're on a river cruise,' said the woman next to him. 'We're berthed here for the night, then we're heading off to Koblenz and the Moselle river. It's the first time we've been on one. It's champion, isn't it, Joe?'

'I'll say it is. You must try it next year, the pair of you,' said Joe.

Dave laughed. 'We'll bear it in mind,' he replied, and Jane felt herself blushing.

It wasn't long before a waitress in a dirndl skirt and peasant blouse came to take their order. Dave ordered two glasses of lager which soon arrived, full to the brim with a frothy head on them.

It was too noisy for any meaningful conversations. The voices around them were mainly English, though they could hear snatches of French, Italian and, of course, German. Jane couldn't imagine why the locals would come here, unless they were from a different part of Germany with different customs, and were on holiday, just as they were.

A little while later a group of men dressed in lederhosen; short leather breeches with coloured braces, thick woollen socks and heavy brogues and wearing green felt hats with a feather in the brim, mounted the stage at the end of the room. There followed an entertainment of dancing, consisting of stamping and thigh slapping, singing along to an accordion, and a comedy routine where they all punched and knocked each other about. It was well received by the audience, who joined in the choruses of the songs, lah-lah-ing if they didn't know the words. Jane felt her inhibitions fast disappearing as she joined in with the rest.

When the entertainment came to an end Dave put an arm round her shoulders. 'Shall we go?' he asked quietly. 'It's an early start tomorrow.'

She nodded in agreement, and he held her hand as they made their way to the door and out into the still busy street. He continued to hold her hand as they strolled back the half mile or so to the hotel, neither of them speaking very much, both deep in their own thoughts.

They collected their keys at the reception desk – they were too heavy to carry around – then they took the lift up to the second floor. When they stopped at Jane's door, Dave took hold of her shoulders; then he leaned forward and, gently and softly, kissed her lips, just once.

'Thank you for a lovely evening, Jane,' he said in a quiet voice. 'See you in the morning.'

'Thank you, too,' she replied. 'I've had a lovely time.'

As she stepped into the room she felt suffused with a quiet joy. She smiled, and almost laughed out loud. Was this really happening to her, the reserved and rather shy Jane Redfern? She couldn't remember when she had felt so happy and care-free; certainly never since . . . since Tom had died. The thought of him subdued her for a moment. She could never, ever forget him; but maybe it was time, now, to look forward and not back.

Seven

Mike had told them that it would be a nine o'clock start the following morning, which was not too early. They must leave promptly although the journey to a little village in the Black Forest, not too far from Freiburg, would not be too long or too arduous.

To some of the party, however, it seemed very early to be up and about. As they stood on the forecourt of the hotel whilst Mike and Bill loaded the cases on to the coach, much of the talk was about the sleepless night that some of them had endured.

'Those blessed trains! No sooner did I drop off to sleep than another one hurtled along the track.'

'All very well having a river view, but nobody told us, did they, that we'd be kept awake half the night by the bloody trains?'

'We were alright; our room was at the back. We were disappointed that we didn't have a nice view, weren't we, Bob? But it seems that we came off best.'

'D'you think they run all through the night?'

'Well, I suppose they must stop sometime, but they start off again too bloomin' early.'

Mike and Bill listened with half an ear to the comments of the passengers. They had heard them all before; it was the same every time. It would serve no useful purpose, though, to tell them beforehand that they might be kept awake by the passing trains. Better to let them find out for themselves. After all, it was only for one night. The rest of the holiday in the quaint little village hotel in the Black Forest would be as quiet as anyone could wish.

Maybe the residents who lived near to the river were accustomed to the traffic noise. Although the scenery along the banks of the Rhine couldn't be surpassed in its beauty and grandeur, it was, nevertheless, an important arterial route in that part of Germany with goods as well as passengers being transported by road, rail and river.

Jane and Dave listened to the remarks of their fellow travellers.

'I reckon we did OK then, having rooms at the back,' observed Dave. 'Did you sleep alright?'

'Very well,' replied Jane, 'once I'd got off. My head was full of the events of the day, especially the music and the hilarity last night. It was a great evening, wasn't it?'

'The first of many, I hope,' he answered.

The other coach party, the one from Yorkshire, was leaving round about the same time. Their drivers, also, were loading their coach; they were bound for the Austrian Tyrol.

There was an enormous stack of suitcases, but it gradually dwindled as the men humped them into the well at the side of the vehicle. They refused help from the men in the parties, although they might well have been glad of it. It was all concerned with health and safety, Bill had told them. If a client injured himself whilst helping, then the company would be liable to pay compensation.

'All aboard now,' shouted Bill when the last suitcase was stacked away. A quick count of heads, then they were off.

It was a pleasant drive along the bank of the river. Bill drove at a leisurely speed as it was not much more than a hundred miles to their destination. They made a morning coffee stop at the side of the river, then, after the lunch break near to the famous town of Heidelberg – unfortunately with no time to view the sights of the 'Student Prince' city – they turned towards the Black Forest region.

They arrived mid-afternoon at the village where they were to stay for the next six nights. The hotel – or Gasthaus – was in an idyllic setting, such as was seen on hundreds of picture postcards. It was a white painted building with green shutters at the windows, situated near a rippling stream that flowed along by the roadside. The village through which they had passed consisted of a cluster of similar guest houses, a church with a spire, and a few souvenir shops and wine bars. The 'Gasthaus Grunder' – the name was on a swinging sign by the door – was a half mile or so from the centre of the village;

there was no other guest house near to it. It would most certainly be quiet – no sound to be heard except the ripple of the stream – a vivid contrast to their hotel of the previous night.

The proprietor, Johann Grunder, came out to meet them, a portly ruddy-faced man of middle-age, clad in a voluminous white apron. He welcomed them in halting English, saying that he hoped they would enjoy their stay. When they had collected their keys there was to be a treat for them to bid them welcome. *Kaffee und Kuchen*: a piece of Black Forest gateau and coffee. And whilst they were enjoying this their luggage would be sorted out and taken to their rooms.

'How very nice!' Mavis remarked to her husband. 'What a kind thought! I must say we've been made very welcome in Germany. I've been pleasantly surprised so far. You can't say any different, Arthur.'

'I'm not trying to,' he answered. 'Aye, it's been alright so far. It's a damn good job we had a room at the back, though, in that last place.' A comment that Mavis agreed with whole-heartedly. She'd never have heard the last of it if he'd had a sleepless night.

The hotel was deceptive, as it was much larger inside than it had appeared to be from the exterior. It was a long low building, stretching back a good way, with bedrooms on the ground floor and on the one above. It was modern and simple in design and there was a pleasant smell of pinewood. Everything was light and bright and scrupulously clean. It was a family-run hotel with a small staff, consisting of the receptionist, three waitresses, and an extra chef who helped Johann Grunder – himself a trained chef – in the kitchen. Marie, his wife, made the pastries and cakes. All this information was gleaned by Mavis who was not shy at asking questions. One of the wait-resses, a language student called Greta, was only too willing to chat and practise her English.

The receptionist, Olga, was a friendly and attractive young woman in her mid-thirties with her dark hair swept back in a chignon. Mavis, who missed very little, noticed that she smiled and nodded at Bill as though she was very glad to see him. He smiled back at her, but he was busy with the luggage. Mavis guessed, though, that they might be well acquainted.

Their cake and coffee was served in the dining room, along a short corridor from the reception area. The room had a cosy, homely feel with floral chintz curtains at the windows, earthenware plates with designs of fruit, flowers, and birds hanging on the walls, and a small vase with fresh flowers in the centre of every table. The tables and chairs were of pinewood, with a tapestry cushion on the seat of each chair.

The six who had shared a table the previous evening sat together now. They all agreed that the piece of Black Forest gateau was the best they had ever tasted. It would be the authentic recipe, of course, moist and rich, oozing with cherry liqueur and whole cherries, covered with chocolate frosting, and served with whipped cream.

'Much better than anything you can get in the supermarket,' said Mavis. 'Even when you have it in a restaurant it doesn't taste like this. It's all so stereotyped and stodgy, not the real thing at all.'

Arthur complained that it would play havoc with his indigestion, but he ate it all the same.

It was whilst they were chatting, having finished their little treat, that Mike came to the table to speak to Shirley. 'Mrs Carson,' he began politely. 'Could you come with me, please? There seems to be a mix-up with your luggage. I'm hoping we can sort it out.'

Shirley sprung to her feet. 'What do you mean? Are you saying that my case is missing? Well, really . . .'

'We're not sure,' Mike answered placatingly. 'Bill's checking again now. So, we'll go and see, shall we? Have you got your room key?'

'Shall I come as well,' said Ellen, sounding very concerned.

'No, best not to, Miss Walmsley.' He smiled at her. 'We're doing our best to sort it out.'

Shirley left the room with Mike; she was looking very cross and anxious.

'Oh dear!' said Ellen to the others. 'I don't like the sound of that. I do hope they find her case. I know I'd be upset if it happened to me. But for Shirley—' she shook her head despairingly – 'I think it would be a major disaster.'

Jane new what Ellen meant, at least she thought she did. She had noticed that Shirley always dressed immaculately and stylishly as well. Even during the day when they were travelling she looked chic; her hair and make-up was perfect and she paid great attention to detail, even with casual clothes. She had never looked the least bit untidy or travel weary. Her trousers looked neatly pressed and she added a touch of style to her tops with a trendy little scarf or a chunky necklace and dangling earrings. And at night she really went to town in long skirts and sequinned jumpers.

Ellen bore out Jane's impression with her next words. 'Shirley tries to look her best at all times, you see. I know we all want to look neat and tidy – at least that is what is important to me – but Shirley loves to dress up, especially when we're on holiday.'

'Yes, I've noticed she always looks elegant,' said Jane. 'I feel as though I need a good wash and tidy-up after the journey today, but Shirley looked as though she'd stepped out of a bandbox.' She laughed. 'Whatever that is; I've never been sure.'

'She's always been the same,' said Ellen. 'Even when we were at school she managed to look stylish in her uniform; she made the rest of us feel a scruffy mess sometimes. I'm not criticizing her; it's just the way she was, and still is.'

'And she'll be surrounded by lovely clothes in the department store where she works, won't she?' observed Mavis.

'Oh yes; she loves her job, and she creates the most wonderful window displays. And she's able to buy her clothes at a good discount,' she added in a confidential voice. 'That's why she has so many. Her suitcase is always bulging with all the stuff she brings. Oh dear! I do hope they manage to sort it out.'

'I expect it's just mislaid – gone to the wrong room, perhaps,' said Jane, trying to be optimistic, although she could imagine how Shirley must be feeling. 'I'm sure the drivers are very careful . . .' But I suppose mistakes happen occasionally, she thought. She had heard of luggage going astray at airports, being missing from the carousel at the end of a flight. She wondered if the Galaxy insurance would pay up if the worst came to the worst.

'It wouldn't matter so much if it was me,' said Ellen. 'I've bought a couple of new things to come away – a summer skirt and a new cardigan – but most of my clothes I've had for ages. They're still good, though; not shabby or worn. I give some to the charity shop now and again, but I've always been thrifty. It's the way I was brought up, you see. My parents weren't short of money – not wealthy but not poor by any means – but they didn't believe in wasting it or going in for luxuries. Actually, my father was a Methodist local preacher, very set in his ways . . . and it's had an effect on me,' she added, almost apologetically.

'I reckon we're all a product of our upbringing, one way or another,' said Mavis kindly. 'And we're all as the good Lord made us. I can see that you're a very good friend to Shirley.'

'As she is to me,' replied Ellen promptly. 'We get on really well, even though we're not at all alike. She's always telling me to clear out my wardrobe and have a fresh start. She says I could make more of myself,' she added in a whisper, 'but I'm quite happy the way I am.'

She probably could, thought Jane. Ellen had a roundish face and dark brown alert-looking eyes, and when she smiled, as she often did, she looked very pretty and younger than she normally seemed. Her grey hair would look better when the newness of the perm wore off. She was prematurely grey; a light brown tint would work wonders. But maybe, as she said, she was content the way she was. After all, it was what we were like inside that mattered. And Ellen was a really nice person. Jane had formed a favourable impression of Shirley, too, but she guessed she might be quite a tartar when riled, as she had seemed when she went off with Mike.

Shirley accompanied Mike up to the first floor. 'That's my suitcase!' she exclaimed when they arrived at her door. 'Oh, thank goodness! It wasn't missing after all. What a fright you gave me.'

'Er . . . no, I'm afraid not, Mrs Carson,' said Mike. 'It looks like it, almost identical, I'd say. I remember seeing yours earlier,

but when we'd sorted them out, this is the one that was left. It's
. . . not yours,' he finished in a halting voice. 'I'm so sorry . . .'

Shirley bent down to look at the label. 'This one says
Richmond Travel.' She stood up, facing him angrily. 'That's
the tour from Yorkshire, isn't it? They were staying at the hotel
. . . Oh, really! This is too bad. I can't believe this is happening.'

'Bill has gone to recheck outside all the rooms. Yours may
have been left at the wrong door.'

'But that doesn't explain why this one is here,' said Shirley.
'There's been a slip-up, a bad one, and you'd better admit it.'

Bill arrived back at that moment, shaking his head. 'No joy,
I'm afraid, I've checked all the rooms.' The drivers looked
dejectedly at one another.

Then Mike spoke. 'We're really very sorry, Mrs Carson. We
can only assume that your case has gone with the luggage on
the Richmond coach. You say your suitcase is just like this
one?'

'Yes, I've already told you that.' Her voice was quiet rather
than loud with anger. 'But how can you have made such a
stupid mistake? The labels are all clearly marked, aren't they?'

Mike ran his fingers through his hair. 'We were loading up
at the same time. We left just before they did. I remember
seeing the two red suitcases; they were near to one another.
That's all I can say. Maybe Jim, the other driver, picked the
wrong one up. Or maybe I did, I don't know. All I can say is
that I'm truly sorry. But don't worry; we'll get it back for you.'

'Don't worry! How can you say don't worry?' Shirley's voice
was shrill with anger now. 'I'm left with only the clothes I
stand up in. Oh . . . this is too bad!'

'We're really sorry, Mrs Carson,' Bill reiterated. 'We try
to be so careful. This has never happened before, at least
not to us.'

'But that doesn't help me, does it?' snapped Shirley. 'It's
happened now. And how long will it be before I get it back
. . . if ever? Where have they gone, the folk on the Richmond
tour? And I suppose some other poor woman will be in the
same boat as me, with the wrong case?' The label had stated
that it was a Mrs and not a Mr.

'Er . . . we're not quite sure where,' answered Mike. 'We

know they've gone on to the Austrian Tyrol. I don't suppose they'll have arrived there yet; it's a longer journey. We don't know the hotel or even the resort, but the receptionist back in Rüdesheim will know.' He crossed his fingers tightly, hoping that this was so. 'We'll do all we can to get it back for you as soon as possible.'

'How?' asked Shirley.

'Well, it would mean one of us driving over there, or their driver coming here, or perhaps we could meet at a point halfway.' He was not at all sure himself, but it would need to be sorted out somehow. It was just one of the hazards of being a coach driver, although one he had not encountered before. 'I promise you we'll do our best. And for now, the least we can do is to offer you a bottle of wine tonight for you and your friends, by courtesy of Galaxy. Just a little gesture of recompense.'

'Well, that's something, I suppose,' said Shirley grudgingly. 'I'll have a look at my room now. At least I've got one or two essential items with me in my travel bag. But I won't be satisfied until my case is back.' She turned the key in the lock and entered her room.

'Phew!' said Bill. 'One angry lady, but you can't blame her. You've remembered, I suppose, that we've got excursions on the next two days? So it's going to be . . . let me see . . . Saturday before we can do anything. Unless Jim is willing to make the journey over here. Oh, what a bloody mess we're in! Let's go and drown our sorrows, mate!'

'In a drink of orange juice?' said Mike wryly, 'or a half of shandy if we really want to go mad. I know it was my fault, for what it's worth – or Jim's – I can't be sure which. But you were nowhere near those blasted red suitcases. Thanks for supporting me, though.'

'No problem, we're in this together,' said Bill, putting a comradely arm round his mate.

There was another matter on Bill's mind. He must have a word with Olga, and try to convince her that it might be better to call it a day.

Shirley entered the room and looked around. Yes, it was a very pleasant room, and in normal circumstances she would have been highly satisfied. It was a good size for one person. There was a single bed with a pinewood headboard, and a duvet with a bright floral cover which matched the window curtains. The pine theme was echoed in the wardrobe, chest of drawers and bedside cupboard. There was a reading lamp, too, and a light over the mirror on the chest of drawers, essential for fixing one's hair and make-up. The room was at the back of the building, and there was a picturesque view of the church spire in the village a little distance away, and further away the verdant rolling hills of the Black Forest region.

She flung her shoulder bag and travel bag on to the bed, then flopped down on it feeling cross and weary. The holiday had been going so well; she had been enjoying it immensely. It was good to meet different people. The two couples that she and Ellen had met – she was already thinking of Dave and Jane as a couple – were interesting to talk to and share points of view. Arthur, admittedly, was a bit of a grumbler; he reminded her of her father who had died a few years ago, both in looks and in temperament. She had not been to this part of Europe before and she had been enchanted by the scenery of the Rhine valley, and now the Black Forest. The food, too, had more than lived up to her expectations, which had not always been so in the past.

It was good to spend time with her old friend, Ellen, as well. She knew that some found it hard to understand their friend-ship; they were so different. But each had found in the other something that appealed to them; maybe it was because they were so dissimilar. Ellen irritated her at times, of course, with her fussiness about getting back to the coach in what she called 'plenty of time', for fear of annoying the driver. (Shirley had sometimes insisted on leaving it till the last minute, just for the sheer devilment of it!) And she knew that she aggravated Ellen sometimes by dressing up 'like a dog's dinner' as her friend might say, and keeping her waiting while she added the finishing touches to her hair and make-up, or making sure that her shoes and bag and scarf matched her current outfit. Whereas Ellen didn't care as long as she looked clean and tidy as she put it, which, of course she always did. Shirley had tried in vain to persuade her to spend some money on herself – fashionable clothes, smart shoes, even a tint on her hair, but you might as well talk to a brick wall.

Shirley sighed, a deep heartfelt sigh that reached down to the pit of her stomach. It was all spoilt now; she had no smart clothes to wear, no high-heeled sandals, floating skirts or stylish culottes – she had recently bought two pairs of those to wear as a change in the evenings. Whatever would she do? She felt like bursting into tears.

There was a knock at the door at that moment, and there was Ellen. She looked at her friend's stricken face and drew her own conclusions.

'Oh dear!' she said – one of her favourite expressions. 'You've not had any luck then? Your case hasn't turned up?'

'No, has it hell as like!' Shirley didn't often swear – she also knew that Ellen didn't like it – but this was enough to make a saint swear. She explained that her case was probably in the Austrian Tyrol by now, and goodness knows when she would get it back.

'Oh dear!' said Ellen again. 'How dreadful! Never mind, though; it could have been a lot worse. You could be ill, you could have fallen and broken your ankle or . . . it could have been raining all the time. It might not be too long before you get it back. Don't let it spoil your holiday. We're having a lovely time. And you always look nice, whatever you wear. And not everyone gets dressed up for dinner. You can wear those trousers and top tonight. You'll look as smart as anyone.'

'Tonight and tomorrow and the day after that!' Shirley retorted. It irritated her how Ellen always looked on the bright side, trying to find the good in everyone and everything – although she knew it was really an admirable character trait, one that she feared she did not possess.

'Yes, I think I can understand how you feel,' said Ellen, her eyes full of sympathy. 'It's such a shame. You wanted to wear all your nice clothes, and you've bought some new ones as well. I know you like to wear something different every night . . . But I've brought loads of clothes with me, far too many. You're about the same size as me, aren't you? You could borrow some of mine.'

'What!' Shirley couldn't believe what she was hearing. This

was adding insult to injury. She didn't stop to think what she was saying as the words burst from her. 'Really Ellen! I wouldn't be seen dead in your clothes!'

Her friend's demeanour changed in an instant. The kindly concern disappeared from her eyes, and her face started to crumple as though she was going to cry. 'Shirley, how could you!' Her voice was faint and trembling. 'What a dreadful thing to say! I know I'm not as attractive as you, but my clothes are always clean and tidy and—'

'Oh, Ellen! I'm so sorry. I didn't mean it to sound like that, of course I didn't. It's just a figure of speech, something people say, but they don't really mean it. And I'm so worked up that I scarcely know what I'm saying.' She put an arm round Ellen as she sat beside her on the bed. 'It was very kind of you to offer, but—'

'Yes, I know,' said Ellen stiffly. 'They're old-fashioned – like me – not all stylish and chic, if that's the right word. But that's the way I am. It was silly of me to even think of you . . . wearing my clothes.'

Shirley was mortified. She felt so ashamed of herself. She had upset her friend really badly and she did not know how to make amends. But she could not let this spoil their holiday any more than she could let the loss of the suitcase do so. Careless words – how quickly and thoughtlessly they were uttered, and once said they could not be taken back. She tried again.

'Ellen . . . I am truly sorry. Please, please forgive me. You know I wouldn't want to hurt you for the world. We've been such good friends, so don't let this spoil things between us. Perhaps I overreacted about the case, but I was so cross, with the drivers or whoever it was, for making such a stupid mistake. I suppose "There are worse troubles at sea", as my mother used to say . . . although I always thought that that wasn't much help to us!'

Ellen gave a weak smile. 'My mother used to say that as well. No, I don't think you've overreacted. It should never have happened. Somebody is at fault, and I know I would have been cross as well if it had happened to me. Although it wouldn't have been such a great disaster to me. Nobody really notices what I wear. I was hurt though, Shirley, it's no use pretending I wasn't, but I know you spoke in haste.' She reached out and put her hand over her friend's manicured one with the red painted nails. 'Let's forget it, eh? Don't think any more about it.'

Shirley felt like hugging and kissing her, she was so relieved, but she didn't do so. There had never been anything like that between them, and she wouldn't want anyone to get that impression. That was one of the reasons why she, Shirley, had suggested that they should have single rooms. She hadn't said that to Ellen, of course. Her friend was very naive about the ways of the world, even in today's climate, and it may not even have occurred to her.

'Thank you,' she said, simply. 'I'll try to watch my tongue in future. There is something you could lend me, though, if you don't mind.' This would be a sop to her own conscience, and no doubt Ellen would be pleased to help in some way.

'Yes, of course. What is it?' asked Ellen.

'Er . . . some underwear,' replied Shirley.

'Underwear? What sort?' Ellen looked puzzled.

'A pair of knickers,' said Shirley, more bluntly. 'I've got a spare pair in my travel bag. I always change them after a journey, but I shall need a fresh pair for tomorrow.'

'Certainly,' agreed Ellen. 'I always change my undies after a journey as well. And I've got lots of spare ones in my case. What about a nightdress? You won't have that either, will you?'

'Oh no, of course not . . .'

'Well, I've brought two with me. They're not all that glamorous, but no one's going to see you in your nightwear, are they?'

'I should be so lucky,' murmured Shirley.

'What did you say?' asked her friend.

'Er . . . no,' she said with a laugh. 'As you say, nobody's going to see me.'

'I'll pop next door and get them for you now,' said Ellen.

Shirley was pleased to see that she was back to her normal, eager-to-please self. Well . . . almost. There was still a little constraint there, but Shirley would work hard to make things right.

What would the garments be like? she wondered. But what did it matter? She was satisfied, though, when Ellen returned with a pair of ordinary white knickers. She had wondered if it might be a pair of what they used to call 'Directoire' knickers such as they sold in old-fashioned draper's shops; voluminous bloomers with elastic at the waist and knees. Her own underwear was of pretty colours. Not thongs – she couldn't imagine wearing those – but briefer ones with high-cut legs. But these of Ellen's would suffice until she could find a shop and buy some more. This was something she could not manage without. The nightdress, too, was plain and serviceable – not like her own garment with lace and ribbons – but she was very grateful to her friend.

'Thank you so much,' she said. 'These are great . . . Shall we go down and have a drink before dinner? It might cheer me up a bit.'

They agreed to meet in half an hour when they had had a wash and tidy-up; and when Ellen had changed her clothes and she, Shirley, had tried to add a fresh look to her daytime trousers and striped top. Fortunately she carried her costume jewellery with her in her hand luggage.

Eight

There was a small, but adequately stocked bar, at one end of the lounge. When Shirley and Ellen arrived there were already a few of their fellow travellers sitting around the small tables at the sides of the room. This area was carpeted, the centre of the lounge being of highly polished wood. Maybe for dancing, thought Shirley, or for evening entertainments. There was a dais at the other end of the room, a low platform where visiting artistes might perform. They had been told there would be entertainment on a couple of nights.

The receptionist, Olga, was serving behind the bar. It seemed that she helped out there when she was not occupied at the desk in the foyer.

'What would you like to drink?' asked Shirley. 'My treat tonight, so put your purse away.' They usually paid their own way on holiday – it saved a lot of arguments as to whose turn it was – but Shirley was doing all she could to make it up to her friend for her tactless remarks; and Ellen seemed to understand this.

'Thank you,' she said. 'I'll have my usual *Apfelsaft*.' It was a sparkling apple juice, popular in Germany and Austria.

'And I'll have my usual Cinzano and lemonade,' said Shirley. 'Oh . . . by the way, there's wine for us tonight, courtesy of Galaxy, for me and my friends, Mike said. It's his way of making amends, of course, for my suitcase.'

'Then make sure you choose one of the best wines,' said Ellen, rather surprisingly.

Shirley laughed. 'If I'm given the choice. They may present me with a bottle of the house white. And I'll make sure you get the tipple of your choice . . . unless I can persuade you to have a drop of wine?' she asked with a questioning smile.

'I'll see,' replied Ellen. 'You never know, I might well do that.'

Pigs might fly, thought Shirley as she made her way to the

bar. The polished floor was rather slippery and you had to watch your step. She was not wearing her high-heeled sandals as she would normally have done; they were a hundred miles or more away with the rest of her smart gear. She had to be careful, though, in the wedge heels she was wearing.

There was no one else at the bar. Olga smiled at her pleasantly, saying that she hoped she would enjoy her stay. She spoke almost perfect English. She was an attractive young woman, possibly in her late thirties, quite tall and slim with dark brown hair and eyes, a contrast to the more usual flaxen hair and blue eyes of many of the German people. She wore a plain black dress, a uniform of a sort, but it was clearly expensive and stylish, the dark shade relieved only by a silver cross and chain around her neck and small earrings.

'Cheers,' said Shirley as they settled down in the comfortable chairs, wicker work ones with bright floral cushions, complementing the pinewood and the light and airy aspect of the guest house. She raised her glass and Ellen followed suit.

'Yes, cheers,' she echoed. 'Here's to a lovely holiday. It will be, you know . . .' She looked intently at her friend. 'You look very nice tonight, as you always do.' Shirley was wearing a chunky necklace of brightly coloured beads that looked well with the plain top she had worn all day. 'Nobody really cares two hoots about what other people wear, you know.'

Shirley did not agree, but she did not say so. For her part, she always looked at other people's clothes, assessing whether the outfit suited them or not. She was just naturally interested, or maybe just plain nosy!

'Anyway,' Ellen went on, 'You could always buy one or two nice things in the shops here, couldn't you? I know it might make a hole in your spending money but . . .'

'Nice things? Here?' Shirley gave a bitter laugh, despite trying to look on the bright side as her friend had urged her to do. 'I'd end up looking like a German hausfrau!' Even as she said it she knew she was being difficult. The young woman at the bar was very smart. 'I'm not likely to run out of money,' she added. 'I've got my credit card with me.' Ellen never used one. She still used the old-fashioned way of paying by cash, or the occasional cheque, when on holiday.

'But I'm not likely to see anything I'd want to wear. Don't let's talk about it any more, Ellen. It's too depressing! Oh look . . . there's Bill. He's on his own. I wonder if they've a room each or if they have to share?'

'Does it matter?' asked Ellen, smiling at her friend. 'You're too nosy by far, that's your trouble,' she added good-humouredly.

'Yes, I admit that I like to know what's going on,' said Shirley. Ellen had voiced what she herself had just been thinking. She liked to know what made people tick.

She noticed now that Bill and Olga were deep in conversation; in fact, it looked as though they might be having an argument. She knew that Ellen would laugh, and probably tell her that it was none of her business, but she couldn't resist commenting on it to her friend.

'Oh . . . yes,' said Ellen, not laughing at all. 'It certainly looks as though they know one another quite well.'

'Maybe they've been friendly,' said Shirley. 'Well, maybe rather more than just friendly. I know that both Bill and Mike have stayed here several times before.'

'Well, it's not really any of our business, is it?' said Ellen. 'As far as I'm concerned Bill and Mike are both very nice young men, very helpful and considerate. I know you may not agree right now, but they're doing all they can to make the holiday interesting, aren't they?'

'Yes, I do agree; they're great,' said Shirley. 'But you never know what problems other people might have, do you? I wonder if they're married? Somehow, I don't imagine that Bill is . . . It's not an ideal job for a married man, is it, being away from home such a lot of the time?'

'You'll have to find out, won't you, about their marital status?' said Ellen with a mischievous grin. 'I'm sure somebody will be able to tell you.'

'You're laughing at me,' said Shirley, 'but I admit I'm curious.'

Bill and Olga were still talking, but not smiling at one another. Then two people from the coach party went to the bar to be served, and Bill walked away, out of the room.

He was quite a good-looking chap, Shirley thought to herself; a bit overweight, though. He had what was termed a good head of hair, an attractive shade of ginger and with a natural wave; such as some straight-haired women might envy, saying it was wasted on a man. He had a cheerful round face, and bright blue eyes. No doubt he would appeal to quite a lot of women . . .

The drivers dined at a small table on their own, away from the coach party, although they were served at the same time. They preferred it that way. They needed a bit of space after dealing with their clients and their problems all day. And the passengers seemed to understand that, and did not pester them at meal times.

'What's up?' asked Mike, as they sat down at their table in a far corner of the dining room. 'You look as though you've lost the proverbial pound and found a penny. Is it Christine? I thought it was all going well.'

'No, it isn't her. Like I told you, we got on famously last night, and she's agreed to have a drink with me tonight as well. I think we'll have a stroll down to the village, away from the busybodies here. No, it's Olga. I'm afraid she didn't like what I had to say, not one little bit.'

Mike looked puzzled. 'I thought you'd agreed, the last time you met, that there wasn't much future in it?'

'So we did, at least that was the impression I got. But it seems as though she's changed her mind. She says she looks forward to me coming every few weeks, and she doesn't see why we can't carry on as we are. I think, between you and me, that she's hoping I'll see a way to making it more permanent. But how can I?'

'I suppose you could if you really wanted to,' said Mike. 'Where there's a will there's a way, as the saying goes. The problem is, women get more serious about these things than men do, depending on the woman, of course. Some are just out for a good time or a casual fling, but a nice well brought up lass like Olga – as I'm sure she is – she probably wants more than just a relationship like yours, here today and gone tomorrow. You can't blame her, Bill.'

They stopped talking as the waitress brought their starter – thick pea soup in deep bowls with chunks of brown bread.

'I've got in too deep, that's the problem,' Bill continued, 'and now it's difficult to back out. I feel dreadful, really; I'm very fond of her. I suppose I've just let it drift on without thinking too much about the future. I thought she felt the same as me, you know – it was good while it lasted, sort of thing.'

'So what are you going to do? How have you left it?'

'It's stalemate at the moment. She was busy at the bar, so I just left her to her work. I'm hoping she'll realize I'm right, that it's best to call it a day. There would always be problems if we were to consider a future together. For a start, she's a Catholic, and that always causes strife in families.'

'I don't see why,' said Mike. 'It isn't as if you are much of a churchgoer, are you?'

'Christmas and Easter if I feel inclined. Olga doesn't go much either, to Mass or whatever it is. But her parents are very keen. She left home to get away from their control – they live in Stuttgart – and she's had a fair number of jobs like this one, living in hotels since she was twenty or so.'

'She must have had a few boyfriends – well, men friends, relationships, surely? She's an attractive woman.'

'Yes, I suppose she has, but I haven't enquired too closely, just as she hasn't asked too much about my past, but I think she's getting rather bored, stuck out here in the back of beyond. She's ready for a change of some sort.'

'And so are you, it seems. Olga doesn't know you've got somebody lined up, does she?'

'Good Lord, no! I've had a quiet word with Christine. I suggested we might go down to the village after dinner. She's a great girl, Mike. I really like her.'

'But you can't possibly know from meeting her just once, that she's right for you.'

'I'm not saying that. But we hit it off straight away. She's from the same neck of the woods, too, from Manchester, like me. Not the same district, but near enough; her home's in Didsbury.'

'Ooh . . . posh, eh?'

'Well, she does speak nicely, and I can an' all – I mean as well! – if I make an effort. It's an advantage, though, living in the same area, not like a friendship with someone in another country.'

'But you wouldn't be in the same town, would you? You'd be working over here. There'd only be the occasional weekends.'

'Yes, I know, but you were saying the other day that there's work in the UK. I might consider that. Some of the lads are dying to get on to the Continental tours. And we don't work during the winter, do we?'

The Galaxy drivers were laid off during the winter months, apart from doing day trips now and again, and a few Christmas tours which were a new innovation. Some of them found other part-time jobs or drew unemployment benefit. They knew that their jobs would be there for them, come the spring.

Their conversation stopped for a time whilst the main course was served. It was a typical German dish; roast pork served with dumplings and red cabbage, an introduction to local cuisine. They did not talk much as they enjoyed the succulent pork and the substantial helping of dumplings.

Bill glanced across at a nearby table where there was the sound of laughter and high spirits. 'Mrs Carson seems to have recovered from the loss of her suitcase,' he remarked. 'Unless she's just drowning her sorrows. That was a nice gesture, offering her a bottle of wine.'

'The least we could do,' said Mike. 'I'll have to get round to tracing the bloody suitcase.'

'Haven't you done anything yet?'

'All in good time, Bill. They wouldn't arrive in Austria till early evening, and then it's all go for the next couple of hours as you know. I'll ring Rüdesheim as soon as we've finished our meal and see it they've got the address in Austria. If not, then it will mean getting on to Richmond Travel in the UK. There are times when a driver's lot is not a happy one!'

At the table a little distance away the six travellers, who were by now good friends, were enjoying the bottle of Riesling wine recommended by the proprietor, Herr Grunder. It was one of the priciest on the wine list and was proving to be a great success with all of them.

'There's not really enough for all of us,' Arthur had remarked. 'I'll order another bottle of the same; no arguments – my treat.'

Dave had argued that Arthur had bought wine the first night in Calais. So after a bit of good-natured quibbling, the two men had agreed to share the cost.

'Ellen won't want any,' said Shirley, 'unless I can twist her arm . . .?'

'Do you know, I think I might!' said Ellen with a sly grin. 'Just a teeny drop, I might not like it.'

Shirley was flabbergasted. 'Well! I'll go to the foot of our stairs!' she exclaimed. The others all laughed.

'Don't ask me what it means,' said Shirley. 'It's one of those old Lancashire sayings my mother used to use. Good for you, Ellen! I bet when you've tasted it you'll want some more.'

Jane wondered if Shirley might be guilty of persuading her friend to act against her better judgement, although Ellen didn't seem the type of person to do anything against her will. 'Why don't you try a mixture of wine and lemonade, Ellen?' she suggested. 'It's called a spritzer. You can have wine with soda water, but it's nicer with lemonade.'

'Thank you; I think I'd like that,' agreed Ellen. She was quite pink-cheeked with excitement, although she hadn't drunk anything yet. And when the drink arrived she said it was refreshing and very much to her taste.

Shirley fended off all enquiries about her suitcase. 'It's a banned subject,' she declared. 'I want to enjoy my meal.'

They all agreed that the first meal at the guest house boded well for the rest of the stay. The main course was delicious, though different from anything they would eat at home. And the *Apfelkuchen* – or apple cake – that followed, served with whipped cream, left them feeling that they could not eat another mouthful.

They retired to the lounge for coffee. Arthur and Mavis, Shirley and Ellen, decided that they had had enough excitement for one day and would stay in the hotel for the rest of the evening. So it was just Dave and Jane who decided to walk down to the village.

They strolled down the leafy country road enjoying the warmth of the balmy evening. It had been another glorious summer day, and the light was just beginning to fade, the sky turning to a darker blue, tinged with golden and crimson streaks. How long could this weather last? Jane wondered. There must be rain in Germany sometimes, though maybe not so much as they had at home. They had been very fortunate so far.

After a few moments Dave took hold of her hand, and she stole a sideways glance at him. He was smiling at her.

'You enjoyed your meal, did you? I noticed you were struggling to finish your apple cake.'

'So I was; and I had to leave one of the dumplings as well. It was all very enjoyable, though a little . . . dare I say stodgy? Satisfying and filling, at any rate. Certainly more than enough for me.'

'I think it may well be the same sort of fare for the rest of the week,' said Dave. 'They don't go in for dainty meals in Germany. Their cuisine has developed from the dishes that the peasants used to eat, especially in the country districts. A meat and potato diet, such as we have at home, but more of the dumplings instead of potatoes. I'm afraid we might go home a few pounds heavier.'

'I don't put much weight on as a rule,' said Jane, 'so I'm not unduly worried. I'm not always watching my weight, like some women do. I should imagine Shirley is very conscious about that sort of thing. She's always so immaculate and concerned about how she looks. It couldn't have happened to a worse person, losing her case . . . I like her though,' she added. 'They're a nice little crowd at our table, aren't they?'

'Yes, so they are, and it makes such a difference to a holiday like this, who you sit with for meals. They very rarely have tables for two; the idea is that they want you to mix and mingle. I've found that it's better to be on a table for six rather than four. If you get stuck with a couple you don't get on with it can be deadly. But we all seem very compatible. Different, of course, but that adds to the interest . . . And I'm so glad that I met you, Jane.' He squeezed her fingers just a little as he turned to look at her.

'Yes, I'm glad too,' she replied. 'I was dreading coming away on my own, although I knew I had to do it . . . to prove that I could. And it's made such a difference, getting to know you. I'm having a lovely time.'

They had arrived at the village, which was little more than a large hamlet. The road widened a little as they approached a row of houses, a church and a few shops. A general store, a pharmacy, a butcher's shop, and what looked like a charity shop such as they had at home, with all sorts of odds and ends in the window. There was a gift and souvenir shop, too; they obviously had their share of tourists passing by.

All the shops were closed, but at the far end of the street there was a beer garden, set back from the road in its own grounds. Strings of lights flickered amongst the trees, beneath which there were wooden tables and benches. Further back there was a white painted building with more seating accommodation inside. There were a few couples sitting outside and a waiter in a long green apron taking an order at a table in the corner.

'Look at that!' said Dave, sounding surprised. 'Just the job! I was doubtful that we would find anywhere open, but this seems as though it might be a popular place.'

'How lovely!' Jane exclaimed. In her present mood everything was delightful. Here was another idyllic scene to store away in her memory along with the other sights and impressions that had followed, one upon the other, these last few days.

They sat down on a bench beneath a spreading lime tree, and Dave handed her a large menu card. They served meals, as well as lighter snacks and a wide variety of drinks. The menu was in German, with no English translation, but it would be easy enough to order as the names of the beers and wines were familiar.

'A beer for me – Helles, I think,' said Dave. 'That's what they call a blond beer, not too heavy. Some of their beers would knock you out, they're so potent. What about you, Jane? White wine?'

'The only German wine I know is Liebfraumilch,' she replied, 'apart from the Riesling we had tonight. And that was quite enough for me, for one evening. Perhaps I could have a spritzer, like I suggested Ellen should have. I rather think it was the first time she'd ever tasted alcohol.'

'It didn't seem to have any ill effect on her,' said Dave. 'A very nice lady. I hope her friend's case turns up, though, or

Ellen may well have to bear the brunt of Shirley's bad moods. She was OK at dinner time – Shirley, I mean – but she was obviously very annoyed earlier on.'

'What an awful thing to happen, though,' said Jane. 'I do feel sorry for her. I should hate it to happen to me.'

'You wouldn't let it spoil your holiday, though, would you?'

'No . . . I'd try not to. But ladies do like to have a change of clothes in the evening, I know I do. And Shirley seems to dress as though she's on a catwalk. Her clothes are jolly expensive, but she was telling me that she gets a very good discount at the store where she works.'

'She's certainly a very elegant lady,' said Dave, 'but there are other things that are far more important than the clothes we wear . . .' He stopped speaking as the waiter arrived at their table.

It was clear that he was quite used to ordering from a German menu, as the waiter seemed to understand what they wanted. Jane commented on this.

'That sounded very competent. Have you been to Germany before?'

'Er . . . yes,' he answered, a little hesitantly. 'Not with Galaxy, though . . . and it was a long time ago. My wife and I went on a couple of Continental coach tours, before our son was born, to Austria and Bavaria. The whole business of coach travel has improved no end since that time. I remember en-suite rooms were few and far between; you had a washbasin in the room, that was all – no shower or loo. And the breakfasts were very meagre: rolls and butter and jam. They have to provide more variety now to cater for tourists from all over.'

'No doubt you have happy memories, though, of your early holidays,' Jane remarked. Dave had sounded a little uneasy when he mentioned his wife. It was the first time he had spoken of her since that first day when he had told her that he, too, was on his own. She thought about the happy times that she had spent with Tom – although these had receded even further to the back of her mind over the last few days – and she guessed it might be the same for Dave. Maybe some poignant memories had returned to him as he mentioned his wife.

He was silent for a few moments before he answered. 'I'm

sorry to say that not all the memories are happy ones. I know from what you have said that you and your husband – Tom, wasn't he? – had a wonderful marriage . . .'

'Yes . . . we did,' she answered quietly.

'But it was not the same with Judith and me. We were happy at first. We were young and in love, or so we thought. I soon realized, though, that we had very little in common, not enough for a satisfactory marriage. Judith was a town girl, and she couldn't get used to the quiet of the countryside, or to being a farmer's wife.

'She had a part-time job in Shrewsbury at first – she was a shorthand typist – and she drove there and back each day. But she had to give up when Peter was born.'

'How old is your son?' asked Jane.

'He's twenty-two, and he's already engaged to a girl he went to school with. I did try to tell him, tactfully, not to rush into things. But he's a sensible young man, and I don't foresee any problems there. Kathryn's a lovely lass, and she's from a similar background. Her father's a market gardener, and she does the bookkeeping for him as well as helping out on the land. She's told him, though, that he'll have to find somebody else next year, because she intends to be a 'hands on' sort of farmer's wife.'

'Are they getting married soon?'

'Yes, next year. They'll live at the farm with me. There's plenty of room, and I shall make sure they have their own space, and plenty of it. I'm sure it will be a happy marriage, as far as one can ever predict such a thing.'

He paused, and Jane made no comment. She did not want to pry. If he chose to tell her more about his own marriage, that was OK. If not, then she would not ask. However, he went on. 'As I said, Judith was not happy as a farmer's wife, and it was worse after Peter was born. She loved him – I never doubted that – but she felt even more tied down. She still had a lot of friends in Shrewsbury, and she wanted go on meeting them the same as before. And I'm afraid that's what she did. We didn't have much of a home life, but I suppose we stayed together because of Peter. I used to worry about her being out late, especially if she was driving.'

He stopped suddenly, and Jane wondered if she had been killed in a car crash. He had not said how his wife had died, and if it had been a road accident it would still be painful to talk about it, even though their feelings for one another might have changed.

'Anyway, that's all in the past, and we have to look to the future. And it's already looking very promising.' He placed his hand over Jane's, smiling into her eyes.

'Yes,' she replied quietly. 'I knew that I had to start enjoying myself again, if it were possible.'

'And you are, aren't you – enjoying yourself?'

'Very much so. It's more than two years since Tom died. And it's longer for you, isn't it?'

'Yes, more than four years since Judith . . .' He sighed. 'But things had not been good for quite some time.' He let go of her hand and took a long drink of his beer. The waiter had put down their drinks unobtrusively whilst they had been talking. Jane sipped at her spritzer and found it very palatable.

'This is nice,' she said cheerfully, hoping to lighten the rather sombre mood that their conversation had evoked.

'Good.' He grinned at her, his good humour restored. He took hold of her hand again. 'Jane . . . I would like to think that I could go on seeing you after the holiday has ended. How do you feel about that?'

The idea had been forming in her mind as well, and she was pleased that he felt the same, but the practicality of it was another matter. So she did not say at once that she would be delighted to see him again, even though she wanted to do so.

'We haven't known one another long, have we?' she said.

'Three days,' said Dave, 'but it seems much longer. I feel as though I've known you for ages.'

Jane felt the same. They had shared so much over the last three days. They had been together constantly, except for the night times. They did get on very well together, but this was a holiday situation. How would they fare when they were back home without the excitement and glamour of new sights, new experiences? Dave lived quite a long way from her own home, and there was her mother to consider.

'Let's see how it goes, Dave,' she said, trying to be sensible and follow her head, not her heart which was urging her to throw caution to the winds. 'We do get on well, and we're having a lovely time here . . . but there would be obstacles at home. Where we live, for one thing; then there's my mother.'

Dave forbore to say that her mother was an elderly lady and would not live for ever, but that would be too unkind, and he did see the problems. 'My mother has been very accommodating,' he replied. 'You might well be surprised. And we're not a million miles apart, are we? And we both drive . . . But you're right; let's see how things go.'

They were both quiet for a little while, each deep in thought. Jane noticed a familiar figure at the other side of the garden.

'Oh, look − there's Bill,' she said. 'And isn't that the lady that sits at the front of the coach? I don't know her name.'

'So it is,' said Dave. 'It looks like another holiday friendship in the making.'

The two of them looked very friendly and happy together as they sat at a table, heads close together studying the menu. 'Good luck to them. Bill seems a decent sort of bloke − well, they both do, he and Mike. But some drivers do have a reputation for getting off with the single ladies.'

'So long as he's not married,' said Jane. 'You never know do you . . .?'

Nine

'Now, Christine, what's your poison?' asked Bill. 'I'm afraid I shall have to stick to a half of lager or Pils, or maybe a shandy. And then it'll be orange juice or *Apfelsaft*. Both Mike and I obey the rules; most drivers do.'

'And do you always obey the rules, in everything?' asked Christine with a sly grin.

'Oh, I think so,' Bill replied easily. 'I'm a pretty straightforward sort of chap. I would certainly not drink while on duty, and that goes for evenings as well. There's too much at stake with a coachload of passengers. We're responsible for their welfare.'

'Yes, I imagine there are problems from time to time, aren't there?'

'You can say that again! We've done alright this time, so far, apart from the missing suitcase. And Mike has managed to trace the hotel in Austria where the Richmond coach has gone. The main problem is when people are late back at the coach. We're not allowed to leave anyone, even though it's a blasted nuisance at times. They usually turn up in the end; they've mistaken the time, or they've got lost. If they're too long we have to go looking for them. Then sometimes people are taken ill and have to be rushed to hospital. Or they complain about the rooms or the food . . . But it's all going well up to now, touch wood.' He tapped on the table. 'What about you? You're enjoying it, are you?'

'Yes, very much, and so is Norah. She made friends with two ladies of a similar age to her. We're sitting with them for meals and we all get on well together.'

The conversation was interrupted as the waiter appeared to take their order – a small Pils for Bill and a glass of Liebfraumilch for Christine. 'I think you will find it far superior to the sort we get at home,' Bill told her.

'There's quite a big age gap between you and your sister, isn't there?' he asked when the waiter had gone.

She grinned. 'That's a polite way of asking how old I am, is it? I don't mind telling you, why should I? I'm thirty-six, and Norah is fifty-two, although she's looked older recently. Her husband was ill for a long while, and she cared for him all the time. I'm hoping this holiday will help her to look to the future again. I'm afraid she's often mistaken for my mother; she did look after me a lot when I was little. I was something of an afterthought in the family. I don't think my parents really intended to have another child! But I was loved all the same.'

'Are your parents still living?'

'Yes, both of them. We're lucky in that respect. We've all got our own homes, of course, not very far from one another.'

They stopped talking again as the waiter arrived with their drinks. Christine took a good sip of the pale golden wine.

'Delicious!' she said. 'You're right. It's far superior to the stuff I buy from Sainsbury's.'

'I think they keep the best for themselves, and export the rest,' said Bill. 'You were saying, Christine, about your home . . . You live alone, do you?'

'At the moment, yes,' she replied with a smile. 'You're asking if I'm single, aren't you?' She knew that the term 'single' no longer just meant unmarried as it used to do. Nowadays it seemed to mean anyone who didn't have a partner at that time, a partner of either sex. Whether you were widowed, divorced, or just on your own you were referred to as being single.

'It's as well to know,' replied Bill, 'so that there's no mis-understanding.'

She nodded. 'I live on my own, and I'm single. By that I mean that I've never been married. Until about six months ago I was in a relationship, but that came to an end, by mutual agreement. I'm not completely on my own, though. I live with my dog, a chocolate Labrador called Monty. He's a great companion, and just lately I've not wanted anyone else.'

'So where is he now?'

'My parents are looking after him; they love having him. My dad takes him for walks in the park, and my mum spoils him rotten. He'll be glad to see me again, though.'

'And what does he do during the day when you're at work?' asked Bill. He was yet to discover her form of employment.

'That's not a problem,' she replied. 'I have a dog parlour, you see, and I live over the premises. I'm able to keep an eye on him, and he likes to make friends with our clients.'

'Good grief! A dog parlour!' said Bill. He had imagined she might be an office worker or a librarian. 'You mean you do shampoos and sets for pampered poodles?'

'There are all kinds of dogs, not just poodles,' she answered, a trifle curtly. 'We do get a fair number of poodles because they need a good deal of care to keep them clean and tidy. But all dogs need a bath now and again, and a bit of a spruce-up. It's something they can't do for themselves, like cats do. Some owners like to bath their dogs themselves, but we're kept pretty busy.'

'So who's looking after the business this week? Or are you closed?'

'No, I have an assistant, Thelma. It's my business, but she's been with me for several years and she can manage very well if I'm not there. And we've got a young trainee girl now, Tracey. She's only sixteen, but she's shaping up very well . . . You look astounded, Bill. You didn't see me as a doggie person, eh?'

'I thought you might work in an office. I'd no idea really. But I'm sure it must be interesting work. Have you always done that sort of thing?'

'No, I had an office job when I left school. I'd always liked animals, though, and I rather fancied the idea of being a vet. But I knew the training would be very long and arduous. I did get a job eventually, working in a veterinary practice, mostly in the office. Then my grandparents died, left me some money, and with help from my parents I was able to start my own business.'

'And that's in Didsbury, is it?'

'Yes, that's right. We get a good clientele round there; some very wealthy people, and others more like my family – just ordinary folk.'

'You get some free time though, don't you? I wondered if we could carry on seeing one another – you know – now and again, when we get back home? I don't live all that far away from you – the other side of Manchester, but that's no problem. I have a car, and I expect you do as well.'

'You're not at home though, are you? You're over here working, most of the time.'

'As a matter of fact, I have a week off when we get back. It's just the way it's worked out. So . . . do you think we could meet? We could go for a meal in Manchester or . . . whatever you like?'

'But I don't really know you, Bill, do I? We've only just met.' Christine felt that she did like what she knew of Bill, so far, but she did not know very much. 'What about you?' she asked. 'Do you live on your own? You haven't told me.'

'Yes, I have a flat in Chadderton, and I live on my own; have done for ages, in between tours, you know.'

'And you are single, too?'

'Yes,' he replied, 'I'm single; and by that I mean that I've never been married. I can't say that I've never had any relationships – you wouldn't believe me if I did – but at the moment I'm as free as a bird; or else I wouldn't be trying to persuade you to give me a chance.'

Bill was metaphorically crossing his fingers that Olga would take heed of what he had said and realize that it was for the best. He had suffered from pangs of guilt from time to time about his simultaneous friendships with Lise and Olga, and neither one knowing about the other. That was why he had decided to break with both of them and have a completely fresh start.

Lise had made it easy for him by her admission that she was already seeing someone else. But it was a different matter with Olga. He didn't want to upset her. They had had some good times together, but he had never thought that she might be looking for something more permanent.

Christine broke into his reverie. 'What's the matter, Bill? That's an ominous silence.'

'Not really,' he replied. 'I'm wondering what you're going to say, that's all.'

'As I said before, I've only known you for three days. I can't say how I will feel when we get back home.'

'But friendships have to start somewhere, don't they? And we have the rest of the time here, in Germany, to get to know one another better. You said that your sister has made friends with two more ladies, so that leaves you free to spend more time with me, doesn't it?'

'You mean . . . during the day when we're on our excursions?'

'Yes, why not? We have a lot of free time at the various places we visit.'

'Don't you spend the time with Mike? What do you do, anyway, when you visit the same places time after time? Doesn't it get boring, hanging around waiting for the passengers?'

'Oh, there's always something to fill the time. If it's a bad day we might have a snooze in the coach. That's when we feel sorry for the clients, having to turn them out in the pouring rain, but there's usually somewhere they can run to – cafes or souvenir shops. But let's hope we have a rain-free week. We've done well so far.'

'But it must rain sometimes?'

'Obviously, or there wouldn't be all these forest areas. It doesn't seem to rain as much as it does at home. They have long spells of glorious weather, but when it rains you think it's never going to stop. We feel sorry for you lot then, when you've paid all that money for a summer holiday. You expect it to be fine all the time, don't you, when you're away?'

'Yes, I suppose so, but it all depends on where you choose to go. If you want endless sunshine you should go to the Costa Brava or the South of France, not to the mountains of Austria or Germany. Where are we going tomorrow? I know it's in the brochure, but just remind me.'

'Well, we start with a leisurely tour of the Black Forest; the part where we're staying, near to Freiburg is said to be the loveliest of all. Then we stop at a shop that sells cuckoo clocks, and lots of other touristy things as well, so make sure you've got plenty of euros. And you'll see what is reputed to be the largest cuckoo clock in the world. Actually, there are a few of them in the area all claiming the same! Then we drive on to Lake Titisee – a silly name, I know – for a lunch stop, and then we'll spend a few hours there before returning home. You'll enjoy it, I'm sure, and if you'll allow me I'd like to show you round the lake area. Not the gift shop – you can browse round there on your own. I've seen enough cuckoo clocks to last me a lifetime!'

'What about Mike? Won't he mind being left on his own?'

'No, why should he? He'll probably stay in the coach after lunch and read a book, or have a nap. We're good mates, Mike and me; it's just as well when we're together such a lot. But we do our own thing when we want to. What we really need for tomorrow's outing is good weather, so we'd best cross our fingers and say a little prayer.'

As Bill was looking round for the waiter, to order a second drink, he saw another couple from the coach at the other side of the garden. They nodded and waved to him, and he and Christine waved back.

'That seems like another holiday friendship that's going well,' he remarked. 'Mrs Redfern and Mr Falconer. They've only met this week, at least that's what Mike and I think. We met them taking an evening stroll together in Rüdesheim the other night.'

'It was last night,' said Christine.

'Gosh, so it was! You tend to lose track of the days when you're dashing from one place to the other.'

'I noticed those two together,' said Christine, 'but I haven't spoken to them very much as yet, only to say hello. Perhaps by the end of the holiday we'll all have got to know one another, but with – how many is it? – thirty odd passengers, it takes time to recognize everyone.'

'Thirty-six, to be exact,' said Bill. 'That's one of the hardest things for us drivers, to recognize all the people from the coach. Especially with the older couples; they all tend to look alike, although we know that they don't, not really.'

He ordered another drink for each of them. True to his promise, he had orange juice, and Christine had the same. She wasn't, in fact, bothered about a second drink, but it was very pleasant sitting there in the twilight. She was enjoying being with Bill. He was an entertaining companion and they had not run out of things to talk about. She had decided – almost – that she would like to spend time with him this week. There could be no harm in it even if, at the end of the holiday, she decided she didn't want to see him again. On the other hand, he might want to call it a day.

Bill was hoping that he would continue to play his cards right. Christine seemed to be coming round to the idea of spending time with him this week. He didn't really know what it was about her that appealed to him. She was not what you might call beautiful, but she was very attractive. Fairish hair in a simple style framed a high forehead and a roundish face; her eyes were a sort of bluey-greyish colour. But when you got to know her there was nothing 'ish' or nondescript about her. She had a lovely smile and a gentle easy-to-listen-to voice. He decided she must be a very nice person because she liked dogs. He hoped she wasn't too obsessed with them, preferring them to human beings as some people said they did. He liked dogs, too, and cats, but his job had prevented him from ever owning one. Anyway, time would tell. He must be careful not to blow it, after such a promising start.

As they strolled back to the guest house he ventured to put an arm round her, and she did not object. When they were just a few yards away he stopped and put both arms around her.

'I'll kiss you goodnight here, if I may?' he said tentatively. 'Just in case there are nosy people around. May I, Christine?'

'Yes, of course you may,' she answered. He kissed her gently on the lips, then let her go. 'Thank you for a lovely evening,' he said.

'Thank you too, Bill,' she replied. 'I shall look forward to seeing you tomorrow.'

Bill gave a gasp, an inaudible one, he hoped, as they went through the door, he with his arm around her. There at the reception desk was Olga. She wasn't usually there at this time of night; in fact, he had never known her to be there. He realized that that was because she had always spent the evenings with him when the tour was staying there. Anyway, there she was now, handing out bedroom keys to the guests. Most people left them at reception as they were too heavy to carry about.

Bill withdrew his arm from Christine as she walked up to the desk. 'Room twenty-five, please,' she said, smiling at Olga. Bill, standing to one side, saw her hand the key to Christine. Olga was smiling, but it was a sardonic smile. She raised her eyebrows as she spoke to Christine.

She pointed towards Bill. 'I see that it did not take him long to find somebody else,' she said, in her almost perfect English. 'Let me warn you: that one, he has had me on a — how do you say it? — on a piece of string since last year. He will tell you all kinds of things, but you will be foolish if you believe them.'

Christine took the key without a word. She turned towards Bill. Her face was grim and her eyes like two grey stones as she hurried past him towards the stairs that led to the bedrooms.

'Christine . . . wait,' he called, hurrying after her. 'I'm sorry. I should have told you; I can explain . . .'

'You have already said quite enough!' She almost spat at him as she dashed up the stairs.

Bill opened the door of the room he was sharing with Mike. His mate was sitting up in bed, engrossed in one of his usual thrillers. Bill flopped down on the other bed, his usually cheerful face a picture of misery.

'I've gone and blown it,' he cried. 'What a bloody fool I am! And I really liked her, Mike. I really thought I was in with a chance.'

Mike put his book down and got out of bed. He was already clad in his pyjamas. 'I'll make us a nice cup of tea,' he said. 'Then you can tell Uncle Michael all about it.'

Ten

Mavis went to the window and opened the shutters. 'Another lovely morning,' she called.

'Arthur, are you listening? It's another nice day. Aren't we doing well?'

She looked out on a pleasing vista of fields and wooded hills, a blue sky with a few fluffy clouds, and the sun already shining at seven thirty in the morning.

All she got from Arthur was a grunt as he turned over in bed. He would come round, though, after his usual early-morning grumpiness. But by the time they had washed and dressed, had their usual morning 'cuppa' and were ready to go for breakfast she realized he was not himself. He was rubbing at his stomach.

'This damned indigestion again,' he said. 'Must have been those dumplings last night, and that roast pork. It was good, though, I must say that.'

'I told you not to eat them all,' said his wife. 'Like my mam used to say, your eyes are bigger than your belly when you see something you like.' She was pleased, though, that he was enjoying the food. He was enjoying everything about the holiday so far, despite being in Germany.

They dined with their usual companions. Jane and Dave were cheerful and happy. Ellen was rather quiet, and Shirley was looking a little downcast after her hilarity of the previous night and her vow not to let the matter of the suitcase bother her. She was, of course, dressed in the same clothes as she had worn the day before.

There was a good choice of breakfast food. Cereals, fruit, different kinds of bread and copious supplies of butter and jam. It looked like home-made jam – strawberry, raspberry and apricot – in glass bowls; far preferable to those pesky little cartons with the awkward tops that they served in hotels at home. There were slices of cold meat and cheese instead of the cooked breakfast of bacon and eggs that some of them might have preferred. But it was certain that no one should go hungry.

Mavis was pleased that Arthur ate sparingly, and after he had taken a couple of Rennies he said that he felt a lot better.

Shirley seemed fidgety and preoccupied. 'I'm going to have a word with Mike,' she said. 'I want to know when I'm likely to get my case back. I'm trying to be patient, but I want to know and that's that!'

'Oh dear!' said Ellen as her friend got up and marched resolutely to the table where the drivers were sitting. 'I do hope she gets a favourable answer.'

'Yes, so do I,' said Jane who was sitting next to her. She feared that Shirley's moods had an effect on her friend. She sympathized with Shirley, too, knowing how lost she would feel if all her belongings had gone astray. 'It's another lovely day, though,' she added. 'I'm sure we'll all enjoy the trip to the lake.'

'Shirley wants to find a shop that sells – you know – underwear,' Ellen whispered confidentially. 'I've lent her a couple of pairs, but it's something you need a lot of on holiday, isn't it?'

'Of course,' agreed Jane, trying not to smile. 'A pair for each day at least.'

Shirley was having an animated talk to the drivers, and when she returned to the table it was clear that she was not too happy.

'Saturday!' she exclaimed. 'Would you believe I can't get my case back till Saturday!'

'And today's Thursday,' said Ellen. 'It could be a lot worse. It's only two days, and at least they know that it's turned up in Austria, don't they?'

'Only two days!' Shirley was not mollified by her friend's remark. 'How would you like to wear the same things all day and all evening as well?'

'No one's bothered, though, about what you're wearing,' said Jane. 'They're all very sorry about what has happened. Why can't they do anything till Saturday?' she asked.

'Because of all these excursions,' retorted Shirley. 'And they've to fit in with the driver of the coach from Yorkshire; there's only one driver, apparently, and he can't get away any earlier. We've got a long trip today, and a long one tomorrow to Baden Baden. On Saturday we go to Freiburg which isn't very far. So Bill will take us there, and Herr Grunder has offered to lend Mike his car so that he can meet the other driver at a halfway point and swap over the cases.'

'That's very kind of the hotel owner, isn't it?' said Jane.

'Yes, I suppose so,' said Shirley a trifle grudgingly.

'And the lady in Austria – at least I assume it's a lady – she'll be in the same position as you, won't she?' Jane went on. 'She no doubt feels just as fed up as you do.'

'Yes, of course she will,' Shirley agreed. She gave a weak smile. 'Sorry I'm such a misery, I'll try to make the best of it, really I will. At least the sun's shining and that makes all the difference, doesn't it?'

They set off at nine thirty for a leisurely drive through the Black Forest. Bill was at the wheel with Mike giving the commentary. It was doubtful if anyone but the people concerned noticed that Bill was somewhat subdued, or that the lady who sat at the front of the coach did not speak to him – or he to her – as she sat down next to her sister.

Mike counted heads and they set off along a route which was one of the most beautiful in the area. At every turn in the road there was another eye-catching vista of the wooded hills and peaceful valleys. They passed rippling streams and waterfalls and an occasional mill wheel – still in use for providing electricity for the industry of the valley – beside a typical Black Forest house, the roof of which reached almost to the ground.

Mike told them they were driving along part of the route that was known as the German Clock road, passing more than thirty places where clocks were made.

They stopped mid-morning at one of the most renowned clock shops which boasted that it housed the largest cuckoo clock in the world. A middle-aged man clad in the form of national dress that was still worn in the country areas – dark green jacket and hat with a feather, knickerbockers and bright red socks – boarded the coach to tell them a little of the history of Black Forest clocks. His English was good, although no doubt well rehearsed after talking to countless visitors, such as themselves.

'We have been making these clocks for hundreds of years,' he told them, in the guttural voice common to so many of his race. 'Ever since the seventeenth century . . .' The clocks were carved by the peasants of the area who were always looking for ways to supplement their meagre income. At first they were simply carved wooden clocks, then, much later, a little house in the shape of a railway station was designed for the front of the clock. No one knows who first put the cuckoo in, but these were the first of the famous clocks that were now sold all over the world. Nowadays, not only cuckoo clocks were produced in the Black Forest, but all types of modern clocks and wristwatches.

'Now, all of you will come with me, please,' he said at the end of his talk, 'I will show you the front of our cuckoo clock, the largest one in the world.'

They followed him to the side of the shop to view the enormous clock with the hands standing at almost eleven o'clock. As they stood there out popped an enormous bird from its huge wooden house, 'cuckooing' eleven times.

'He measures one metre from his beak to his tail,' their guide told them. 'Now, if you follow me, please, I will take you into the shop.'

They entered the large store and were confronted with a display of fantasy and colour that had to be seen to be believed. It was a fairyland of delights from floor to ceiling; so much merchandise that at first they could only stand and stare.

'If you wish,' said their guide, 'you may come with me to see the mechanism of the large cuckoo clock. It is worth a few minutes of your time.'

It was mainly the men, and a few of the women, who accompanied him up the stairs. Most of the ladies wanted to spend as much time as possible amongst the tempting goods that were calling out, 'Come and buy me!' They did not need the company of the menfolk, especially the ones who might say, 'Good grief! Look at the price of that!' or, 'Come on, you don't really want that, do you?' No, they just needed a purse full of euros and time to indulge themselves to their heart's content.

The pre-eminent goods for sale were, of course, the clocks. Cuckoo clocks of all sizes, some quite garishly painted in bright colours, others of dark wood, intricately carved, and most of them ticking away merrily, a constant accompaniment to the voices of the shoppers. There were other kinds of clocks as well; small mantel clocks, kitchen clocks, and larger timepieces, even a few grandmother and grandfather clocks standing against the wall.

They all walked around, up and down the aisles, examining the price tags, pondering what they could afford to buy, or what to take home for a present for a friend or relative. Some of the articles were inexpensive trifles – souvenir pens and pencils, bookmarks, simple wooden toys or cheap pottery vases and mugs – costing only a few euros. But they were in the minority. Amongst the goods for the more discerning were wood carvings of peasant folk, animals – mainly bears – and birds; brightly painted wooden nutcrackers, bottle openers, screwdrivers, salt and pepper pots in the shape of comical characters; cute Hummel figures of children; calendars for the forthcoming year with glossy pictures of the region; dolls in national costume; wooden puppets; soft toy animals, mainly teddy bears, some with the Steiff button in the ear.

'Hello,' said a voice at Jane's ear. 'Are you enjoying yourself?' It was Dave who had been viewing the workings of the cuckoo clock. Some of the men had joined their wives now, others of them had gone outside for a smoke or a chat.

'Yes, I'm quite mesmerized,' replied Jane. 'There's such a lot to look at, most of it very tempting. You could easily spend a fortune – on things you don't really need!'

'That's the idea,' said Dave with a laugh. 'To make you part with your money. You have to treat yourself, though, sometimes . . . and I must buy something for my mother and my son and his fiancée.'

'Yes, so must I, for my mother,' said Jane. 'I've been looking at the cuckoo clocks, but I can imagine her saying that the cuckoo gets on her nerves, popping out every hour! So I've almost decided on a wood carving. There's one of a deer that I think she might like; it's quite small so she should be able to find a place for it. And I shall treat myself to a little carved bear. I like bears, although I know these are really very fierce in the wild. I much prefer teddy bears! And I'll get a calendar for next year; it'll bring back happy memories.'

'Yes, my mother would like a wood carving,' said Dave, 'and I'll get a cuckoo clock for my son and his fiancée . . . but that's not really very personal, is it, seeing that we all live together? Never mind; we can all enjoy it . . . I'll get a beer stein for Peter as well, and a little Steiff bear for Kathryn.'

They went their separate ways, each of them to choose their purchases. Jane took a little longer wandering around, deliberating about this and that. There was quite a long queue at the cash desk. Most of the people from the coach – mainly the women – were carrying one of the store's baskets containing several items. The lady assistant packaged all the goods up very neatly, placing them in a distinctive carrier bag, along with a picture postcard of the cuckoo clock as a thank-you token.

Dave was waiting for her. He smiled as he handed her a bag. 'A little present for you. As you said about the calendar, it will bring back happy memories.'

'Oh, Dave . . . thank you so much!' she exclaimed. She almost said, 'You really shouldn't,' then she realized it was something he wanted to do – because he liked her? – and she must accept the gift gratefully. She peeped inside the bag, and there was a little Steiff bear with golden fur and a blue satin bow round his neck.

'Oh . . . how lovely!' She was almost crying with delight, and she wanted to put her arms round him and kiss him – they had exchanged a few kisses by this time – but of course she didn't do so.

'I'm glad you like it,' he said. 'I got one for Kathryn as well.'

Mike and Bill had come into the shop and were talking to the lady at the till.

'They'll be sorting out their commission,' whispered Dave. 'They'll get a small percentage for everything we buy. One of their perks, but you can't blame them . . .'

They all stood outside for a few moments enjoying the sunshine. Mavis had a bulging carrier bag.

'I thought she was going to buy up the whole shop!' said Arthur. 'Not that I mind what she spends if she enjoys it.' He chuckled. 'She deserves it for putting up with me!'

'How's your indigestion?' asked Jane. Arthur was not one to suffer in silence, and they had all known of his discomfort. 'Much better, thanks,' he replied. 'I'm looking forward to my lunch. I had hardly any breakfast.'

Shirley and Ellen were both holding carrier bags. Shirley looked far happier than she had been earlier. 'I've bought a couple of colourful scarves,' she said, 'They'll add a touch of glamour to my top, till I get my case back. I was looking at the sweaters, but they're not my sort of thing, far too countrified and homespun. Anyway, it's too hot for jumpers.

'And we've each treated ourselves to a little teddy bear, haven't we, Shirley?' said Ellen, as excitedly as a little girl.

'We have indeed,' replied Shirley. 'Steiff ones, no less!'

Jane smiled to herself. It seemed that all women liked teddy bears, even the sophisticated Shirley. Dave was not near them – he was talking in a group of men a little distance away – so she could not resist telling them.

'I've got one as well!' she said, a little coyly. 'Dave bought it for me.'

'Oh, isn't that nice!' said Ellen. 'You must be thrilled. You're getting on very well with him, aren't you?' she whispered.

'I think so,' said Jane, wondering already if she'd said too much. 'We'll see. It's early days yet . . .'

'All aboard,' called Mike coming out of the shop. They all climbed on the coach and stacked their carrier bags containing their purchases in the compartments above the seats.

Mike sat down behind the wheel to take his turn at driving, and Bill did a quick count of heads. 'Two missing,' he remarked. 'It's not surprising, though; it's a very tempting place to linger. They'll soon realize everyone else has gone.'

He knew who was missing. It was Christine and her sister from the front seat. They appeared after a couple of minutes. 'Sorry, everyone,' called Christine as she boarded the coach.

'No, it was my fault,' added Norma. 'I got into a muddle with my euros.'

'Never mind, it's easily done, love,' said Bill. 'We'll forgive you, won't we, Mike?'

'Sure,' said Mike. 'We'd better get moving though now, ladies and gents. We want to get to the lake in good time.'

Christine and Bill were forced to exchange glances now. He half smiled at her as her sister settled down in the seat by the window.

'I hope I'm forgiven, too?' he said, leaning down to speak to her. 'It's all over with me and Olga, really it is. If you'll let me explain . . .'

Christine nodded. 'OK,' she said briefly. 'See you later.'

What the heck! she thought. The chances were that it wouldn't come to anything with Bill, but she had enjoyed his company so far, so why not continue to do so? By the time they had arrived at their destination, the oddly named Lake Titisee, she had decided to give Bill a chance to explain if that was what he wanted to do, but not to let herself get too involved. She had been happy enough recently with just her faithful friend Monty for company, and had not even considered embarking upon another relationship. On the other hand, she did not want to turn into a 'doggie' person, a middle-aged spinster with only a canine companion. Bill had seemed amazed on finding she owned a dog parlour. She must try to rediscover her more human and feminine side.

Mike stopped the coach a little way above the village at the spot where he would pick them up again in three hours' time. So they had ample time to shop and browse, to enjoy a meal, or even to stroll all the way round the lake if they wished to do so, which would take about an hour and a half.

There was a chilly wind blowing when the passengers alighted from the coach. The lake was situated some 850 metres above sea level and the air was fresh and keen. The road which led down to the small resort of Titisee Neustadt became more crowded the nearer one got to the lakeside. There were shops and cafes aplenty, most of which catered for the tourist trade. Here were cuckoo clocks, wood carvings and souvenir items such as they had already seen in the home of the largest cuckoo clock, but many of these were of an inferior quality. It was an appealing street in spite of the touristy overtones which, for some, only added to the holiday atmosphere. The women lingered to stare into shop windows whilst the menfolk strode ahead.

There was a pleasant lakeside promenade and a landing stage from which pleasure boats left for a trip round the lake. There were a few brave souls swimming near to the edge of the lake, and further out a few waterskiers and yachts sailing in what appeared to be calm waters.

They were feeling peckish by that time. It was ages since breakfast time, but there was no shortage of eating places to choose from; posh and no doubt expensive hotels down to kiosks selling hamburgers and different kinds of wurst. (They soon recognized that the word meant sausage.)

All the lakeside cafes had their menus prominently displayed. You could dine inside away from the crowds or outside under a colourful umbrella that provided a shade from the midday sun. The problem was knowing which place to choose. There were so many serving identical dishes – bratwurst, goulash, Black Forest ham, pork with the inevitable dumplings – so how could you tell which of them had the best chef?

'You find that the busiest ones are usually the best,' Mavis remarked to Arthur. 'If there's hardly anyone there it might be a sign that the food's not up to much.'

'Well, for goodness' sake, let's sit down somewhere,' groaned Arthur. 'My belly thinks my throat's cut! I'm famished. It's ages since breakfast, and how can I keep going on a bit of bread and jam?'

'Now, you know you couldn't eat anything else. You had that bad indigestion,' Mavis reminded him.

'Well, it's gone now. Let's go in here or we'll be wandering around all day.'

'Yes, there's a table by the window, and it's nice and quiet inside.' There was a goodly number dining outside and the food looked appetizing.

The table was covered with a green and white checked cloth, and the waitress, who handed them the large menu, wore a green dirndl skirt and a white peasant-style blouse embroidered with green flowers and leaves.

'It's all in German,' said Arthur, but Mavis pointed out that the English was written in italics at the side.

'Now, nothing too heavy, Arthur,' she told him. 'You may well be hungry but there'll be a big meal tonight.'

They settled on a platter of cold meats including the Black Forest ham – which lived up to its reputation of being the best in the country – served with a simple salad of lettuce and tomatoes tossed in oil, and crisp bread rolls and butter. Arthur would have preferred his usual Heinz salad cream, but said he was comfortably full again after his meal and a half of lager.

They were not the only ones from the coach who had decided to lunch there. There was a couple whose names they didn't know who waved to them from across the other side of the room. Then Mavis noticed Bill sitting down at a table outside. But he wasn't on his own, nor was he with Mike. He was with that young lady who sat on the front seat, right next to him.

'Look, Arthur,' she said. 'There's Bill, over there, see. And he's with that nice young lady who sits at the front of the coach. It looks as though there's something going on there.'

'Don't stare at them, Mavis. It's nothing to do with us, whatever they get up to.'

'No, perhaps not, but I like to know what's going on.'

'You mean you're just nosy!'

'No, I'm not. I'm . . . interested, that's all. Jane mentioned to me at breakfast time that she and Dave had seen the two of them last night – Bill and that lady, whatever she's called. They were having a drink at a wine bar in the village.'

'Well, good luck to them then,' said Arthur. 'I dare say it'll just be a holiday fling. Coach drivers have quite a reputation for that sort of thing. Let's hope the lass has got her head screwed on the right way.'

'Oh, I think today's young women are a lot wiser about the ways of the world than we were,' replied Mavis, 'I wouldn't like her to get hurt, though. She seems a nice young woman. Bill seems a pleasant sort of fellow, too. I saw that receptionist, Olga, smiling at him when we arrived, and I thought it looked as though they might be . . . well, friendly, you know. I hope he's not playing fast and loose with the pair of them.'

'For heaven's sake, Mavis, give it a rest!' said Arthur. 'I've told you, it's nothing to do with us. Now, have you finished eating, or do you want a piece of that Black Forest cake?'

'Gateau . . . No, I don't think so, Arthur. It's very tempting, but it'll be coming out of our ears by the time we get home if we eat much more of it. Let's have a coffee to finish off with.

It's very pleasant here watching the world go by. Then we'll have a nice stroll by the lake. We're having a lovely holiday, aren't we, Arthur? Aren't you glad we came to Germany?'

'Maybe I am,' he replied, a trifle grudgingly. 'The hotel's OK, and the food, and we've seen some nice views of mountains and what have you. But I don't know about the folk, I haven't made up my mind yet. I think they have long memories; they can't forget that we won the war.'

It was Mavis's turn then to tell Arthur to shut up. She caught the waitress's eye and ordered two coffees. Arthur gave her a sheepish look. He knew by the set of her mouth that she was annoyed with him. But she would come round. She always did.

Outside on the terrace, Bill and Christine were studying the menu; at least Christine was doing so. Bill had decided that he would have Weisswurst.

'What on earth is that?' she asked. With her limited German she could work out what the word meant. 'White sausage?' she queried. 'It sounds awful. Is it really white?'

'You'll see when it arrives,' said Bill. 'What about you? Do you want to try some?'

Christine grimaced. 'No, thanks! I'll stick to the normal bratwurst, and just a few chips, or whatever they call them here.'

'*Pommes frites*, the same as in France.'

When the meals arrived, however, there were more than just a few chips. When the waitress had gone, Christine looked at the Weisswurst and shuddered.

'That looks disgusting!' she said.

Bill laughed. 'It's an acquired taste, but I've got used to it. It's a dish from Munich, really.'

The fat white sausages, made from veal had been brought to the table in a tureen of hot water. They were flecked inside with parsley, and were eaten with sweet grainy mustard. Christine watched as Bill slit the sausage along the middle, separating the edible meat from the skin.

'Don't you eat the skin?' she asked. 'We always do at home, don't we? And our sausages are pink or pale brown.'

'It's really very tasty,' he told her. 'No, you don't eat the skin. Another way to eat it is to open one end and suck out the contents. That's what the locals do, but I'll use a knife and fork.'

He laughed at her bemused expression. They had made up their differences now and were enjoying one another's company.

'I should have told you about Olga,' he had said. 'I had decided to finish it before I met you. I thought she would agree that there's no future in it. But . . . you saw how she reacted when she saw me with you.'

'And I can't say I blame her,' said Christine. 'I'll spend some time with you this week, Bill. But nothing too heavy, eh? And then we'll see.'

'Suits me,' replied Bill; but he was finding that he liked her more and more.

Everyone agreed on boarding the coach a couple of hours later that they had enjoyed the day immensely. Shirley was still feeling cross, though, as she hadn't been able to find a shop that sold underwear, let alone any decent clothing. Surely the German women had to buy knickers and bras?

'They probably do their clothes shopping in Freiburg,' said Ellen patiently. 'We're going there on Saturday, and we're going to Baden Baden tomorrow. There's sure to be a large store there that sells panties. Until then I'll lend you two more pairs,' she whispered. And with that, Shirley had to be content.

Mike put on a tape of well-known German songs as they drove back, and those who didn't doze off joined in with the singing of 'Valderee, Valderah . . .' The holiday was going well.

Eleven

The dining room was filled with the noise of excited chatter as the folk of the coach party discussed the events of the day with their table companions. It seemed as though they had known one another for ages although it was really only four days. Some, maybe, would form a friendship, exchange addresses and send a card or letter at Christmas. For others it would just be a holiday acquaintanceship, good while it lasted, but receding to the back of the mind when they were home again. Mike and Bill agreed that they were a good crowd this week; passengers that seemed to 'gel' and get along well together.

'Sounds like a bloomin' aviary in here,' Arthur commented. 'All these women chattering away like budgerigars.'

'Not only the women, Arthur,' his wife reminded him. 'The men are doing their fair share. Now, it's veal cutlets tonight for the main course, according to the menu. You'll be alright with that, so long as you go easy on the dumplings.'

'Oh, I'll be fine. Stop fussing, Mavis. That onion soup was watery. I'm ready for something more substantial.'

The veal was tender and very palatable; small cutlets in breadcrumbs served with noodles and pickled cabbage. Arthur pushed the cabbage to one side.

'Can't say I'm right keen on that. Why can't they serve it like you do? Spring cabbage with nice tasty gravy.'

'It's called sauerkraut, Arthur. Not entirely to my liking either, but you know what they say. "When in Rome . . .'''

'Aye, but we're in Germany, aren't we?' He sat back in his chair, and Mavis noticed that he winced and put his hand to his stomach.

'What's the matter?' she asked. 'Have you got that pain again?'

'Just a twinge, that's all. I've told you not to fuss. I'll just sit quietly and happen it'll go away.'

Mavis looked at him anxiously. His face was pale, almost

ashen. He sat motionless and closed his eyes as the waitress cleared away the plates.

'You'd better not have the pudding,' Mavis whispered to him. 'It's pancakes and they'll be rather indigestible. What about a little portion of ice cream?'

'No, I don't want anything,' he mumbled, as he suddenly clasped at his stomach and fell forward on to the table, knocking over a couple of glasses and making the cutlery jingle. The sound of that and of his groan of agony silenced the people on the nearby table.

Mavis sprang to her feet. 'Help him! Please help him, somebody . . .'

Dave was at his side at once, and a man from the next table. Mike and Bill were soon at the scene and together they lifted Arthur and carried him out of the dining room into the lounge area. They laid him on a settee. His face was deathly pale but he was still breathing, in strangled gasps, as he struggled to get air into his lungs.

Mike rushed to the reception desk where Olga, fortunately, was still on duty. 'An ambulance,' he told her. 'Ring the hospital, Olga. Quickly, please. A man has collapsed. It looks like a heart attack.'

Mavis sat at her husband's side, holding on to his hand. 'Arthur, I'm here with you. You're going to be alright . . .'

He could not speak to her. He looked at her pleadingly, then closed his eyes again, still gasping and struggling for breath.

'I should have known it was more than indigestion,' she whispered to Dave. 'He's having a heart attack, isn't he? Oh, dear God! Why didn't I realize what was the matter with him?'

'You couldn't have known,' said Dave. 'The symptoms are so similar. Mike's rung for an ambulance so you won't have long to wait. See . . . he looks a little easier now; he's stopped gasping for breath.'

Arthur was laid full length on the settee with cushions supporting his head. His eyes had closed and it seemed as though he had lost consciousness.

'He's not . . . he's not gone, has he?' Mavis murmured. 'Oh God, please don't let him die . . .'

Dave took hold of Arthur's wrist, feeling for a pulse. 'No,' he said. 'There's a pulse there, and it looks as though the spasm, or whatever it was, has passed. We're all here with you, Mavis, all your new friends.'

The rest of the people from the table – Jane, Shirley and Ellen – had come into the lounge. It would have been unfeeling to eat the dessert course; besides, they had all lost their appetites. The rest of the company carried on as normal with the delicious raisin pancakes in lemon sauce, but the hubbub in the room had dropped to a murmur.

It seemed a long time as they waited for the ambulance, but it was really only ten minutes before the two men hurried into the hotel with a stretcher and blankets. They talked together quietly as they examined Arthur, then they lifted him on to the stretcher, fitted an oxygen mask to his face and covered him with a red blanket.

One of the men spoke to Mavis. 'You are his wife, ya?'

'Yes, I'm Mrs Johnson,' she replied. 'You're taking him to hospital?'

'Ya . . . We will take good care of him. Frau Johnson, you come with us, please? Come with your husband. We take him to hospital, in Freiburg.'

'Oh . . . oh yes, of course. I didn't realize . . .'

'Yes, you go along with him, Mrs Johnson,' said Mike. 'He'll be in good hands there. And they'll see that you get back safely, or one of us will come and get you. Try not to worry too much.'

Jane and Dave and the two drivers went with the little party as Arthur was carried outside into the waiting ambulance. Mavis climbed into the back looking scared and bewildered, but she smiled and waved bravely to them as the vehicle drove away.

'What a shock!' said Jane as she and Dave sat down in the lounge. They had missed the pudding but there was no point in going without the coffee as well. 'How awful for this to happen on their holiday. They were enjoying it so much. Oh dear! It casts a gloom over everything, doesn't it? And it was all so lovely . . .'

Dave took hold of her hand. 'Let's hope for the best,' he said. 'At least he was still breathing. My father died of a heart attack. It was very sudden, just like it was with Arthur. But Dad had gone, straight away. There was nothing anyone could do. It was a tremendous shock for us all. I don't know, of course, but I should think there's every chance that Arthur will recover.'

There was no longer the happy chatter that there had been earlier in the evening. There was a far more subdued atmosphere in the lounge. Little groups sat together talking quietly, a few playing cards, and others reading a book or magazine.

Shirley and Ellen joined Dave and Jane, all of them concerned about Arthur but trying to look on the bright side.

'I'll tell you something,' said Shirley in a thoughtful, almost penitent voice. 'I'm feeling quite ashamed of myself. Making all that fuss because I have to wear the same clothes for a few days! Whatever must you think of me?'

'We understand,' said Jane, reaching over and patting her hand. 'The women do at any rate. We all like to look our best, don't we, wearing the nice new things we've bought for our holiday? But I do know what you mean. Something like this puts our own little problems into perspective, doesn't it?'

'Yes, that's what I meant,' said Shirley. 'Poor Arthur! And Mavis, too. She thinks the world of him, doesn't she? You can tell she does.'

'And he of her,' added Ellen. 'Such a nice old couple; though I'm sure they don't think of themselves as old.'

'No, and it's a lesson for all of us,' said Dave, 'to make the most of the time we've been given. Seize the moment. You never know what's round the next corner.'

Jane was aware of Dave looking at her, and they exchanged a brief and rather sad smile. Shirley and Ellen left them before long, both deciding they would go to their rooms and read. It wasn't long before the other two decided that they would do the same.

'I'll go and read my adventure story,' said Dave. 'It might help to take my mind off things.'

'And I'm in the middle of a Maeve Binchy,' said Jane. 'A nice comforting read.'

He kissed her fondly as they said goodnight at her bedroom door, and she clung to him for a moment.

'Try not to worry,' he told her. 'There's nothing we can do . . . except to say a little prayer. And I'm sure we'll have a lovely day again tomorrow. Goodnight, Jane . . . my dear.'

It was after eleven thirty when Mavis arrived back from the hospital. The staff there had been very kind to her and had sent her back in one of their smaller vehicles as there was a temporary lull at that time.

The hotel was in darkness apart from one light shining in the reception area. Fortunately she had her key with her, and she crept along the corridor towards her room at the far end. Then she stopped in her tracks. She didn't feel like going into an empty room, not just yet. Surprisingly she was wide awake, not tired by the events of the day, and relieved, of course, that there was now slightly more encouraging news of Arthur. It would be good to have a chat with someone, and perhaps a cup of tea before turning in for the night.

Jane! She would go upstairs and see if Jane was not yet in bed. She had told Mavis that she sat up late reading before going to sleep. Jane's room was on the first floor. There was, in fact, only one floor above the ground level. The light was on a time switch, allowing only just enough time to climb the stairs before you were plunged into darkness again. Jane's room, too, was at the end of the corridor, and Mavis hurried along before the light went out again. Everything was dead quiet and a little eerie with no one around. There was a fanlight above each door, so you could tell whether the occupant was still up or had gone to bed.

Good. There was still a light shining in room thirty-two; Mavis had noticed the number on Jane's gigantic key. She lifted her hand to knock, then she hesitated. Supposing Jane was not alone? Supposing . . . Dave was with her? She knew that the couple were getting very friendly, and she had seen the way they looked at one another. Unless she was very much mistaken the two of them were falling in love. They had known one another for only four days, but feelings could be heightened in the free and easy holiday atmosphere. And who could blame them if . . .

Mavis prided herself on being broad-minded. She had a

daughter a few years older than Jane, happily married, fortunately, and a son two years older who had been married, divorced, then married again. So she had been with them in their various joys and sorrows. She guessed though, that Jane was a very circumspect sort of woman and would not commit herself until she was very sure.

The corridor light went out, and she decided to take a chance. She knocked at the door. A moment or two passed before she heard the sound of quiet footsteps. Then the door opened just a fraction and a nervous voice whispered, 'Who is it?'

'It's me . . . Mavis,' she answered. 'Sorry if I'm disturbing you, but your light was on and I felt as though I needed to talk to someone before—'

'Oh . . . Mavis, of course!' Jane interrupted as she opened the door fully. She was wearing a pretty pink housecoat and matching slippers. 'Come on in. I was startled for a moment, wondering who it was. Anyway, how is Arthur? That's the important thing.'

'He's recovering quite well, at least that's what I'm trying to tell myself,' said Mavis as she entered the room. Then she suddenly burst into tears. Jane put an arm round her and guided her across to the bed, where they sat down.

'Oh, Jane, I'm so sorry,' she began. 'It's been such a worry and I've been trying to be brave. I thought he was dying, really I did.'

'But he's getting better?' Jane asked encouragingly. 'He's come round now, has he?'

'Yes, he regained consciousness when we got to the hospital. He recognized me, but he didn't speak. It was a heart attack, like I thought. Well, I thought it was just bad indigestion at first. We'd no idea that Arthur had a bad heart. He's had palpitations in the past, and his blood pressure is high at times; he takes tablets for that. But we never expected this.'

'He's in the best place now,' said Jane. 'And they've let you come home . . . well, come back here. It's not home – no doubt you wish you were there – but you've got friends around you here. They must be satisfied with his progress.'

'Yes, he's in intensive care at the moment, or whatever they call it here, and he'll have to stay in hospital for a few more days. We'll have to take a day at a time with regard to the holiday and everything. I shall go back there and stay with him tomorrow; they said it didn't matter about sticking to visiting hours. I can be there with him till we see how things go. I'm afraid we've rather spoilt the holiday for everyone, haven't we?'

'We're all very concerned,' said Jane. 'And they'll all be pleased that Arthur's recovering. Now, Mavis; how about a cup of tea?'

'That would be lovely,' she replied, 'if you're sure it's not too late for you?'

'I was on the last chapter of my Maeve Binchy,' said Jane. 'That's why I was up late. I'll finish reading it tomorrow. I'm ready for another cuppa now.'

Mavis stayed a little while with Jane, until they both realized that they were trying to suppress their yawns. It had been a long and eventful day, especially for Mavis. She kissed Jane on the cheek as she said goodnight, as though she was an old friend.

'May I ask, do you go to church?' she enquired. Jane replied that she did, not all the time, but that she did believe in God.

'Would you say a little prayer, then, for Arthur?' asked Mavis. 'I believe that it might help.' Jane assured her that she would do so, straightaway, before she got into bed.

Mavis switched on the corridor light and made her way along the passage and down the stairs to her own room. Whatever had happened – or was still to happen – on this holiday, she felt that she had made a few good friends, ones that she hoped would stand the test of time.

Twelve

Mavis was touched and overwhelmed at breakfast time the following morning by the enquiries about Arthur. Almost everyone from the coach came to ask about him and send their good wishes. And at the end of the meal Mike gave her a 'Get Well' card signed by them all, to take to him. She guessed that this sort of thing had happened before, a passenger being taken ill and rushed into hospital. It was a very thoughtful gesture that she appreciated and she knew that Arthur would, as well.

She hoped that what she was telling them all – that he had come round and was recovering nicely – was true, and that he hadn't had a relapse during the night. She would know soon enough; she would be returning to the hospital in a little while, while the rest of the company prepared for the day's excursion to the spa town of Baden Baden.

Mavis was pleasantly surprised when Herr Grunder, the proprietor, offered to run her to the hospital. She had intended taking a taxi, but he insisted on taking her. It was above and beyond the call of duty, and very kind of him. Everyone was being so kind and thoughtful. She hoped that Arthur might be changing his mind about this country and its inhabitants.

The trip to Baden Baden would be the longest excursion of the week, and so the coach party set off at the rather earlier time of nine o'clock. It was some seventy miles away – or 110 kilometres, if you had got used to the metric calculation – and it was hoped that they would arrive in time for lunch, after a morning coffee stop en route.

Bill was at the wheel, and the now seasoned travellers settled back comfortably in their seats. Mike gave the commentary as they drove along. Most of them listened, especially if they wished to learn and – hopefully – remember as much as they could about their holiday. Others dozed off after a little while, but not really because they were tired. The motion of the coach had a soporific effect.

They were travelling northwards along the route which led, eventually, to France and Switzerland. The spa town was situated in the most northerly foothills of the Black Forest.

'Baden Baden is so good they named it twice, like New York!' said Mike.

He told them that it had originally been know just as Baden, but had been given its double name later partly because it was the town of Baden in the state of Baden Wurtenburg but also to distinguish it from other towns with the same name: Baden near Vienna and Baden in Switzerland.

It had long been a celebrated resort visited by the rich and famous, partly for health reasons – its hot springs had been known about since Roman times – but also because it was the popular place to be, the premier European capital of pleasure in the nineteenth and early twentieth centuries. Queen Victoria had stayed there. So had her son Edward the Seventh, lured there by his love of horse racing and gambling at its famous casino, and by his pursuit of lovely ladies!

Kaiser Wilhelm, and the Emperor Napoleon, had stayed there too; the composers Berlioz and Brahms; and several of the Russian writers. Tolstoy's novel, *Anna Karenina*, had been set partly in Baden Baden, although it had been given a different name in the story.

Jane, listening to the commentary, thought to herself that that was one of the books that she had always intended to read, but had never got round to it. It was not so much the length of it that had put her off, but the unfamiliarity of the Russian names. She found her mind wandering a little until Mike started to tell them of the attractions of the town and the places of interest.

'You ladies will think you're in Wonderland today,' he said. 'I hope you haven't spent all your euros, although credit cards are very acceptable, of course, provided you don't get carried away. I'm rather glad my wife isn't here! You'll find shops there to rival those in London or Paris; boutiques and jewellers and antique shops, whatever takes your fancy.' He laughed. 'Bill and I will be heading for one of the taverns. Not to drink, I assure you – you know our strict rule about that – but to have a jolly good meal. You'll find plenty of eating places to suit every pocket. I know you're all going to have a great day. Now, I'll shut up for a while and let you enjoy the scenery.'

He put on a tape of 'easy listening' music, some of the lighter pieces by Beethoven, Brahms and Mozart.

Shirley, also, started to listen intently when Mike told them about the shops in Baden Baden. She nudged her friend.

'Did you hear that, Ellen? It sounds as though it might be my lucky day, that is if what he says is true. We've seen nothing so far that I'd look at twice.'

'Yes, I heard what Mike said,' replied Ellen resignedly. Thank goodness for that, she thought to herself, for something to put a smile back on Shirley's face. They had both been pleased to hear the news about Arthur, but Ellen knew that it still niggled at Shirley and hurt her pride that she was unable to look her best each day in her smart holiday clothes.

'We'll have a good browse round the shops, Shirley,' she assured her. 'I might even treat myself if I can find something that I like.'

'To wear, you mean?'

'Yes, why not? I rather like the nice trousers and tops that some of the ladies wear. I've never really liked to wear trousers. My father used to say that they weren't for women; that trousers were only for men.' She chuckled. 'What he really meant, of course, was that he had to be the only one in the house to wear the trousers!'

'Very true,' agreed Shirley. 'Your father ruled the roost, didn't he? And you and your mother had to toe the line, if I remember rightly. You were a good obedient daughter, Ellen. I know jolly well that I'd have rebelled; but it's time for you to please yourself now. We can't live in the past, none of us.'

'Yes, I'm realizing that,' said Ellen. 'We're having a good time, aren't we? We were all upset about Arthur, and it's hard to go on enjoying yourself when someone else is in trouble. There's not much we can do, but I said a little prayer for him . . .'

Shirley smiled at her fondly. 'You're a saint, Ellen.'

'No, I'm not!' her friend retorted. 'Far from it. I had some very un-Christian thoughts about my father sometimes, and my mother, too, for kowtowing to him like she did. But I knew that I mustn't upset them . . . I know I'll never get married, not now,' she added in a whisper. 'That was something I really wanted at one time, but my father disapproved of the young man I liked. But I've got used to being single now, and I'm quite happy with it.'

'Why shouldn't you be?' Shirley laughed. 'Who needs men, anyway?'

It seemed a long way to their destination. They had a brief stop after a couple of hours, what Mike called a coffee and comfort stop, then arrived at Baden Baden at twelve o'clock.

'Now, we have a nice long stay here,' he told them. 'Be back at the coach for half past four, and please try to be on time. I've arranged for us to have our dinner a little later tonight, so that we can make the most of our day here.'

He showed them the way to the town through the Kurhaus gardens, a place where they could linger on the way back. They were all anxious, though, at the moment, to get to the town to have a meal and to savour the delights of the shops, particularly so for the ladies.

'You won't want to spend all day with me,' Jane said, tactfully, to Dave. 'I remember how my husband used to get bored with the shops after so long. I'll stay with Shirley and Ellen, if that's OK with you?'

'That's fine with me,' Dave assured her. 'I shall find some antique shops to browse around, or book shops. I may not understand the language, but they usually sell all sorts of other things as well. You go and have a good time with the ladies.'

Christine also had a word with Bill. 'You spend today with Mike,' she told him, 'and I'll go with my sister and our new friends. I'm sure boutiques and jewellers are not much in your line. I'll see you later tonight . . . that is, if you still want to?'

'Of course,' replied Bill. 'Off you go and spend your money. We'll have a drink together after dinner.' They had been getting along well together since they had sorted out the problem with Olga. The receptionist seemed to have got the message now, and Bill had to accept that she was ignoring him. He would have preferred them to part more amicably, but he knew that he had only himself to blame. He might, unwittingly, have given her false hopes. He decided that he must not make the same mistake with Christine. It must be one girl at a time from now on for Bill. He had a feeling that this one might well be the right one for him.

Jane had decided at the outset that she must not be too 'clingy' with regard to Dave. Besides, she would welcome a day with 'the girls'. She suggested to Shirley and Ellen that she might spend the day with them, if they didn't mind, and they seemed delighted at the idea.

Dave walked on ahead, catching up with Mike and Bill. There didn't appear to be any other men on the coach tour who were on their own; but Jane was sure that Dave was the sort of man who would not be bored with his own company.

The extensive gardens of the Kurhaus housed the famous casino and conference centre which attracted people from all over the world. They walked through tree-lined avenues and flower beds ablaze with colour at the start of the summer season. Those that were able walked at a fast pace to reach the town and find a place to eat.

Baden Baden did not disappoint them. It was a mixture of the old and the new. There were wide streets with all kinds of modern shops, whilst the old town was a maze of picturesque cobbled streets and narrow lanes. There were exclusive boutiques, and small quaint shops selling all manner of things – jewellery, antiques and other 'collectibles', second-hand books, handmade chocolates, perfumes and body lotions – as well as bistros and taverns, and cafes with seating both inside and out.

Shirley had to be discouraged from stopping and staring in every shop window.

'Lunch first,' the other two told her. 'We'll come back afterwards,' said Jane. 'If we start shopping we'll have no time to eat.'

Shirley was reluctantly steered away from a very tempting boutique. 'I only hope we can find it again later,' she said, as they walked up one little lane and down another. 'We must try and remember where it is.'

'I feel it might be rather expensive anyway,' remarked Ellen, 'and there are plenty of other shops in the modern part of the town.'

'It depends on what you want to buy,' said Shirley, with a longing glance at an emerald green trouser suit at the front of a shop window. There was no price ticket on it, though, which was sure to mean that she couldn't afford it.

She sighed. 'OK then, girls. Lunch first, as you say. Look, there's a place over there that looks promising. Let's go and see, or we'll be wandering around all day.'

The bistro looked clean – which was an important consideration – and inviting, with gaily patterned tablecloths and attractive menu cards with the items written in English and French as well as German. There were several people dining there which, again, was a good sign, but there was still plenty of room.

They opted to go inside rather than dine out on the street as the pavement was not very wide and the streets were crowded. They chose a table by the window, then pored over the menu. There was an extensive range, as there seemed to be in all these places, but their choice was simple. Pizzas for each of them, though with different toppings, sprinkled liberally with Parmesan cheese, accompanied with a drink of fresh orange juice.

They decided against a sweet, as the pizzas were enormous, and they would, no doubt stop for refreshment again later in the afternoon. They did, however, have coffee to end the meal, strong and fragrant, such as they rarely had at home, but to which they were becoming familiar. It was a pick-me-up that was favoured on the Continent more so than in the UK. When they had sorted out the bill and worked out how much the tip should be, they set off for their afternoon shopping spree.

Closer scrutiny of the garments in the boutique windows proved that the prices were way out of their range, so they decided – reluctantly on Shirley's part – not to venture inside the little shops. They bought some handmade chocolates, though, for themselves, and some as a little treat for Mavis, from the three of them. It was such a shame that she was missing today's trip and would, possibly, have to forgo the other excursions as well.

They fared better – as Ellen, in her practical way had suggested they might – in the larger shops in the more modern

part of the town. There were numerous shops there selling
ladies clothing, and Shirley was forced to admit that she had
been wrong. The clothes were not of a fuddy-duddy style,
suitable for German hausfraus. They were, in the main, very
stylish and modern.

Besides being able to replenish her stock of necessary underwear, Shirley, as was only to be expected, had a whale of a
time.

'Go steady, you'll get your suitcase back tomorrow, won't
you?' Ellen reminded her. But she took little notice. She was
like a child in a sweet shop.

When their shopping spree was finished she had bought a
pair of flared trousers in royal blue, and two snazzy tops, one
striped and one with polka dots that would go well with the
trousers. Also, a floaty chiffon skirt in pastel shades, a pair of
high-heeled blue sandals, and a blue and white shoulder bag
that was suitable for day or evening wear.

'Now, come along, Ellen,' she kept urging her friend. 'You
said you wanted some trousers. I'll help you to choose them.'

Ellen could not be persuaded to buy flared ones. She
preferred the straight style, and the others admitted that they
suited her better. She felt she was being extravagant as she was
coaxed, though not unwillingly, into buying two pairs, one in
navy blue and the other in fawn. She bought two pretty tops
as well, not as bold as the ones her friend had chosen, but in
colours that she liked, lemon and coral pink.

'And for heaven's sake, ditch those old-fashioned cardigans
of yours,' Shirley told her, 'and buy a nice smart jacket.'

She did as she was bid, choosing an edge-to-edge terylene
jacket which, she told herself, was a serviceable colour and would
go with most things. Never had she spent so much money all
in one day. Never had she used her credit card so much. Her
parents had paid for everything in cash, with the occasional
cheque, and she had always done the same. She was surprised
that she did not feel guilty, but she knew she had money in the
bank to cover the expense. She knew she must watch herself,
though, and be careful not to turn into a spendthrift.

Jane, not to be outdone, treated herself as well. She enjoyed
watching her new friends choosing their clothes. She didn't

very often have the chance to go shopping for clothing, and when she did she invariably went to her favourite store, Marks and Spencer, or to Debenhams.

With Shirley's help she chose a floral dress in a silky fabric, in shades of green and blue, ankle-length with elbow-length sleeves – she did not like to show too much bare arm – and a neckline that was not too low. 'For those special occasions,' as Shirley told her.

There had not been too many of those recently, but Jane was hopeful that there might be in the future. She also bought some green summer sandals and a bag to match. Then she decided that that was enough; but she couldn't remember when she had enjoyed a shopping expedition so much.

Mike and Bill invited Dave to join them for lunch in a little place they knew of near to the main square of the town. It was a tavern, rather than a restaurant, with subdued lighting and wood panelled walls, giving it a more masculine feel. They assured him that the food, and the drink, too, was excellent, although the two drivers restricted themselves to a small glass of lager each, then went on to apple juice. Dave indulged himself with a pint – or the equivalent – of Dunkles, a strong dark German beer. At their recommendation he dined, as they did, on goulash, so full of vegetables that you could stand a spoon in it, with crusty bread rolls (*brutchen*) and butter.

Dave found the two men very affable and easy to get along with. In their forties, he guessed, as he was, but possibly a few years younger. He learned that Mike was married, as he had thought, and that Bill was single and had not yet taken the plunge into marriage, as he put it.

'But he's hopeful, aren't you, Bill?' said Mike. 'He's met the girl of his dreams this week.'

Bill laughed. 'I wouldn't go so far as to say that. It's early days, and I nearly messed it up at the start. I'd been seeing Olga, the receptionist, you see, and Christine wasn't too pleased when she found out – neither was Olga! But enough said about that. Yes, she's a really nice girl; well, young woman, I should say.'

'You've been let off the leash today, haven't you, Bill?' teased Mike.

'Well, I spent yesterday with her at the lake, and we'll have a drink together tonight. But, like I said, it's too soon to . . . well, you know. She wanted to go shopping today with her sister and their new friends, so I thought that was a good idea.'

'Yes, so did Jane,' replied Dave. 'I've . . . er . . . got friendly with the lady who sits next to me. It was totally unexpected. I wasn't looking for anything, neither was she, but we just seemed to hit it off.'

'Yes, we'd noticed, hadn't we, Bill?' said Mike. 'Not that we're being nosy, but we are aware of what goes on with the passengers, to a certain extent. None of our business, of course, any of it, but we have to try to get to know them all, one way or another. Not always easy, is it, Bill?'

'Good grief, no!' replied Bill. 'It's the elderly ladies, all with grey hair and glasses. I do get them confused, but that's usually on the tours at home. Over here the clientele is rather different, younger on the whole. We do get elderly couples, though, like Mr and Mrs Johnson. And it's not the first time we've had to deal with someone being rushed into hospital. All in a day's work, isn't it, Mike?'

'Yes, that's true. We have to be prepared for anything and everything.'

'You mean . . . like somebody dying?' enquired Dave.

'Yes, it does happen, occasionally. It's only happened to me once, thank the Lord! Bill wasn't with me. I was on my own, doing a tour at home – in Torquay, actually – so it wasn't quite so complicated as being abroad. Traumatic, though; it puts a downer on the holiday. We're just hoping the old chap will be OK, aren't we, Bill?'

'I'll say we are! For his sake, and his wife's, of course. Anyway, let's look on the bright side, eh? This lady you've met – Mrs Redfern, isn't it? – she seems a very pleasant person. Are you hoping to go on seeing her when we get back? Not that it's anything to do with me . . .'

'I certainly hope so,' replied Dave. 'I intend to say something before the holiday comes to an end. It's complicated, though. Family issues, you know . . .'

'You're single, though?' enquired Bill.

'Oh yes. I've been married, but I'm not now. But we live

miles from each other. Not Land's End to John O' Groats, but far enough. Jane's in Lancashire and I'm in Shropshire.'

'Not far on the motorway . . .'

'No, but Jane has an elderly mother; rather a harridan from what I gather! And there are other things on my side that I haven't mentioned yet.'

Dave didn't explain any further, and Mike and Bill knew better than to ask.

'I hope it works out well for you, Dave,' said Mike. 'And for Bill here, of course. But that's a different problem. It could put an end to gadding about on the Continent . . . That reminds me, I must ring Sally tonight and see how things are at home. She's not too happy about me being over here so much.'

They talked for a little while about the pros and cons of working abroad, then when they had settled the bill they went their separate ways.

Dave mooched around the old part of the town, enjoying himself in his own quiet way. He had never been bored with his own company; sometimes he liked to be entirely on his own for a while. It would be good to meet up with Jane again, though. And Mike's remark had reminded him that he must ring up his son that evening and see if everything was going well at home.

They were all walking back through the Kurhaus gardens at roughly the same time, making sure they did not arrive back late at the coach. Dave caught sight of Jane with the other two ladies and hurried to catch up with them. They were all laden with carrier bags and were chatting and laughing together.

'Oh, hello Dave,' said Shirley. 'We've had a great time. Mind you, we'll have to live on bread and corned beef when we get back!'

'So I see,' said Dave, laughing, knowing full well that all of them had good jobs and could afford to indulge themselves occasionally. He guessed that for Jane it would have been a real treat. 'You'll be dressed in your new finery tonight, will you?' he asked Shirley.

'You bet I will!' she replied, 'But we've all had quite a spree.'

He and Jane smiled at one another, glad to be together again even though it had been only a few hours. He offered to carry her bags, and she agreed to let him take the heavier one.

'Have you bought anything?' she enquired.

'A book with photos of the region in the last century,' he told her, 'and two CDs – Mozart concertos for woodwind, and German overtures.'

The four of them stopped at a cafe near to the casino to refresh themselves with lemon tea and a slice of gateau. Then they had to step on it so as not to be late back for the coach.

Mike, also, stepped on the gas for the return journey, taking a more direct route. The passengers chatted for a while, then some of them dozed and some looked out of the window at the now familiar scenery. Dave took hold of Jane's hand and held it for the whole of the journey. She smiled contentedly to herself.

Thirteen

Shirley caused quite a sensation in the dining room that evening in her royal blue flared trousers and her eye-catching white top with blue polka dots. Everyone had sympathized with her over the missing suitcase and were pleased to see her looking so smart again – although she always did, whatever she was wearing.

Ellen wore her new beige trousers and the coral pink top, feeling a little self-conscious about 'the new you', as Shirley had called her. Ellen was aware that she looked different – quite modern, and younger, too – but she didn't want anyone to comment too much about her changed appearance.

The four of them at the table were delighted when Mavis joined them for the meal. She had spent all day with Arthur, and the news was encouraging. He was now in the normal ward for heart patients, in a little side room on his own. He would need to stay in hospital for at least another day, but all being well he would be able to travel home with the rest of the party. A relief to everyone, not least to the drivers. His heart attack had not been as severe as it had at first appeared to be, but it was a warning that he had to take extra care of himself.

'So you will go and stay with him tomorrow, will you?' asked Jane, full of concern for the woman she now regarded as a friend. 'It's a shame you're missing the excursions, and Arthur is as well.'

'His health is far more important, my dear,' replied Mavis. 'Freiburg tomorrow . . . I'd like to have seen the shops there, but we have a free day on Monday. Perhaps by then . . . But Arthur says I must definitely go on Sunday to Lake Constance and that island where there are all those gardens. Anyway, we'll see. Now, tell me all about your day. Did you enjoy it?'

It was clear from the happy chatter in the room that they had all had a most enjoyable day. Dinner was later that evening because of the long excursion, and they did not finish until after nine o'clock. The five of them sat together in the lounge. Most of the passengers were all too tired to venture out to the village or even to take a little stroll, but it was pleasant to just sit and relax. Both Jane and Dave said that they had to make phone calls to relations. Mavis had been in two minds as to whether to ring her son and daughter to tell them about their father, but she had decided against it. He was recovering, thank God, so there was no point in alarming them.

The hotel phones were busy that evening. Many of the group had mobile phones but it wasn't easy to get a satisfactory signal in the mountainous region. 'And about time too!' was Alice Rigby's opening remark when she went to the phone to receive her daughter's call. 'I was wondering when you'd remember to ring and see how I'm getting on.'

Jane sighed quietly to herself. But had she really expected anything any different?

'Sorry, Mother,' she said. It came naturally to her to apologize even if she hadn't done anything wrong. 'I didn't think it had been all that long, and I didn't promise to ring every day. Anyway, how are you going on? You've settled in OK, have you?'

'Yes, I suppose so. I've been here five days now, and there's another five to go. I'll be glad to get home, I can tell you. There's nothing like your own bed or your own armchair.'

'But it's a comfortable place, isn't it? I thought the lounge looked very nice and homely, and there's that big television set . . .'

'Yes, I suppose it's alright – could be worse.'

'And what about the other people there? Are you getting to know them?'

'Some of 'em aren't so bad. I've got friendly – well, sort of friendly – with a woman called Flora. She's a bit younger than me, but we get on alright. She's had the life of Riley, though; more money than she knows what to do with. She's OK, though.'

'And are there some men there as well?'

'Of course there are. More women, though. It seems as though women live longer. But there's Henry and Jack – they're not so bad. A bit argumentative, like, but I give as good as I get.'

'Yes, I'm sure you do, Mother.' Jane smiled to herself.

'What's that supposed to mean?'

'Nothing at all . . . I'm glad there are some people you can talk to. They're not all zombies, then, like you thought they might be?'

'No . . . no, I have to admit that they're not losing their marbles. Funny ideas, though, some of 'em. I don't always agree, and I'm not afraid to say so. There's Henry, for instance. His son comes to see him, with his latest lady friend. He's been married twice already, so Henry says, and this one – well, he might marry her or he might not. Living in sin, they are – that's what they used to call it in my young days – but it doesn't seem to matter any more. Henry doesn't think it's important.'

'I suppose we have to move with the times, Mother.'

'Well, some of us don't want to move. I'm old-fashioned about marriage, and I don't care who knows it.'

'But it's really none of our business, is it? I don't know why we're even talking about it.' Jane was getting cross. There was her mother, wittering on about the views of some old chap, and this phone call was costing her an arm and a leg. 'Aren't you going to ask me about my holiday?'

'Oh . . . yes, of course I am. I haven't forgotten you're gadding about in Germany. Enjoying it then, are you?'

'Yes, very much, thank you, Mother. I'm having a lovely time. Germany's a beautiful country, and the people are nice and friendly, too. We've been on some interesting trips, and this hotel is very good, especially the food, and that's one of the main things of course. Some of it is rather like we would have at home . . .' Jane stopped, realizing she was beginning to sound like a travel brochure. 'Yes, it's all very nice.'

'I'm glad you're having a good time. Make the most of it while you can.' Was her mother inferring that it might be her one and only such trip? 'What about the folk on the coach? Are you getting on alright with them?'

'Oh yes, they're a very friendly crowd. You don't get to know everyone, of course, but I've got friendly with two ladies and . . . some others as well.' Now was not the time to tell her mother about the very attractive man she had met, or about the elderly man who had had a heart attack. 'Yes, it's all turning out very well, Mother. I think that's all we can say now, isn't it? You're OK, and so am I. So I'd better say cheerio. It's costing quite a lot to ring from here, but I'll call you again, perhaps after the weekend.'

'Are you on that mobile thing?'

'No, it's the hotel phone. The signal's not good here, for mobiles. So . . . 'bye for now, Mother. Take care of yourself, and I'll see you soon.'

'Yes. You take care of yourself as well. I'm glad you're having a nice time. You deserve it.' Her mother's last words were uttered quietly, and Jane wondered if she had misheard them. Then, 'Goodbye, Jane . . . love,' she said. 'See you soon.'

She heard the phone go down, and she, too, hung up. That hadn't gone too badly. It was hard to tell with Mother, but, reading between the lines, it seemed as though she might well be enjoying herself at the Evergreen home, more than she was letting on.

'Hi there, Dad,' said Peter. 'Great to hear from you. Are you having a good time?'

'Wonderful, thanks,' said Dave. 'Yes, I'm really enjoying it all. But tell me about you and Kathryn, and the farm. All going well, is it? No problems?'

'No, none at all. Everything's going well. Kathryn's been helping me with the cooking, not my strong point, you know. And she's coming to stay for the weekend. Her dad said she could have a couple of days off, so she'll be here till Monday. Everything will be nice and shipshape when you return.'

'Very good,' said Dave. He had a relaxed attitude regarding his son and his fiancée. Kathryn sometimes stayed the night with Peter, and he knew it would be considered stuffy to make an issue of it nowadays. They were sensible young people and well, it seemed to be the norm these days. 'I know you won't let things go to pot on the farm. It's your livelihood as much as mine, isn't it?'

'Yes, and it means a lot to Kathryn as well. Anyway, like I

said, it's all OK here. What about you? You're having a great time, then? You certainly sound on top of the world.'

Yes, everything's just fine. The scenery, and the hotels, and the food. Germany's a lovely country. A good crowd on the coach, too. Nice, friendly people. And . . . I've met someone, Peter. Somebody I like very much.'

'Well, well! I take it you mean a lady?'

'Of course I mean a lady!'

'Come on then, Dad. Tell me more.'

'There's not a great deal to tell at the moment. She has the seat next to me on the coach. She got on at Preston – that's where she lives – so we met when I joined the coach at the next stop in the Midlands. She's called Jane; a few years younger than me, and she's very nice. We just seemed to click, if you know what I mean.' Dave laughed. 'That's an old-fashioned word, "click." It's what they used to say ages ago when you got off with a girl.'

'So, you and this Jane have clicked, have you?'

'I'm hoping so, Peter.'

'Well, good for you, Dad. I've been telling you for ages that it's what you should do – find someone to share your life. There's no point in dwelling on the past, especially as it wasn't very happy. So, do you think it will go any further with Jane? Have you said anything to her?'

'I think she knows I'm getting fond of her, and she of me, at least I hope so. Yes, I'm sure she is.'

'And does she know about the circumstances? About . . . Mum?'

'Er . . . no. I must confess I've not told her everything, not yet. She thinks I'm a widower, although I didn't actually say so. She probably assumes I am because she's a widow. Her husband died two years ago. They were very happy together, from what I gather. So, it's rather different for her, you see.'

'But you deserve some happiness now, Dad. Why don't you tell her how things stand? It's not your fault that my mother's being so damned difficult.'

'I like to think I might have a future with Jane, although it's early days yet. We've known each other for less than a week, although it seems much longer. But she's the sort of girl – woman, I should say – who would want something permanent, if it ever got that far.'

'But you don't really know until you ask her, do you?'

'No, but another problem is that she has an elderly mother, an awkward so and so, from all accounts! They live together, but the old lady's staying in a home this week, very unwillingly.'

'You never know, she might decide she wants to stay there. Gran did.'

'I rather think Jane's mother is a very different kettle of fish from your gran. Anyway, we'll see. It's my problem, but I don't want it to be too much of a problem right this minute because we're having such a good time together, Jane and me. She's a lovely person. I know you'd like her.'

'Yes, I'm sure I would. But listen, Dad – nothing ventured, nothing won. Put your cards on the table and see what she says. You might be able to sort it out.'

'I'll wait for the right moment. I don't want to spoil things. Perhaps towards the end of the holiday. I'll be more certain then about how we feel about each other.'

'Yes, you do that, Dad. We'd better say cheerio, hadn't we? You're running up quite a bill. Anyway, all the best . . . to both of you. Take care, and I'll see you soon.'

'Yes, you take care as well. Good to talk to you. Love to Kathryn, see you next week. 'Bye for now.'

'Hello there, Sally. Sorry I've been so long ringing you, but you know how it is. I've been so busy, what with one thing and another.'

'What do you mean, I know how it is? How should I know what you're getting up to over there, Mike? You promised to ring, and it's five days now. And here I am, over here, tearing, my hair out.'

'Hey, steady on, Sal. What's the matter? This isn't like you.' His wife sounded really uptight and Mike was concerned. She was normally quite a placid person, took things in her stride, although she had been getting on to him lately about being on her own with the children, and the problems she had with them, at least with Tracey.

'What's up, Sal?' he asked again. He was even more worried when he heard Sally, at the other end of the phone, give a sort of choking sob.

'It's our Tracey, isn't it?' she managed to gasp. 'She's only got herself excluded from school.'

'What! She's been expelled?'

'No, not expelled, excluded, I said. Just for a few days, her and two friends of hers. But it's bad enough. I'm so ashamed, and she seems to think it's all highly amusing. At least she did until I grounded her. She's not allowed out, and I've confiscated her telly and phone until she goes back to school on Monday. Oh, Mike! I don't know what I'm going to do. I've told you, it's getting too much for me to cope with on my own.'

'Yes . . . yes, I can see that, love.' Sally sounded really distraught. 'So what's she been doing to get excluded? I'm sure it can't be anything too dreadful. Not our Tracey.'

'She's only been stealing from the Tuck Shop near to the school, hasn't she? Her and that Nicky and Kim. I never did like those two girls! They were caught red-handed by the chap that owns the shop, and he marched them right back into school. And of course Miss Fielding sent them home right away, when she'd written all the parents a severe note – that we had to reply to to prove we'd received it – saying how they'd let the school down and all that. Honestly, Mike, I've never been so ashamed in my life.'

'Yes . . . yes, I can see that it's quite serious, it really is,' said Mike. He was remembering, though, the time when he and his mate, Colin, had pinched some sweets from Woolies. They'd not got caught, and they'd had a real good laugh about it. But Mike, secretly, had felt ashamed. He had been brought up to be honest and trustworthy. His dad would have belted him if he'd found out, though he had never done so, only threatened it. He appreciated, though, that it was regarded as a serious offence by the school and by Sally as well. 'What has she to say for herself?' he asked.

'She says they only did it for a dare. Some other girls egged them on. She's really getting out of hand, but maybe this will teach her a lesson.'

'What did they pinch?'

'Oh, a packet of crisps and two Mars bars. What the heck does it matter what it was! It's the humiliation of it. I'll never be able to lift up my head again, everyone knowing she's a thief.'

'Now come along, Sally love. It's not as bad as all that. Get it into perspective. It's just a silly prank, very childish really, for girls of fifteen. Now if she'd been bullying other girls I'd have been more worried. They had an incident of that not long ago at the school, didn't they?'

'Yes, they did. And Tracey wasn't involved, thank God. No, she would never do anything like that. She's always been a kind-hearted girl. She's just got rather out of hand recently.'

'Well, try not to worry too much, love. I'll be home on Wednesday, then I've got a day or two off until the next tour; that's to Scotland, for a week. But I'll see what I can do about staying in the UK permanently. Bill and I have been discussing it.'

'So how's the tour going?' Sally sounded a little calmer now. 'No problems?'

'Well, just a few. We mislaid somebody's suitcase. It went off to Austria on another tour, so I've to go and collect it tomorrow at a halfway point. And an old chap had a heart attack and was rushed to hospital, but they think he's going to be OK.'

'Good grief! It sounds as though you're earning your money this week. There might not be so many problems if you stayed in the UK.'

'I wouldn't say that. There's always something to cope with. But I'd be home more often, that's for sure. Bill's thinking of packing in the Continental tours as well. He's met a lady on the coach this week. He seems really taken with her.'

'So he's decided it's time to settle down, has he? Goodness knows what you coach drivers get up to! Somebody said that to me, but I told her I can trust my husband.'

'And so you can, love . . .'

'I just want to see more of you, Mike. And so do the kids. I'm sure Tracey would be better if you were over here.'

'I'll see what I can do, I promise. Now, are you feeling a bit calmer? It's not the end of the world, you know. It'll be a nine day's wonder at the school, and I'm sure Tracey will have learnt her lesson.'

'Yes, I'm feeling a bit easier now I've told you about it. It was all getting on top of me.'

'Yes, I know. Try not to worry any more. I'll see you soon. Love to Tracey and Gary. Don't tell Tracey her father's cross with her, or anything like that! You know I've never been hard on them, but I will try and be there with you more of the time. Anyway, I don't think we can say any more at the moment. 'Bye for now. I love you, Sal . . .'

'Love you too, Mike. Take care, won't you? See you soon . . .'

Fourteen

The coach party would be setting off later on the Saturday morning as the excursion was a half-day one to Freiburg, just a short distance away. They would leave at ten o'clock, have lunch in Freiburg, then set off back at half past two, leaving them free for the rest of the afternoon to do as they pleased.

Mike had already set off in Herr Grunder's car to meet the driver of the Yorkshire coach at a halfway point and retrieve Shirley's suitcase. Bill was left in sole charge of the group.

'Now, don't forget it's our al fresco meal tonight,' he told them. 'We will be having a barbecue meal outside, weather permitting, and it hasn't let us down so far. Then we're being entertained by a group of local lads and lasses with dancing and singing and all manner of jollity. We'll have a rare old time, I promise you. So, ten o'clock at the coach this morning, please, ladies and gents.'

Bill suggested to Mavis that she should travel to Freiburg with the rest of the group and spend some time in the town before going to the hospital to see Arthur. 'I'm sure he won't mind you spending an hour or two with your friends, will he?' he said, 'especially as he's feeing so much better.'

'I'd love to,' agreed Mavis, 'and of course he won't mind, but he might be expecting me to come earlier.'

Bill offered to phone the hospital and say that she would be there at around two o'clock. She would get a taxi to take her the short distance and spend the afternoon with him.

Arthur was, indeed, feeling much better. It had been a heart attack, sure enough, but milder than they had thought at first. He was vexed, though, that he was still stuck there in hospital – albeit in a little room to himself – instead of enjoying the holiday with the rest of the group. And Mavis was missing the trips as well, although she didn't seem to mind about that, bless her. She was full of concern for him, spending hours each day with him and trying to keep him cheerful.

'Could you imagine I'd be stuck here at the mercy of a load of Germans,' he had complained to her, though half jokingly. 'Who'd have thought it would come to this, eh?'

He had to admit, though, that he was being treated with kindness and consideration and the German doctors and nurses seemed to know what they were doing. They spoke good English, too.

'And that's more than you can say for us,' Mavis told him. 'Us speaking German, I mean. We haven't a clue.'

'They learnt it at school,' said Arthur, a trifle dismissively. 'They had to when we won the war; they were a conquered nation and our troops were over here. Still, I can't complain about the treatment I'm getting.' He was finding that there was very little to grouse about.

He was greeted on Saturday morning at about ten o'clock by a young nurse whom he hadn't seen before.

'Good morning, Mr Johnson,' she said, which was unusual for a start. They usually used the title of 'Herr', rather than the English version. 'I have a message for you from your wife. She will be coming to see you, but it will be later, at two o'clock. She is spending some time in Freiburg with her friends . . . I think the message is correct. You understand it, yes?'

'Yes, that makes sense,' he replied. The nurse was a pretty young woman, neat and trim in her blue uniform which matched the colour of her eyes. Her dark hair waved attractively under the brim of her little cap. She reminded him rather of Mavis when she was young; Arthur could still appreciate a pretty face and figure. From her name tag he read that she was called Ingrid Hoffman.

He smiled at her. 'I haven't seen you before.'

'No, I have just returned after a few days' leave. I will be looking after you now. You are recovering well, I am told?'

'Yes, I'm doing nicely, thanks,' he replied. 'I must say that you speak good English. The others do, but yours is very good indeed.'

She laughed. 'Yes, thank you. That is because I am part English. Just . . . a quarter English. Oma, my grandmother, was from England – from Yorkshire. She married my grandfather after the war. He was there, in England, you see.'

'You mean they met during the war?' Arthur was beginning to understand what she meant, but it was difficult to put it tactfully.

'Ya . . . yes. He was prisoner of war.' Whilst she tidied his bed, checked his temperature and his pulse, and made him comfortable she told him more.

'My grandfather – Opa, I call him – he was in the Luftwaffe, air force, you say, and his plane was shot down. He was not hurt, that was lucky. He was in a camp, then he worked on a farm. And there he met my Oma. She worked on the farm, too. So they were friendly, you see?'

'She was in the Land Army, was she?'

'Yes, she said she was a land girl. My grandfather, he stayed in Yorkshire after the war. They were married, two years later, I think, and they lived there for a little while. But he wished to come home. The hills in Yorkshire were very lovely, but they were not the hills of home. That is what he said to Oma. So she came with him to Freiburg, to his home, and they had their family. My father, then my aunt . . . then I was born. So, you see, I know a little about England. My grandmother, she tells me, and she speaks to me in English, sometimes. She is a lovely lady.'

'So your grandmother is still living?'

'Yes, and my grandfather. They will be same age as you, I think.'

'Yes, they would be, I suppose.' Arthur nodded thoughtfully. 'You talk about the war . . . I was in the war, in the army though, not the air force. I spent some time here afterwards. But it is all a long time ago now.'

'Yes, and we are all friends now, are we not?' said Ingrid. 'We have the European Union. And your Tony Blair, he likes to – how do you say it? – keep us on our toes.'

'You can say that again!' answered Arthur, but he did not want to be drawn into politics.

'He is good ambassador for your country, I think . . .'

'We could do worse,' said Arthur, thinking again that his new nurse had an excellent command of English.

'I am very pleased to meet you, Mr Johnson,' she said. 'Now I leave you in peace. I bring you your lunch in a little while.'

A very pleasant young woman, he mused, when she left him. And that was very interesting, her grandfather bring a prisoner of war in Yorkshire. He had heard that they were very well treated, and many of them had met and married English girls. He felt that he would not have liked it if his sister, for instance, had decided to marry a German. She hadn't, of course, but if she had he would not have approved.

All the same, it seemed to have worked out well for this family. This Ingrid was a lovely young woman. What age would she be? he wondered. Probably in her mid-twenties; the same age as one of his granddaughters.

She returned with his lunch at twelve o'clock; a sort of hamburger with a small amount of mashed potato and cabbage.

'I have an idea,' she told him. 'You go on eating while I tell you. Do not let your lunch go cold. My Opa – I tell you he was in camp in Yorkshire – I think he would like to meet you. He lives here, in Freiburg, with my Oma. I finish here at six o'clock and I will phone and tell him about you. It is coincidence, I think, very good coincidence. I ask him to come and see you, yes?'

Arthur was nonplussed, but how could he refuse? She was such a nice friendly girl and she was doing her best to please him. 'Why not?' he answered, smiling at her. 'It will be good to have a visitor, but don't pressure him. Do you know what I mean? Make sure he really wants to come.'

'Yes, I understand, but I know he will be very pleased to meet you. Now, you eat your lunch. I bring you cup of coffee soon, then your wife, she will be coming to see you. Yes?'

'Yes, so she will. Thank you . . . Ingrid. May I call you Ingrid?'

'Yes, of course you may. It will please me very much.'

Mavis spent an enjoyable morning in Freiburg with Shirley and Ellen who had insisted that she should accompany them. Most of the people on the coach continued to enquire about Arthur, and she felt that she was amongst friends. Now that he was improving she decided that she must try to relax and make the most of the day. It was a pity he couldn't be with her, but she would see him again soon.

They found that Freiburg was a delightful medieval city with a modern shopping area as well. They wandered through the narrow streets of the old town, alongside fast flowing rivulets at the sides of the road. They had once been sluices carrying away the sewage, but were now perfectly clean and added to the charm of the place. They admired the Rathausplatz with its early Renaissance town hall, and the Zum Roten Baren – the Red Bear Inn – which claimed to be the oldest inn in Germany.

When they were tired of wandering they ended up in the Munsterplatz, the main square of the city. They looked in admiration at the Munster, reputed to be one of the most splendid medieval minster churches in Germany. Its 380-foot tower loomed over the square. In its shadow was the picturesque town market, buzzing with activity, especially on a Saturday morning. The tourists mingled with the housewives doing their weekly shopping, stopping now and again to listen to the street musicians and hearing the ranting of an itinerant preacher near to the church.

The stalls were a wondrous sight, a medley of rich colours and appetizing smells against the background of chatter and laughter and the cries of the stall vendors. There were fruit and vegetable stalls galore, with all manner of produce. Piles of oranges, and apples in russet, green and red; luscious strawberries, raspberries and gooseberries, figs and fresh dates; enormous cabbages and cauliflowers; strings of onions, lettuces, tomatoes, huge bunches of radishes. The tourists, in the main, did not want to shop there, but they gazed in wonder at the tempting displays which seemed, somehow, to be more attractive than they were at home.

Farmers' wives were selling the produce of their farms – eggs, cheese, butter, jars of jam and marmalade, pickles and chutneys. There were flower stalls, too, the fragrance of the lilies and roses, and the more pungent dahlias and chrysanthemums scenting the summer air. Pot plants as well – begonias, fuchsias and geraniums, sturdy and healthy looking blooms – but the ladies decided they would be impractical to transport all the way back to England.

Across from the fruit and vegetable stalls were stalls of possibly more interest to the tourists. Here were all sorts of gifts and handicrafts, many of them produced locally. Pottery mugs and plates; wooden toys; floppy dolls, clowns and furry animals; embroidered tablecloths, napkins and mats – probably machine made but still most attractive – and dried flowers fashioned into posies and garlands to hang in a kitchen.

The three ladies meandered amongst these stalls for a while, trying to decide what they would like to buy. There were so many things to tempt them. They met others from their coach tour, notably the women, wandering around like children in a toy shop. The menfolk, on the whole, had decided it was not much in their line and had drifted away to have a smoke or to partake of a beer in one of the many cafes and bars around the square. Not surprisingly they bumped into Jane, on her own for once.

'Where's Dave?' asked Shirley. 'Not far away, I guess?'

'No, he's having a mooch round on his own. There are some old Dinky cars and some old German toys on a stall over there, and ancient postcards and books. More to his liking than this sort of thing. Some of it's a load of tat, isn't it?' she remarked, lowering her voice. 'But I must admit I like those tablecloths, and the floral arrangements are very attractive.'

'Yes, so they are,' agreed Shirley. 'But you have to be discriminating or you'll end up buying a lot of junk! You arrive home and ask yourself why on earth you bought it.'

After another ten minutes or so of lingering and pondering they all decided to buy a dried flower arrangement, of varying designs, and embroidered tablecloths for that special occasion, such as Christmas or a birthday. Jane chose some dressing table mats for her mother, maybe a little old-fashioned she thought. They were not used so much now, but Mother liked that sort of thing and they had a rose design and a pretty crocheted edging.

Jane was meeting Dave for lunch at a cafe they had already picked out, overlooking the market square. The other three went with her, and found him already sitting there enjoying an ice-cold lager. Jane joined him under the shade of the large green umbrella, and the others sat at a vacant table nearby.

They were glad to escape from the heat of the sun and to rest their aching feet.

After they had enjoyed the lunch of their choice – as usual the menu was vast and varied – it was time for Mavis to leave the others and find her way to the hospital. Shirley and Ellen went with her to locate a taxi at a rank not far away, leaving Jane and Dave to enjoy a refreshing lemon sorbet, then a cup of strong coffee to fortify them for the rest of their time in Freiburg. The city streets, quaint and charming as they were, felt claustrophobic in the midday heat.

'I've enjoyed it, but a half day here is long enough,' said Jane. 'We're not used to this heat, are we? It will be nice to get back to the hotel and rest for a while.'

Dave agreed. 'Yes, and it's party time tonight. I wonder what they've got in store for us?'

'Whatever it is, I'm sure I'll enjoy it,' said Jane contentedly.

Dave knew what he intended to do. Tonight he would ask Jane if she might consider planning a future with him.

Mavis found Arthur much improved. His colour was better; the pale grey pallor had gone and he was in good spirits. She told him about the pleasant morning she had spent in Freiburg.

'It's a lovely old town, Arthur. I'm so sorry you missed it. It was tiring, though, walking round in the sunshine. We kept trying to find patches of shade, so it might have proved a bit too much for you. Anyway, I'm pleased to see you looking so much better. Is there any news about when you can come home? Come out of here, I mean. We'll be able to travel back on the coach on Tuesday, won't we? Or would the journey be too much for you?'

'For goodness' sake, Mavis! We've got to get back somehow, haven't we?' A touch of the old irritable Arthur showed for a moment, then he grinned again. 'The alternative would be to fly, and you know I won't do that. They wouldn't let me anyway, not after I've had a heart attack, The doctor's coming to see me this afternoon while you're here, so he'll tell us when they're going to let me out.' He chuckled. 'Sounds as though I'm in jail, doesn't it? But I can't complain. They're treating me very well.'

And that, coming from Arthur, was praise indeed! Not even a remark like, 'Considering that they're Germans!'

Mavis had another surprise when a pretty young nurse came into the room and greeted Arthur as though she had known him for ages.

'Hello again, Mr Johnson.' She beamed at him. 'And this is your wife, yes?'

'Yes, this is Mavis, my good lady wife. Mavis, this is Ingrid. She's looking after me now.'

The two of them shook hands. 'I am very pleased to know you, Mrs Johnson,' said Ingrid. 'Your husband, he tell me about you. And I understand because, as I tell Arthur, my grandmother – my Oma, I call her – she is English. And so we have – what is it you say? – some things in common?'

'That's good,' replied Mavis. She was certainly a pretty girl. No wonder there was a gleam in Arthur's eye! 'Thank you for looking after him.'

'It is no problem. And tonight he will have a visitor. I already ring my Opa, Mr Johnson, and he say yes, he will be pleased to come and see you.'

Mavis was mystified. 'What's all this about?' she asked.

Arthur explained, a little apologetically, she thought. 'Ingrid's grandfather – her Opa, she calls him – he was in the war, like me. He was . . . er . . . his plane came down, in Yorkshire, so he was a prisoner, you see. He worked on a farm, and he met an English girl. Then he married her after the war; she's Ingrid's grandmother. And Ingrid thought . . . she wondered if I would like to meet him. So I said yes, I would.'

'Good for you, Arthur!' said Mavis. My goodness! she thought to herself. That was a turn up for the book. Arthur agreeing to meet a former enemy! She couldn't make any comment, though, with that nice young nurse being there.

'I hope you have an interesting time together,' she said, 'reminiscing about . . . everything. I'm sure you'll have a lot to talk about.'

'Yes, I'm sure will,' said Arthur, with a touch of irony, or had she only imagined that?

'So I won't come and see you this evening, then you can have a good chat with your visitor, just man to man.'

'Aye, I suppose so.' He nodded thoughtfully. She could tell he was none too sure about it.

'Anyway, there's a party on at the hotel tonight,' she told him. 'I was feeling guilty about being there without you, but now I won't feel so bad.'

'Yes, you go and enjoy it, love,' said Arthur. 'What sort of a party? I don't suppose it will be a wild abandoned affair, will it?'

'I doubt it.' She smiled. 'It's what they call an al fresco meal. You know, a barbecue sort of thing, eaten out of doors. Then there's an entertainment by a local group, singing and dancing and that sort of thing. It'll be a nice change.'

Ingrid didn't stay long. She took Arthur's pulse and temperature again before saying goodbye to Mavis.

'It is a pleasure to meet you, Mrs Johnson. Now, you look after Arthur when you get back to England. I am hoping he will be well, for a long long time.'

'I hope so, too,' said Mavis. 'Goodbye, my dear. Lovely to meet you.'

'I couldn't very well refuse, could I?' said Arthur, 'when she asked me if I'd like to meet this chap. What have I let myself in for, I wonder?'

'It will be fine, Arthur,' she told him. 'He married that English girl, didn't he? So he must have got to know quite a bit about life in our country. You'll be polite and friendly towards him, won't you, Arthur?'

'Of course I will! What d'you think I'm going to do? Start an argument as soon as we meet? I'll be as nice as pie, I promise you.' He chuckled. 'Who'd have thought it, though, eh? Me having a tête-à-tête with a German!'

The doctor who was in charge of Arthur came to talk to them soon after Ingrid had left. He was far more impersonal than the nurse; friendly to a point, but with an abrupt way of speaking.

'We are satisfied with your progress, Herr Johnson,' he said. His English bore scarcely a trace of an accent. 'Your condition is not so bad as we at first thought it to be. The heart attack was quite a mild one, made worse, I believe, because of your fear of being ill in a strange place. It is a warning, though. You must take care. You must not try to run before you walk.' He managed a brief smile.

'Thank you, doctor,' said Mavis. 'So. we'll be able to travel home with the others, will we?'

'Yes, of course. You may leave here in the morning, Herr Johnson. We will make arrangements for you to travel back to your hotel. Then you enjoy the rest of your stay here, in our lovely Black Forest. You behave quietly, though. You must not get too excited.'

He shook hands with Arthur, then with Mavis, giving a curt bow and a nod of his head. 'Goodbye, Frau Johnson. You look after your husband, yes?'

'Yes, of course I will, Doctor. Thank you very much for all you've done for him.'

She stayed for a little while longer, then took a taxi back to the hotel, feeling, for the first time since it happened that all would be well. It had been only two days since Arthur had been taken ill, but it had been the longest two days of her life. She knew they would not live for ever, but she would thank God every day now for the time they had left together.

Fifteen

Arthur was feeling a little apprehensive as he waited for his visitor that evening. He had combed what little hair he had and straightened his crumpled pyjamas. Fancy greeting a visitor in these old pyjamas! But at least they were his own, not the awful regulation nightwear from the hospital. Mavis had brought them in for him, with his shaving tackle and the book he was reading; a war story, but not about the last lot, but the exploits of Sharpe in the Napoleonic wars.

There was a knock at the door at just after six thirty, then a nurse entered – not Ingrid, she had gone off duty – accompanied by a tall distinguished-looking man.

'Here is your visitor, Herr Johnson,' she said. 'This is Herr Hoffman. I hope you have good time together.'

The man approached the bed, smiling and holding out his hand. 'Herr Johnson,' he began. 'I am delighted to meet you. Ingrid told me about you, and of course I said yes, I would be pleased to see you. So, how are you, my friend?'

'Not so bad, thanks,' replied Arthur. 'Much better actually. I've had a scare and it put the wind up me, I can tell you. But they say I'll be alright.' He smiled. 'I'll be here for another few years, please God! I'm pleased to meet you too, Herr . . . er . . . Herr Hoffman. Ingrid's told me about you. Sit yourself down then. There's a chair over there.'

Arthur was feeling more conscious than ever about his appearance now, compared with the spruce-looking gentleman who had come to see him. He was a tall upstanding man, with not the trace of a stoop. He had a good head of silver grey hair, and blue eyes that did not look the least bit faded behind rimless spectacles. A handsome chap with classic Germanic features. He was wearing a smart grey suit with a blue shirt and a striped tie, the picture of elegance.

Especially so compared with me! thought Arthur, clad in boldly striped 'old man's' pyjamas, and wearing glasses with heavy frames. He was used to them because he had had them for years, and he refused to change them for a more modern design. But the man seemed pleasant, and the first hurdle was over with.

His visitor pulled the chair closer to the bed and sat down. 'Now, you will allow me to use your first name, yes?' he said. 'I cannot go on calling you Herr Johnson. I believe my granddaughter said you are called Arthur?'

'Yes, that's right. And your name is . . .?'

'I am called Wolfgang,' he replied, with what sounded like a touch of pride.

'Same as the composer,' said Arthur. 'Yes, I like that name. I like Mozart as well.'

'Just as I do,' said his visitor. 'So, we already have something in common. Now, tell me, Arthur, where do you live, in England?'

'My wife and I live in Blackburn,' said Arthur. 'It's in Lancashire. That's just over the Pennine hills, the next county to Yorkshire. It's an ordinary little town, not what you'd call a beauty spot, but we live on the outskirts, and there's a nice view of the hills from the back windows. Ingrid said that you were . . . that you lived in Yorkshire. It's a lovely county, one of the best in England, I reckon, though happen I shouldn't say that, being a Lancashire lad, born and bred.'

'Yes, I agree. It is a most beautiful part of your country, although I haven't seen all of it. My wife and I, we have visited London, and many years ago we travelled to Scotland. And, of course, we visit Yorkshire again, several times.'

His English was perfect, but then it would be with his wife being from England. They had no doubt done their courting in her language, thought Arthur. She wouldn't have known any German until the two of them had met.

'Where were you when . . . where was the farm you worked at?' asked Arthur, trying to choose his words carefully. 'I believe you were at a farm in Yorkshire during the . . . er . . . the war?'

'Yes, so I was.' Wolfgang smiled. 'Do not be afraid to mention the war, Arthur. I tell you, I was glad when I knew it was all over for me, when I became a prisoner. I did not know how

I could carry on much longer with all the dreadful bombing raids. But the way I see it, the good Lord, he rescued me. I could not admit that to my fellow Germans, but I believe that many of them felt the same about the war. It was frightful, horrific.'

Arthur nodded. 'Yes . . . yes, so it was.' His visitor was shaking his head, gazing into space unseeingly. But he soon recovered.

'Yes, the farm. It was near a town called Settle. A very beautiful place, but lonely as well. Those hills, so wild and bare, they seem to close in on you. As I say, I was glad of an escape from the war. No more worry about the next time we go up in the air, what we had to do. But then I feel sad and depressed as well, missing my family at home here in Freiburg. They would not know, perhaps, what had happened to me. Then it all changed . . .' He smiled. 'Because I met Elsie.'

'Your wife? The girl you married?'

'Yes, of course. My dear Elsie. She came to work as land girl at the farm. She lived there, she and her friend, Paula, with the farmer and his wife, Mr and Mrs Strickland. They were very kind people. They treat us well, my friend Johann and I. But Paula, I think she did not like me very much. She did not approve, you understand, of Elsie and me being friendly.'

'Yes, I see. I suppose there might have been some bad feeling.' said Arthur. 'The war would be at its worst perhaps, then?'

'Yes, it was 1942. I joined the Luftwaffe, as so many young men did, at the start of the war. We felt we must, you understand? I expect it was the same for you. There was unrest in Germany. The older people felt it was not good after the first war, the treaty and everything. Then the new regime, it seemed at first as though it could be the answer to the problems. We were carried along with it all for a time. By . . . Herr Hitler.' He spoke the name scathingly. 'We did not know until afterwards, when it was too late. Such dreadful things; we did not believe they could happen. So many of us, we felt the same after the war when we heard about it. We felt guilty, ashamed that they were our people, that they were Germans who had done all that. And I think we had bad reputation for a long time.'

'Yes, there was bad feeling for a time,' said Arthur. 'And some of us, we saw too much. I was at Dachau, when it was all over . . . but I never talked about it, not to anyone.'

Arthur knew, though, that it had influenced his feelings about Germany and the German race as a whole. He had always known, deep down, although he would not admit it, that there were many decent peace-loving Germans who had not wanted to be a part of it all. Like this gentleman, Wolfgang. He was, indeed, a perfect gentleman. Arthur felt that he would be pleased to have him as a friend, if that were possible. He knew now that it was time to set aside his prejudices. He knew, also, that he had exaggerated them at times for effect, sometimes just to be awkward.

'I must admit I didn't want to come to Germany,' he said now. 'I still had bad memories, and I wouldn't let myself forget the past. But my wife persuaded me to come, and I'm very glad I did.' He looked into the eyes of his new acquaintance and smiled at him. 'And I'm very pleased to have met you, Wolfgang.'

'You are glad you came. In spite of being ill?'

'Yes, maybe the heart attack was a wake-up call. It's made me see things differently. Anyway, it might have happened at home. Who can tell? These things happen at our age, quite unexpectedly. We've got to make the most of our years now, haven't we? I'm damned sure I'm going to enjoy mine, what's left of 'em.'

'You must not do too much, though, Arthur. You must be careful for a while. My Ingrid says that is what you must do.'

'Yes, I know that. She's a grand lass, isn't she, your Ingrid?'

'Yes, and she is the image of my wife, Elsie, when she was young, of course. I sometimes feel I am seeing my young Elsie again. But my wife is still a very lovely lady. She is eighty now, but still beautiful, I believe.'

'And . . . what did her family think,' asked Arthur, 'about their daughter and you? Was there any opposition, any trouble about it?'

'I did not meet Elsie's family until the war ended,' said Wolfgang. 'Her home was in York, a good distance from the farm where we worked, and she did not go home very often. But she told them about me, when we fell in love. We did so, soon after we met. We both knew how we felt, but it was difficult at first to admit that it had happened. I was afraid to do anything, to say anything to upset Elsie. But in the end I took hold of my courage and I told her. I said that I loved her. And it was the same for her. She had been waiting for me to tell her.'

'So you were married in England, were you, after the war ended?'

'Yes, that is so. When I left the camp it was a little while after the end of the war. I went to live at the farm with Mr and Mrs Strickland. Elsie and Paula had gone home, and I had a small room in the attic. The farmer had asked me to stay and work for him, as a paid worker this time.' He smiled. 'I was happy there, I enjoyed working on the land. It was very new to me. Here, in Freiburg, my work was in an office, very boring job. But I knew now that this was what I wanted, to work outside.'

'So you changed your job, did you, when you came back here to Germany?' Arthur felt that he was asking a lot of questions, but it was an interesting story and it seemed as though Wolfgang wanted to tell it.

'Yes, that is correct. Elsie and I were married in York the year after the war. When her parents met me they decided I was not so bad.' He laughed. 'We lived in Settle. We had two rooms rented to us by a family. I was working at the farm, and Elsie, she had a little job in a shop.

'But then, it was in 1947, I knew I wanted to come back home. I was missing my family and they missed me, too; and they wanted to meet my new wife. And Elsie, she wished to please me, and so we came back here. I found work with a man who had a small farm, just crops and vegetables and a few chickens. Then, later, I had a small place of my own. And so we stayed and were very happy. We have two children, Karl and Eva, and four grandchildren – you have met Ingrid – and now there is another little one on the way, our first great-grandchild.' He smiled contentedly.

'But I talk too much, all about myself. Now, you tell me about you, Arthur. You were in the air force, too?'

'No, not me,' said Arthur. 'I was a soldier – in the army. Joined up when I was eighteen, didn't wait for them to call me up. Like you said, we felt we had to do it. I didn't see much action for a long time. It was after Dunkirk, you see, and all the troops were back in England, just waiting. So I went out with the D-Day lot, and managed to get through it all without any injuries, thank God! Then, well, I told you about Dachau . . . then eventually I was demobbed. My war was quite uneventful, I suppose, compared with a lot of chaps. You, for instance. It must have been hair-raising being part of a bomber crew. Did you pilot the plane?'

'Oh no, not at all!' Wolfgang shook his head. 'I was not an officer, you understand? I was just an ordinary flyer. But we had lost so many men – just as you did – and the rest of us, we took their place. I was a navigator . . . not a very good one, I fear.' He gave a wry smile. 'Our plane got lost, crossing the hills, and we were shot down. There were no casualties among the crew, but we were all taken as prisoners. A happy escape for me, as I told you. Now, that is enough about the war. You tell me, Arthur, about your work in England and your family.'

The nurse who had brought Wolfgang to the ward came back with cups of coffee and biscuits. They chatted together like old chums for another half hour or so. It was not an official visiting time, but an allowance had been made as a favour to Ingrid. Arthur found, when talking to his new friend, that his tendency to grumble and to look on the gloomy side was not apparent. In fact he found himself looking at things from a more positive point of view. It became clear that Wolfgang was an optimistic sort of man, one to whom the glass was always half full, rather than half empty, as it often was with Arthur. He made up his mind to watch himself in future, starting with a determination to enjoy what was left of his holiday in Germany.

At the end of the visit the two men exchanged addresses and promised to keep in touch. Arthur was not much of a letter writer – he left all that sort of thing to Mavis – but at least they would be able to send a Christmas card, if nothing else. And who could tell? He might even get round to penning a few lines himself.

The al fresco meal at the guest house was most enjoyable. They all sat around at small tables, helping themselves when they felt inclined to a variety of food, both hot and cold. There were sausages – bratwurst – and chicken legs; chunks of beef, pork and veal cooked on the barbecue; large platters of cold meats, and dishes of sauerkraut, potato salad and lettuce and tomatoes tossed in oil; and crusty brown bread and butter. And it you were still hungry following that, there was a choice of the inevitable Black Forest gateau, *apfelstrudel*, or ice-cream.

Despite it being an informal meal the ladies had dressed up to look their best. Particularly so for at least three of the ladies, who had purchased new clothes in Baden Baden. Shirley and Ellen wore their new trousers and tops, and Jane wore her floaty dress in shades of green and blue, and her green high-heeled sandals.

She knew that Dave kept glancing at her admiringly during the meal, and when their eyes met he smiled tenderly and knowingly at her. She felt that tonight would be a turning point in their friendship. She was sure now that she was falling in love with him.

Following the meal there was an entertainment by a local group of men and women all dressed in national costume. This took place in the lounge, where the tables and chairs had been pushed to the sides leaving a large empty space in the centre. There the troupe danced and sang and played musical instruments, putting on a show very similar to the one that some of them had seen in Rüdeshiem, on their first night in Germany. A lady played a huge piano accordion that was almost as big as herself and a man blew down an alpenhorn more than six feet in length. There were fiddlers, too, and harmonicas to accompany the thigh slapping knockabout dance by the men, then the gentler landler, danced by the men and the ladies.

There was enthusiastic applause as they finished their act, then departed with smiles and waves to the audience. After a short interval a local disc jockey played recorded music for the company to sing along and dance to, or just listen. It was not the ear-shattering sound such as was heard in the clubs and discos frequented by young people, but more gentle nostalgic tunes considered suitable for the clientele from the coach tour. Familiar songs, mainly from a bygone era, though not so very far distant. Hits by the Beatles, the Pet Shop Boys, Boyzone, Simon and Garfunkel, the Beach Boys . . . And the haunting songs of Nat King Cole, Matt Monro, and Andy Williams.

'Do you dance?' Dave asked Jane. They had been sitting quietly, hand in hand, contented in one another's company.

She laughed. 'Are you asking me?'

'I'm just wondering if you do . . . if you did? It's something we haven't talked about.'

'Well, if you're asking me, then I do,' she replied. 'At least I used to dance; I'm afraid I'm rather out of practice.'

'Well, that makes two of us,' he said. They took to the floor to the strains of 'Unforgettable', sung by the truly unforgettable Nat King Cole.

Dave held her close to him, her head resting on his shoulder. She was just a few inches shorter than he was. The foxtrot had never been her forte, but they glided rather than danced, their steps in time with one another. Jane was sure that their minds, also, were attuned to one another and that Dave felt just the same as she did.

There were several couples dancing, but not all of the company had taken to the floor. Mavis was sitting with Norah and the two new friends she had met that week, and Norah's younger sister, Christine, was dancing with Bill, the driver. Norah confided to Mavis that the two of them were getting very friendly.

'I worry about her, you know,' she said. 'My little sister, she's quite a lot younger than me, and I feel responsible for her. I thought it would just be a holiday fling, but they seem to be quite taken with one another. Anyway, time will tell. He seems a decent sort of fellow, though, from what I've seen of him.'

They certainly seemed very 'lovey-dovey' together, thought Mavis as she watched them dancing. How lovely it was to be young, she mused, although there were always problems to be encountered along the way. She hoped that all went well for them, and for Dave and Jane. The two of them were oblivious to everything but one another as they swayed in rhythm to the sentimental melody.

Shirley and Ellen were dancing, too. Not with one another but with two men from the coach tour. They were brothers, both widowed and in their sixties, holidaying together. They had been seen in company with the two ladies, not that there would be any romantic notions there, thought Mavis. But it was good to see Ellen's face light up at the unaccustomed attention.

The evening's festivities ended at eleven thirty. Dave and Jane danced again as Engelbert Humperdinck sang of the last waltz with you, the song that told of two lonely people together. Jane thought how lovely it would be, never to be lonely again. But was that just an impossible dream?

Dave's next words surprised her. 'Let's go to my room,' he said. 'I've got a bottle of wine, and we can have a nice quiet drink together to finish off the evening.'

Jane burst out laughing. She couldn't help it. 'Well, that's a good chat-up line if ever I heard one!'

Dave laughed too. 'Yes, I suppose it sounds like it, but I didn't mean it like that . . . I don't intend to seduce you,' he added in a whisper. 'Everyone's going now, and we can't very well stay down here. Besides, I want to talk to you, Jane.'

They went up the stairs to their rooms. 'Oh dear! There's only one glass,' he said. 'You'd better bring your own.'

Jane felt bemused as she went along the corridor to Dave's room with the glass provided by the hotel. She had already had quite enough to drink, but she knew that what Dave had said would be true. She knew he was not the sort of man to take liberties with her.

It was the first time she had been in anyone else's room. They were almost identical with regard to decor. Not elaborate, just homely and functional with pine furniture and folkweave curtains and cushions. Dave had already drawn the cork from the bottle of Riesling and he poured out a glass for each of them.

'It's been a good evening, hasn't it?' he began, as they perched together on the edge of the bed. There was nowhere else to sit apart from one semi-easy chair at the other side of the room, and she felt it might look rather stand-offish if she sat there.

'Cheers.' He raised his glass and she did the same. 'Here's to the rest of our wonderful holiday. It's been a very happy one, unexpectedly happy, thanks to you, Jane.'

He put his glass down on the bedside table and put an arm around her. She put her glass down as well, welcoming his embrace and his tender kiss. But he did not continue kissing her. He took hold of both her hands, looking earnestly into her eyes.

'Jane,' he began, 'I've only known you for a few days, but I feel that I already know you so well; that we both know each other really well . . . and I believe that I love you. No . . . I'm sure that I love you. And . . . dare I hope that you feel the same?'

'Yes . . . yes, I do,' she answered. 'But it's less than a week since we met. I've been trying to tell myself that it's just a holiday thing; that we've been thrown together and that it was inevitable that we should get friendly.'

'But if we'd disliked one another on sight we wouldn't have even tried to be friendly, would we?' said Dave. 'There are spare seats on the coach; one of us could have moved. But we didn't, because the attraction was there, right from the start.'

'Yes, so it was,' said Jane. 'And I do believe I'm falling in love with you.'

He kissed her again. 'It sounds corny to say that I've never felt like this before, but it's true, I haven't . . . well, not for ages. And I've been very cautious about showing my feelings to anyone. But now, I would like to think that we might have a future together, don't you, Jane?'

'Yes, I do,' she replied. 'I know that we're both single, as they say nowadays. I'm a widow, which is what they used to say, and so are you . . . a widower. But it isn't quite so simple, is it? There are other commitments.' She shook her head. 'What on earth would I do about Mother? She depends on me so much. And you have your farm to run, and we live so far apart.'

'Not so very far, love,' he said. 'A hundred miles or so. What's that? Yes, I know there are difficulties, but I'm sure we could carry on seeing one another. We both drive, it shouldn't be too impossible.'

He did not kiss her again, not just then. He picked up his glass of wine and she did the same. He knew that he was not being entirely truthful with her, in fact he was allowing her to believe something that was a lie. What was more, he had had the chance to tell her the truth, and he felt he couldn't do it, not after they had spent such a lovely evening together. Jane believed that his wife had died. He had said that he had lost his wife, and Jane had presumed that she was dead. But Judith was very much alive. She was in a relationship with another man, as she had been ever since she had left Dave, but she refused to consider a divorce because of her Catholic upbringing.

'Is something the matter?' asked Jane. 'You've gone very quiet.'

'No, not really,' he replied. 'I was just thinking about what you said, mainly about your mother. There must be some way round it all. She wouldn't be so heartless as to deny you a chance of happiness, would she?'

'I don't know. If she met you I feel sure she would like you. Let's just wait and see, shall we, Dave, and enjoy the rest of our holiday? We have to return to reality in a few days' time. This is an unreal situation in a way, isn't it? A carefree holiday, no worries, no decisions to make. Let's see how things go when we get back home. Of course I want to carry on seeing you. I shall do all that I can to make sure I do, so long as we both feel the same?'

'I will, my darling. I assure you, I will.' It was the first time he had used the endearment. He kissed her again and again. Their embraces became more passionate until they both realized it was time to call a halt.

Jane stood up rather abruptly. 'I must go, Dave.' She kissed him lightly on the cheek. 'Don't let's worry about it, not just yet. Goodnight, sleep well.'

'Goodnight, my dear, See you in the morning.'

He would tell her tomorrow, Dave decided. Tomorrow night when they had returned from the excursion. He didn't want to spoil what promised to be one of the best days of the tour. Maybe she would understand and not think it too much of an issue. There was a much more relaxed attitude now about couples living together out of wedlock. It was something Dave had thought he would never do; he was a trifle old-fashioned in that respect. He knew now, though, that his life had not been complete. He had been contented enough on his own, with his work and his family . . . and then he had met Jane. He did not want to miss out on the chance of being happy and fulfilled again.

Sixteen

There was a resounding cheer on Sunday from the company of the Galaxy tour, when Mike entered the dining room carrying Shirley's missing suitcase. They had all sympathized with her, understanding how they might feel if parted from their possessions. As it turned out she had managed quite well. She had come to realize that there were others with far worse problems and, on the lighter side, she had enjoyed a good spending spree and had persuaded Ellen to do the same.

The Sunday excursion was to Lake Constance, a large lake, almost an inland sea, which bordered on three countries, Germany, Austria and Switzerland. The distance from Freiburg was around a hundred miles, so they would need to make an early start.

Arthur was due to come out of hospital that morning and, to Mavis's delight, the doctor had said that he might be allowed to go on the excursion with the rest of the group, provided he took very great care. He would be facing a long journey home in a few days' time, so this would get him used to the coach travelling again.

Both the hospital staff and the coach drivers did all they could to help. He was taken back to the guest house in an ambulance, and Mike delayed the start of the journey for fifteen minutes to make sure he was comfortably settled in his seat.

'By heck! This is grand,' he said to his wife as the coach sped along the road. They were using mainly the Autobahn route as the journey was quite a long one. 'I'd never have believed that I'd be out and about again so soon. They've worked wonders at that hospital. I tell you, Mavis, I was scared to death when I came round and realized where I was. I thought I'd had it, really I did.'

'Well, thank the good Lord you're still here with us.' Mavis took hold of his hand and squeezed it gently. 'I was worried, too, that night when I left you in hospital. You seemed to be recovering, but I was scared that you might have a relapse. But it wasn't as bad as we feared, after all.'

'No, and I'm still here to tell the tale.' Arthur laughed quietly. 'It was quite an experience meeting that German fellow last night. He's a grand chap, Mavis, and he did me a world of good. I'm sorry you couldn't meet him an' all.'

'Yes, I'm sorry, too. You were able to swap stories then, about the war?'

'Aye, but we didn't dwell on it too much. He felt the same as I did, that it was horrific, just . . . dreadful.' He shook his head sorrowfully. 'He said he was relieved when he was taken prisoner, so that he could escape from what he was being forced to do. All that bombing and destruction . . . He didn't want to be a part of it at all, especially when he realized what was going on. They didn't know, Mavis, a lot of 'em, not till afterwards. They weren't to be blamed. It was just that Hitler and his cronies.'

'So you're changing your mind about the Germans, are you?' Mavis smiled at him understandingly.

'Aye, I suppose I am. I've had to, haven't I? The ones I've seen so far, they're great folk. A bit humourless, maybe; a bit prim and proper. Not Ingrid, though, she was a real lively young lass. She reminded me of our Melissa, she was so bright and cheerful. She made me feel tons better, same as Melissa always does. Well, like all our grandchildren do. We've a lot to be thankful for, haven't we, Mavis?'

'We certainly have,' she replied. Arthur sounded like a different person since his traumatic experience. She couldn't help but wonder if the old Arthur might surface again when they got back home. What did it matter, though? She still cared deeply for him, warts and all.

'Just relax now, Arthur,' she told him. 'Look at the scenery, or have a little doze. It'll be a long day, so just take it easy now.'

They had a coffee and comfort stop mid-morning, and arrived at their destination, the lakeside town of Constance – the same name as the lake – in time for lunch. It was a pleasant town with a new pedestrianized zone as well as the old town with narrow cobbled streets and alleyways, similar to other German towns they had already visited. From the harbour there was a magnificent view across the lake to the Swiss and Austrian mountains.

They stayed only a short time in the town, to have a stroll around or a quick bite to eat if they so wished. The main part of the tour was to the flower island of Mainau, situated in the German part of the lake and reached by a causeway from the town. They were to be there for three hours to see all the sights that the island had to offer. A short enough time, and they all agreed afterwards that they could have spent a whole day there and still not seen it all.

When they arrived at the island Mavis discovered to her relief – she had been rather worried – that wheelchairs were available and, what was more, there was no shortage of men who were willing to push Arthur around. It was finally decided that Trevor and Malcolm, the two brothers who had formed a casual friendship with Shirley and Ellen, were to take turns with the wheelchair. And so the six of them set off together to view the delights of the island.

They had already been told by Mike, in his commentary, that the island had been created by Frederick the First, the Grand Duke of Baden in 1853. He had been responsible for the planting of the arboretum and for the building of the Baroque summer palace.

Throughout their stay there the people from the coach tour kept encountering one another at the various places of interest: the gardens, hothouses and numerous cafes. The island was an enormous flower-filled park with enchanting vistas at every turn.

The little group of six stopped to take a rest in the Italian rose garden, a fairyland of pergolas, sculptures and fountains, containing, it was reputed, more than five hundred varieties of rose. Their fragrance scented the air, and the varied hues of the flowers, from purest white to lemon, gold, delicate pink, scarlet and deep purplish red, were a wondrous sight to see.

They strolled through the Mediterranean terraces, a haven for palm trees, colourful pot plants, and purple bougainvillea cascading from gigantic urns. At every turn there were rhododendron and azalea bushes, coming to the end of their flowering period. The hothouses were filled with exotic blooms too delicate to exist out of doors, and in one of the conservatories there was a myriad of butterflies flittering amongst the flowers.

At the end of the afternoon when they arrived back at the coach they could not stop enthusing about all that they had seen.

'We've had some wonderful tours this week,' said Dave, speaking for them all, 'but I think this one beats the lot. Thanks very much, Mike and Bill, for bringing us to this lovely place.'

Mike laughed. 'Don't thank us, thank Galaxy Travel. They arranged it all. We're glad you enjoyed it. By the way, it's the last trip you'll take with Bill and me, apart from the journey home, of course. Tomorrow we have to take a rest day – the company is very strict about that – so that we're in good shape to travel back to the UK. So it's a free day for you folks tomorrow to do as you wish. You could take a bus into Freiburg again, or have a saunter round the countryside. We'll tell you later on about the starting off time on Tuesday. Now, relax and enjoy the journey back. It's full speed ahead now, back to our hotel.'

Several of them felt dejected thinking about going back home in two days' time. Jane was one of them. It was all coming to an end. It had been so exciting, such a happy time, just like a dream, and all so unexpected. She thought about what Dave had said last night. Could she dare to hope that they might have a future together? She hadn't rung her mother for a few days. She was loath to burst the bubble of happiness that enclosed her, She decided it would be time enough to break the news to Mother – if she could ever find the courage to do so – when she saw her again.

Dave, also, was deep in thought. He knew that he would have to talk to Jane again, later that evening, and this time he would have to be absolutely truthful with her. He was in a quandary. He could not ask her outright to be his 'mistress', an outdated expression that he would not use, but it amounted to the same thing. But he had to make it clear to her that he wanted her to be more than a friend, although he was unable to promise her the security of marriage. Did it matter, though, nowadays? He was coming to the conclusion that living together – not straight away, of course, but sometime in the future – was the only solution. He was sure that he and Jane could be happy together. But how would she feel about it?

Dinner was a little later that evening to give everyone a chance to freshen up after the tiring day. After the meal Dave asked Jane if she felt like taking a stroll down to the village, if she was not too tired.

'We could have a drink at the beer garden, like we did the first evening,' he suggested. 'That is if you feel up to it?'

'Of course I do,' she replied. That had been a memorable evening, with the feeling of a developing romance. Dave had kissed her a few times on the way back to the hotel, and she had known that she was growing very fond of him. She was sure now that she would like to think – to hope – that they could have a future together. But was that all that it amounted to, just a forlorn hope?

They walked hand in hand down the country road that led to the village, and to the beer garden they had discovered the first evening. There were a few others from the coach party sitting in the garden area, including Bill and Christine. Jane and Dave said hello to them then found a secluded table at the other side. Not that they wanted to be unfriendly but they both knew that there were personal things that they wanted to talk about, and their time together was growing shorter, only two more days and they would be on their way home. It was clear, as well, that Bill and Christine were very contented on their own.

'White wine for you?' asked Dave when the waiter appeared.

'Yes, please . . . Well, a spritzer, I think,' she replied. It would last longer, and more than a couple of glasses of wine – which she had already drunk at dinner time – made her feel woozy. Dave ordered the drinks – lager for himself – then they sat quietly until they arrived.

When he had taken a good gulp of his lager Dave looked intently at Jane and took hold of her hand. 'Jane,' he began, 'I have to tell you something.'

She guessed by the serious tone of his voice that it was something of importance. She wondered for a brief moment if he was beginning to regret what he had said about them sharing a future together. Maybe she had not seemed enthusiastic enough about the prospect, putting obstacles in the way, chiefly the problem of her mother. She looked at him in silence, waiting for what would come next.

'I haven't been entirely honest with you,' he went on. 'You are under the impression that I am a widower, and I know that it is my fault. I have let you go on believing so, when I should have told you. The truth is . . . I'm so sorry, Jane . . . I still have a wife. Judith is very much alive.' She gave an involuntary gasp, and Dave leaned closer to her.

'I feel dreadful about this, my love, please believe me. It wouldn't be so bad if I could say we are divorced, but we're not.'

Jane shook her head in bewilderment. 'But . . . I don't understand. What are you saying, Dave? You are separated . . . living apart, aren't you?'

'Yes, of course we are. Judith left me four years ago to go and live with someone else, someone more exciting than I am who can give her the sort of life she wants to live – glitter and glamour, parties and exotic holidays. She's still with him – I've never met him – but according to my son, Peter, they're very happy together.'

'Then why are you not divorced? That's what you said, isn't it? Surely there are grounds for divorce?' Jane was stunned. This had come right out of the blue. She could scarcely take it in. She was so sure that he had said his wife had died. Now she remembered that what he had actually said was that he had lost his wife. So what else was she to think? That was what the words implied; that the woman was dead. And he had let her go on thinking so.

Dave sighed. He let go of her hand and took another good drink of his lager. 'Yes, there are grounds for divorce, ample grounds; anyway, divorce is so much easier now than it used to be. It is what I want and she knows it. The problem is . . . Judith is a Catholic. Not even a practising one any more. That's what makes me so mad. She hasn't attended Mass, or whatever, for years. But she insists that it's her conscience, what she was brought up to believe. They still don't accept divorce, and she's going along with their teaching. Her parents are still living, and I guess that has a lot to do with it. They are more Catholic than the Pope, as the saying goes. They never approved of her marrying me. We had to be married in a register office because there was no other way round it. I refused to be married in her church, nor she in mine. I admit I don't go to church all the time, but I'm a believer, Jane, and I would always say with pride that I am Church of England. So, I suppose our marriage got off to a shaky start with regard to that. And it was never really a satisfactory marriage, I soon realized that.'

'But if you were only married in a register office . . . Sorry, perhaps I shouldn't have said 'only'. It's still a marriage, isn't it? What I mean is, do Catholics – people like her parents – regard it as a proper marriage? Why haven't they objected to her living with this other man who she's not married to, if they are so strict about everything?'

Dave shook his head. 'I honestly don't know, Jane, my dear. I know it doesn't make sense, but she's sticking to it like grim death. I know that the top and bottom of it is that she's being damned awkward. She refuses to think about a divorce, and that's that. She's very happy living with this chap Roger – that's what he's called. Maybe he still has a wife, I don't know because I haven't asked.'

He was silent for several moments and so was Jane, trying to take in all that he had said. Eventually, after what seemed ages, she said quietly, 'I wish you had told me at first, Dave. Right at the start . . . you should have told me then.'

'I know – I know I should,' he almost shouted. 'But it doesn't alter how I feel about you. I love you, Jane. I know I do. As I said before, I would like to think we might have a future together. Not right away, of course, but sometime, maybe in the not too distant future.' He took hold of her hand again. 'Does it really make so much difference, my dear, that I'm not free to get married again?'

'I don't know, Dave,' she said, quietly. She was remembering something her mother had said when she spoke to her on the phone a few days ago. Something about a man in the home whose son was 'living in sin'. Those were Mother's exact words, and that was how she regarded it and always would as far as Jane could see. This fellow had been married twice, and was now living with another woman, and they might or might not get married. Some such tale, the subject of gossip in the home. Jane hadn't taken much notice, but it all came back to her now. Mother was so set in her ways. She would never understand.

'Maybe . . . maybe we might be able to go on seeing one another when we get back home,' she began. 'But as far as anything else is concerned, I just don't know. You say that we don't live all that far apart, and I suppose that is true. With the motorway and everything a hundred miles isn't the obstacle it used to be. But you must admit there would still be problems. Your farm for a start. You can't keep taking time off, can you, no matter how well your son can cope in your absence? And, of course, there is . . . my mother.'

Yes, your mother! thought Dave, but he did not give voice to his somewhat uncharitable thoughts. From what he could see, Jane's mother was always going to be the stumbling block if Jane continued to go on regarding her as such.

'Bring her over to meet me,' he said impulsively. 'You could easily get to Shropshire and back in a day, if you set off early. And she would enjoy a day out, wouldn't she? My daughter-in-law – well, she isn't yet, but she soon will be – Kathryn, she would cook a nice meal for us all. You don't need to say any more than that I am a friend you met on holiday, for a start, that is. Then we would just have to see how things worked out.'

Jane looked pensive and a little sad. Dave knew he had dropped a bombshell that had been a tremendous shock to her. He felt truly sorry that he had disappointed her, as he knew that he had.

'I'm really sorry, Jane,' he said again. 'I can't tell you how much I regret it now, not telling you about my wife. My ex-wife – that's all she is. But even if I had been widowed, as you assumed, there would still have been problems, wouldn't there? Exactly the same problems regarding where we live, and the question of your mother.'

'Let's not think about it any more now, Dave,' said Jane. 'Going over and over it only makes it seem more complicated. Let's forget it, shall we? Well, put it to one side, at any rate.'

He nodded. 'Very well then. As you say, we're not getting anywhere, just mulling it over. But we won't let it spoil the rest of our holiday, will we?'

'No, I hope not,' Jane replied.

'We still have tomorrow, a free day for us, before we set off for home on Tuesday. Let's try and make the most of it and not think about the problems. I know I've upset you, but you'll forgive me enough to spend the day with me, won't you?'

Jane smiled, a little ruefully. 'Of course I will. After all, we've only known one another for a week, haven't we? That's all it is. Tomorrow it will be exactly a week since we met.'

'And what a fantastic week it has been,' said Dave. 'Whatever happens, I know I shall look back on it as one of the happiest weeks of my life. And that is thanks to you, Jane. We've had a wonderful time together. And I do hope it is something we can build on, not just look back on as a memorable week.'

'Yes, I hope so, too,' she replied. But she knew, and Dave knew, too, that her words lacked conviction.

They did not talk very much on the way back to the hotel. They walked hand in hand, but they did not stop to kiss from time to time as they had done before. When they reached Jane's bedroom door he kissed her gently on the lips.

'Goodnight, Jane, my dear,' he said tenderly. 'See you in the morning.'

'Yes, see you, Dave,' she replied. She hurried inside quickly and closed the door.

She did not burst into tears. Her mother had always been a stiff upper lip sort of person, and a lot of it had rubbed off on Jane. She felt sad, though, unutterably sad that her dream – or maybe it had always been an impossible dream? – might be coming to an end.

Seventeen

'Checkmate!' cried Henry with obvious delight as he moved his last piece into the strategic place.

'You've done it again!' said Alice, sounding vexed, but smiling at the same time. 'I shall beat you one of these days, Henry Collins, just you see if I don't!'

'Well, you'll have to hurry up about it, won't you?' replied Henry. 'You've only a few days left, haven't you? When is your daughter coming to pick you up?'

'Oh, I think it will be Thursday morning. She gets back on Wednesday, but I expect it'll be late by the time she arrives home. Yes, Thursday. That gives me three days to get even with you.'

'You're doing very well,' said Henry, just a trifle patronizingly. 'You wouldn't want me to let you win now, would you?'

'Let me win? I should think not! I shall beat you fair and square or not at all. Now, how about a cup of tea before we call it a day?'

'Good idea. Let's go and join Jack and Flora.'

Henry led the way across the lounge to where his mate, Jack, was talking to Flora the woman with whom Alice had become friendly since coming to stay at Evergreen. The four of them were often to be seen together, chatting or watching TV, or playing a board game that required more than two people.

Alice, during the week she had been there, had been relearning how to play chess.

She and her husband, Joe, had used to play. It was Joe who had taught her to play and she had become proficient, though never as good as he had been. Since he died there had been no one for her to play with. Jane, for some reason – although she was very intelligent – had never taken to the game, although her father had tried to teach her. Anyway, Alice realized that the lass was tired when she had done a day's work, as well as the shopping and cooking. It was little wonder that Jane wanted to relax, watching the TV or reading a book, or, on rare occasions, going out with a friend.

Whilst she had been staying in the home Alice had been thinking about how much her daughter did to make her life so much easier. She found, to her surprise, that she was missing Jane very much and was looking forward to seeing her again. She appreciated now, more than ever, that the two of them, mother and daughter, had needed a break from one another. They had spent far too much time together, apart from the time when Jane was out at work, and Alice knew that that had been her own fault. Her daughter had tried to encourage her, many times, to join this or that.

She remembered Jane saying, 'There's a branch of the Townwomens' Guild not far from here, Mother. Why don't you go and join? It would be just up your street. Intelligent ladies that you could chat to, and I believe they do all sorts of interesting things.'

Or, 'There's an Over Sixties group at church, Mother. They meet every Tuesday for a social afternoon – a talk by a visiting speaker, and a cup of tea and a chat. Mrs Evans down the road goes there. I could ask her to come and pick you up in her car. I'm sure she wouldn't mind.'

But Alice had always had an excuse for why she wouldn't do this or that. How would she get there, with Jane working all the time? And she wasn't going to be beholden to people giving her a lift. Yes, she knew there were taxis, but she wasn't going to spend her money on taxi fares, they were far too expensive. Anyway, she didn't know any of the people, and she'd heard that they could be very 'cliquish' in these organizations. Yes, she knew some of the women at church, but they weren't really her cup of tea. From what she had seen of them they spent all their time gossiping about one another.

The truth was – and Alice could see it only too well now – that she just couldn't be bothered. She had got into a rut and hadn't wanted to make the effort to join anything or to make new friends. And so after a time Jane had stopped trying to persuade her to do anything. She remembered how she had taken a great deal of cajoling to even consider coming to stay at Evergreen.

But how glad she was, now, that she had agreed to Jane's suggestion. She had been determined, after she had finally given in and said yes, that she was not going to like it, but her resistance had been broken down, even on the first day. She sat at ease now, on the Sunday evening, enjoying a cup of tea with Flora, Henry and Jack, the three people she had come to know best whilst she had been staying there.

'Well now, did you manage to beat him this time, Alice?' asked Jack.

'Did I heck as like!' she replied. 'No, I'm beginning to realize that Henry is streets ahead of me. If I had more time I'd catch up with him, you mark my words. But I'll be going home in a few days' time.'

'We'll miss you, Alice,' said Flora.

'Aye, we will that!' echoed Jack.

'There's nothing to stop you coming back for a visit, is there?' said Henry. 'We could have a game of chess, you and me. You could swot up on your moves at home. I'd look forward to another session.'

'I've no one to play with at home,' said Alice, sounding regretful. 'Our Jane's never learnt to play. Besides, she's too busy. I'm glad I've got into it again, though. It's jolly good exercise for the brain cells, isn't it? I think mine were beginning to stagnate with lack of use.'

'You certainly seem a lot brighter than you were when you came here,' said Flora. 'I could tell you were here under sufferance, but we soon jollied you up a bit, didn't we? We made you realize it wasn't all that bad living here.'

'Yes, so you did,' replied Alice thoughtfully. 'I must admit I've changed my mind about old folks' homes, and I never thought I'd say that. But you can't really compare this one with the majority of homes, can you? My daughter told me it was more like a residential hotel, but I didn't believe her. I was determined not to like it, but she was right.'

'Aye; you don't like to admit you're wrong, do you, Alice?' said Henry with a chuckle.

'Less of your cheek, Henry Collins!' she retorted. 'I thought

just the same about you when I first met you. He's a bloomin'
awkward so and so, I thought. Then I realized that you're a
lot like me, aren't you?'

'Well, it takes one to know one,' he replied.

'Yes—' Flora looked at Henry and then at Alice – 'you two
make a good pair, you're two of a kind. Hard on the outside,
but quite soft underneath, like those hard chocolates with a
creamy centre.'

'Aye, maybe we are, but I'm not right keen on those soft
centres meself. I like a nice chewy caramel, at least I did until
my teeth started sticking to 'em. I know this about Alice and
me; we haven't much time for folks who won't make an effort
to help themselves.'

Rather like I was before I came to stay here, Alice thought,
with a sharp twinge of guilty conscience. But Henry had not
seen that side of her, and she was determined that she would
never go back to the way she had been before.

'. . . and who won't have a go at summat new,' Henry went
on. 'You're never too old to learn. Look at Alice now, how
she's got the hang of chess again. She's nearly as good as me,
and all it needs is a bit of perseverance.'

'Oh, shut up Henry, for goodness' sake!' said Jack. 'You and
your flippin' chess! Just because Flora and me don't want to
be bothered to learn. It doesn't mean that we're stupid.' He
winked at Flora to show that he wasn't really as cross as he
sounded.

'I never said you were. Don't be so damned touchy, Jack
Perkins! But there's a few of 'em here who are content to sit
around and let life pass them by. I'm going to make the most
of it till I draw my last breath, and I reckon you will an' all,
won't you, Jack?'

'Yes, I hope so. But I've never got the hang of that chess
game. Draughts is exacting enough for me, and dominoes.
Flora and me, we'll stick to our draughts, and leave the chess
to you and Alice.'

They all retired to their rooms soon afterwards. Alice's room
was on the ground floor, something she was pleased about. It
was getting more and more difficult to climb the stairs, and
she hated having to use a stick, even for walking. Jane had

suggested that they should have a stair lift installed at home – which was very thoughtful of the lass, she supposed – but she had refused to even consider it.

'Do you want me to lose the use of my legs altogether?' she recalled saying, rather snappily. 'That's what it would come to if I got one of those contraptions. No, I'll get upstairs even if I have to crawl on all fours.' Which was what she had to do sometimes . . . And, there again, Jane had stopped making the suggestion.

Alice had also refused, so far, to have an operation on her knee. 'It would make a world of difference to you,' several people had told her. All about Mrs Whatsit who had had a knee replacement and she was a changed woman. You wouldn't believe the difference it has made to her. And so on and so on . . .

Her doctor had told her that her heart was strong, and that was the main issue, even though she was turned eighty. That had been a few years ago, but still she remained obdurate. So long as she could hobble about what was the point of putting herself through the trauma of an operation? And the more people tried to persuade her the more she dug her heels in. She was not going to be told what she must or must not do.

The truth was that Alice had an irrational aversion to hospitals. She had had the good fortune never to have been ill enough to stay in one. When she had given birth to her daughter she had insisted on staying at home. At that time there had been a lot of home births. Her husband had died, quite suddenly, at home. But she had seen both her parents go into hospital and die there. Her father had died when Alice was ten with a lung complaint, the legacy of a gas attack he had suffered in the trenches in the Great War. Her mother had died from cancer many years later.

She knew that conditions had improved drastically since those days, with the availability of new drugs and up-to-date procedures with anaesthetics. And hospitals were much more patient-friendly than they had used to be, or so she was told. But she remembered the stark clinical feel of the wards, and the rows of iron beds. The hospital staff, too: the stiff and starchy matron, the sisters and nurses, all immaculately dressed without a hair or a button out of place. Like prison warders, she had thought, remembering one particularly brusque sister with whom she had had words regarding her mother's condition.

She knew they were much more relaxed nowadays with regard to dress and their relations with patients and visitors, much more friendly and approachable. Possibly too familiar, though. She did object to being called Alice by some chit of a girl young enough to be her granddaughter . . . if she had one. That was how doctors' receptionists addressed you now, instead of affording you the courtesy of your proper title.

'So what exactly do you want, Mother?' Jane had asked her, not long ago, when she had been telling her about the casual attitude of the dental nurse, her use of Christian names and the way she was dressed, in what looked like a pink romper suit. And the dentist as well, Alice had complained about. He was dressed in a pale blue tunic and trousers, as though he was about to break into a song and dance act.

'You object to being called Alice,' Jane had said, 'but she's only being friendly and it's what they do today. It doesn't bother me, it makes me feel younger. But you say that the old-time nurses were unfriendly. There's no pleasing you sometimes, is there, Mother?'

But Jane had been laughing, so Alice had been forced to admit that she was perhaps being a mite unreasonable. 'Yes, I'm a contrary devil, aren't I?' she had agreed. 'Nothing's ever right, but things have changed so much, Jane, and not often for the best.'

'Hospital treatment has changed,' Jane had told her. 'That's why I think you should have that operation while you can. You can't afford to wait much longer, timewise, I mean. Or you could even afford to have it done privately.' But Alice had refused to budge. Now, as she looked around her room at Evergreen she realized she had been stubborn and pig-headed about a lot of things. This was a pleasant room and it was beginning to feel almost like home. The owners had certainly done all they could to give an individual feel to each room. She had been in Flora's room, and hers was similar in many ways, but with a different style and colour scheme.

Alice's room looked out on to a pleasant garden at the back of the house. The curtains at the double-glazed windows were a Laura Ashley design, patterned with spring flowers in shades of green and yellow, and there was a matching duvet cover on the bed. It was a fair-sized room with a green carpet, a wardrobe and dressing table in light wood, and a small television set on a corner cupboard. There was a comfortable chair with plump yellow cushions and an upright chair as well, and two framed prints on the wall of paintings by Monet, floral scenes to match the decor.

Opening off the room was a cubicle containing the toilet, washbasin and a low bath with grab handles and a handheld shower. Alice was glad about the bath. She could still get in and out of a bath, provided it was low enough, and she much preferred that to a shower.

Flora's room had more of an autumnal feel, although it was equally attractive with curtains of a William Morris design in brown and orange, a rust-coloured carpet and prints of paintings by Constable.

Alice decided to make herself a mug of hot chocolate to drink in bed. Another bonus was the provision of a kettle and a beaker, also tea bags, sachets of coffee and drinking chocolate and packets of biscuits, just the same as you would get in a hotel. Alice had been very surprised to find this facility here, in what she had originally thought of as a home for old people. She had found out, however, that a kettle was only provided for those guests who were capable of using it without any chance of an accident. There were several who were incapable, but, by and large, Evergreen's guests were still quite active and mobile.

Alice undressed and had a wash, then settled herself in bed with the mug of chocolate on her bedside table. There was a reading lamp provided, too, also an alarm bell to ring if assistance was needed during the night. She was contented, much more so than she had imagined she could ever be, away from her home in a place full of strangers. But that was one of the best things about her stay there, the people were not strangers any more. She could even class some of them as friends.

She opened her book, intending to have a good read before

she went to sleep, as she did every night at home. It was the latest Ruth Rendell book, one of her murder mysteries involving Inspector Wexford. She loved watching them on TV as well; George Baker personified him so brilliantly. She had also brought a Barbara Vine book – Ruth Rendell's alter-ego – usually more creepy and psychological, and another mystery by P.D. James.

She had thought that she would spend a good deal of her time reading, as she did at home. She did little else at home, reading avidly, or watching the television. Her TV viewing habits had changed since she had been living with Jane. At one time she would have scorned the 'soaps', but now she was a great fan of *Coronation Street* and *Emmerdale*. She enjoyed *Midsomer Murders* too, and *Foyle's War*. That was possibly her favourite of all; a contradiction, really, as she had often said she had seen enough of the war to last her a lifetime. But this was more about the Home Front, not the war that had been raging in Europe, and the characters were so convincing.

She had become engrossed in this make-believe world but, when all was said and done, it was not real life and, however well it was portrayed, it was just a form of escapism. The TV programmes and the books she enjoyed had become a substitute for her lack of friends and human companionship. She hardly ever conversed with anyone, apart from Jane. She spoke briefly to people at church and to shop assistants, to her doctor – on rare occasions, to the milkman, maybe, or the postman. Her life had become sterile and empty, but she hadn't realized it until she had spent a few days at Evergreen.

She read a page or two of her book – she was only halfway through it although she had been here for a week – but she found that her mind was wandering . . . That had been a jolly good game of chess tonight, with Henry. She knew, though, that however much she said it, she was unlikely to beat him. Henry was a 'whizz' at the game. That seemed to be the term they used nowadays.

He was very good company, too, and she enjoyed talking to him. She had made up her mind at first, in her usual forth-right way, that this was a man she was going to dislike. He was so argumentative, always so sure that he was right. Then she had come to see that he was very much like herself. And the twinkle in his eyes when he was arguing that black was white, showed that he didn't mean the half of it.

To her surprise she found that he kept coming to talk to her, actually seeking her out as though he enjoyed her company, and they didn't always argue. Then he had asked her if she played chess – there was no one in the home who could give him a decent game – and this had become a shared interest for them.

She found herself smiling as she thought about Henry. Never since she lost Joe had she found anyone – let alone a man – with whom she was so compatible. But then she hadn't wanted to meet anyone; she had missed Joe so much and knew there would never be anyone else to compare with him. Pull yourself together, Alice! she told herself sternly now. Having silly thoughts about a man, at your age! She wasn't falling for him. Of course not, the very idea was ridiculous! All the same it was very encouraging to feel that someone, especially a man, should want to be with her.

She had learned, during their many conversations that week, that Henry Collins had been a joiner by trade. He had retired, of course, many years ago.

'I left school when I was fifteen,' he told her, 'I had to because my parents needed me to go out to work and earn some money. There were four of us; me and my brother and two sisters, and I was the eldest. It was just after the war started, 1940, and my dad had been injured. He'd lost a leg early on in the war, so he was never able to work again. Anyway, I was lucky enough to get apprenticed to a good trade, and I've done all right; had my own business in the end, and my eldest son took it over when I retired.'

Alice knew that although he had left school at an early age he had a keen brain and had done what he could to further his education.

'I didn't have the chances like you had, Alice,' he had said. 'No sixth form and college and all that for me, but I was determined to do what I could to make up for it.'

He had attended night school to obtain the qualifications for his carpentry and, years later, he had studied French and learnt to speak the language quite fluently as he and his wife had used to travel abroad each year.

Henry was five years younger than Alice. He had just celebrated his eightieth birthday, but didn't look anything like his age. His hair was grey, of course, a silvery grey and he had not lost any of it. He was tall and upstanding, with no sign of a stoop, and he walked without the aid of a stick, something that Alice found very galling when compared with herself. This, above everything else, made her feel her age.

'You've no sign of arthritis then, Henry?' she had asked him. 'You're lucky if you haven't.'

'At my age, you mean? No, that's something I seem to have escaped, thank goodness. I can walk nearly as well now as I could when I was thirty. Not that I was ever a great walker, fell walking and all that. But I used to cycle, and I played a fair game of cricket, and bowls as well. I still have a game of bowls now and again. Jack goes with me sometimes to the green down the road, and there are one or two fellows there who play with us.'

Alice had been surprised at the number of residents at the home who still got out and about to follow their various interests. Flora had told her about her own activities, and there were others of them who were just as active. There were some, though, who preferred to stay put and do very little. They were the ones who were more difficult to get to know.

'The least you do, the least you want to do,' Flora had remarked. It was true that the least active folk among them tended to become insular and preoccupied with themselves and their problems and ailments.

'Thank God there's nowt very much wrong with me,' Henry had said. 'A bit of chest trouble; I get bronchitis in the winter and I have to keep an eye on my blood pressure. Apart from that I'm as fit as a fiddle.'

'Then may I ask, what are you doing here?' Alice had enquired in her usual outspoken way, 'Why did you decide to come and live with a lot of old folk?'

'Age is an attitude of mind, Alice,' he replied. 'You are just as old as you want to be. You can be young at heart even at our age if you take an interest in what's going on around you.

I know I'm a bit crotchety and I like to argue, but I've always been like that. I don't know how my wife put up with me. She was a very patient lady, one in a million, my Esther.'

Not very much like me then! thought Alice to herself. And it had struck home to her what Henry had said about age being an attitude of mind. She was realizing that she had allowed herself to become old in her mind – set in her ways – even though she still prided herself on looking younger than she was.

'She looked after me too well,' Henry went on, and I missed her so much when I lost her. Not because of what she did for me, being a good housewife an' all that, but the house seemed so empty without Esther. I didn't know how I would ever stand being there on my own. I stuck it for about eighteen months, then I found this place and thought I'd give it a try, and I've never looked back.'

'Wasn't it a big wrench, though, leaving your home – all your possessions and everything?' Alice asked.

'In a way I suppose it was. It felt strange at first, but I reckon that sort of thing might be worse for a woman than a man. It was Esther who made the house into a home; she was the one who was interested in furniture and colour schemes and what-have-you. She was a real homemaker, and it was never the same after she'd gone. And apart from all that I was never much good in the kitchen.' He laughed. 'I could make a cup of tea and boil an egg – although they're damned tricky things to get right – and put bread into the toaster. Apart from that I was pretty useless.'

'So what did you do when you were left on your own?' she asked.

'Oh, I managed the best way I could. Meals for one from Marks and Spencer or Sainsbury's that I could put in the micro-wave, or I went to the local chippy. My son asked me round for a meal now and again, him and his wife . . . I told you he's been married twice, didn't I? The last one was a rotten cook, though; happen that was part of the problem, I don't know.

'But I could never have gone to live with Barry – he's too much like me – not that he's ever suggested it. It doesn't always work out, does it, living with a son or daughter?'

Alice had learnt that Henry's daughter lived in the south of England, and he had another son who had emigrated to New Zealand, so he was pretty much on his own.

'No, perhaps not,' Alice had replied. 'It isn't ideal living with Jane, but I knew it was the best thing to do at the time. And I must admit she's made me feel that it's my home just as much as hers. I took a lot of my own belongings with me. I suppose she might miss me if I wasn't there . . . I don't mean if I died – if I was to leave.'

'Why?' asked Henry. 'Are you thinking of coming and living here permanently?'

'No,' she answered decidedly. 'No, of course I'm not . . .'

Eighteen

The guests at Gasthaus Grunder awoke on the Monday morning – their last day in Germany – to grey skies and lowering clouds. There was no sign of the sun that had blessed them all week, and it was already starting to rain.

Jane opened the shutters, then felt her heart plummet as she looked at the dismal scene. She was already feeling downcast following the revelations from Dave the previous evening. They had not fallen out about his disclosures, but she felt very let down and disappointed in Dave, whom she had thought of as such an honest and straightforward man. But they had agreed that they would spend their last day – that was the last day apart from the journey home – together, and try not to think too much about what the future might hold for them.

She made a cup of tea, which always brought her round and made her feel more able to face the day ahead. She was like her mother in that respect. Alice said she only felt half alive before she had drunk her first cup of tea.

Jane found herself thinking almost fondly about her mother now. It would be good to see her again, although it had been great to have these ten days away from her. She would ring her later today and see how she was faring at Evergreen, and assure her that she would pick her up on Thursday to take her home. She could imagine her mother saying, 'About time too!' or some such remark, although Jane had a sneaking feeling that she might have enjoyed her stay at the home rather more than she had let on.

The two of them would then have to settle down again to their life together. Perhaps it had been just an impossible dream to imagine that it could be otherwise. How could she go off and live her own life when her mother was so dependent on her? Dave still seemed convinced that there was a way round it, but Jane was trying to become reconciled to the fact that this last week had been a lovely idyll, a memory

– lots of memories – to look back on with pleasure and
nostalgia when she was back in her normal routine.

She washed and dressed, putting on a cardigan because the
day felt chilly, something she had not needed to do since the
start of the holiday. Dave was already seated at the breakfast
table, and he greeted her cheerily, ready to carry on as though
everything was hunky-dory.

'It's a miserable sort of day,' she commented, but Dave was
determined to be cheerful. 'It'll probably clear up later,' he
said. 'We can't let it spoil our last day here. We've done very
well so far, and a drop of rain won't hurt us. It isn't as if we're
not used to it back home.'

They helped themselves to cereal and fruit at the breakfast
bar. Then Mavis and Arthur arrived, both of them looking
happy to be together again. In reply to Jane's question he said
that he was feeling fine, and was glad to know that his condition was not as bad as he had feared. He was looking forward
to being home again, when they had got through the long
journey back.

Shirley and Ellen were the last to arrive at the table. 'Our
last breakfast together,' said Ellen. 'It's rather sad, isn't it?'

'It isn't our last breakfast,' Shirley told her. 'We'll be here
tomorrow morning, then we'll have a breakfast in Calais on
Wednesday before we cross the Channel.'

'Yes, I know that,' said Ellen, 'but I mean it's the last real day
of our holiday. We'll be travelling for the next two days, and
we'll be having our breakfast at some unearthly time tomorrow
morning. What time did Mike say we were setting off?'

'Eight o'clock,' said Shirley. 'Cases packed and ready to load
by seven. Yes, I agree it's damned early, but there's a heck of
a distance to cover from here to Calais.'

They were doing the return trip to France in one day instead
of the two more leisurely days they had taken on the outward
journey.

'So, what are we all going to do on our last day?' Shirley
asked the others. 'Have you anything planned?'

Jane and Dave looked at one another uncertainly. It was
Dave who answered.

'Take a bus into Freiburg, I should think; that's the nearest place. I know we've already been there, but there's a lot to see.'

'And shops to go into if it keeps raining,' said Jane.

'Oh, it'll stop, you'll see,' answered Dave, a shade impatiently. 'We've got to look on the bright side of life, like it says in that song.'

'My mother used to say, "Rain before seven, fine before eleven,"' said Arthur. He turned to look out of the window. 'It's still pouring down, but I think it might be getting a bit lighter.'

Mavis turned to look out as well. 'Is there a little patch of blue?' she said. 'No . . . I can't see one, but it might clear up. My mother used to say that if there's enough blue in the sky to make a sailor a pair of trousers it will be a fine day.'

Arthur laughed out loud. 'It looks as though your sailor will be without his pants at the moment, love. But never mind, eh? I don't mind if we have to spend the day here. We can get some lunch here at the hotel.'

'Yes, I think Arthur and I will have a quiet day here,' agreed Mavis. 'We're just relieved that everything has turned out so well for Arthur. What about you two?' She was speaking to Ellen and Shirley. 'How are you going to spend your last day here?'

Shirley grinned mischievously. 'Well now, Ellen and I have got a date, haven't we, Ellen?' she said, rather to her friend's discomfiture.

Ellen blushed and looked warily at Shirley. 'I wouldn't say that we could call it a date. We're not exactly teenagers, are we?'

'It doesn't matter how young or how old we are,' Shirley replied. 'Don't be such a spoilsport, Ellen. What would you call it then, if it's not a date?' She laughed as she turned to explain to the others. 'We sat with Trevor and Malcolm in the bar last night – you know, those two brothers. Yes, of course you know, how silly of me. They helped to push Arthur along in the wheelchair, didn't they? Well, they've asked Ellen and me to have lunch with them today. We'll probably go into Freiburg. I expect most of us will end up there. It's no big deal, but Ellen's getting all of a fluster about it.'

'Well, isn't that lovely?' said Jane. 'I hope you enjoy it. They seem to be very nice friendly sort of men, from what I've seen of them.'

Shirley started talking to Mavis who was sitting next to her, so Jane spoke in a quiet voice to Ellen. 'You look very attractive in your new top and trousers,' she said, 'and it's great for you to have a change of company. You don't need to get all worked up about it. I'm sure you'll have a lovely time.'

'It's ages since I went out with a man,' Ellen whispered. 'Well it's not really 'going out' is it, because there are four of us? Not a proper date, like Shirley was saying, but I know she was just teasing me. I've not had a lot to do with men, you see, except for those I work with, and they're married, of course, just colleagues. I had a boyfriend once,' she added in a confidential tone, 'when I was about twenty. My parents were very strict, you see, so I hadn't been out with many young men. But I really liked this one and we were getting quite fond of one another, but my parents disapproved of him because he liked to go for a drink, and they were afraid he would encourage me to do the same. So, it just fizzled out. There was never anyone else after that. And then, of course, I looked after my parents when they became ill.

'I'm not complaining, though.' Ellen smiled so brightly that Jane felt sure she meant it. 'I've enjoyed my job at the bank, and I have some good friends, as well as Shirley. And this week – it's been just wonderful. I do hope we'll all be able to keep in touch, Jane.'

'I'm sure we will,' replied Jane. 'We'll exchange addresses before we say goodbye.'

She was sure that these words had been said many times before by people who met on holidays such as this one. Maybe some kept up the friendships – though possibly by email or phone these days, rather than the conventional letter – whilst others lapsed apart from the odd Christmas card. For her part, Jane felt that she would like to keep in touch with Ellen. She experienced a kinship with her, knowing that Ellen, like Jane herself, was somewhat diffident when it came to friendships with the opposite sex. Ellen had been discouraged, even prevented, it seemed, from forming any meaningful relationships, until now she assumed it was too late.

Jane could not complain about her parents in that respect. She had never had the close bond with her mother that she could have wished for, but neither of them had ever objected to her having boyfriends. There had been one or two, but no one of any importance until she had met Tom. She understood how Ellen must feel now, nervous and unsure about getting friendly with a man, as she had felt after Tom died. Jane did not know, in fact, whether the four of them had formed themselves into two couples. Probably not, at least not so far. But it might work out that way, she thought to herself; foursomes usually did. Maybe it would just be a holiday companionship, not leading to anything afterwards. But however it turned out, Jane hoped that Ellen would forget her fears and have a really enjoyable time.

As for herself, she had soon overcome her shyness on meeting Dave. It had seemed that their friendship might be going somewhere, but now the future looked more unsure than ever.

The two drivers had breakfast together rather later than usual. As a rule they liked to dine before the guests appeared. They were glad of a complete day of rest, which was what the management insisted on before they embarked on the long journey home. They were not allowed to drive at all on this rest day. On the UK holidays the drivers were permitted to do an extra tour, usually a half day, and this was regarded as a bonus for the driver; he was allowed to keep the fare money for himself, less the amount used for the fuel. This little tour on the last day rounded off the holiday nicely, but on the Continental tours the clients were left to their own devices.

'So, what do you have planned for today?' Mike asked his co-driver. 'Are you seeing the lovely Christine?'

'As a matter of fact, I am,' said Bill. 'You don't mind, do you?'

They had sometimes spent the last day together, mooching around doing not very much at all, glad of the time to be on their own without the responsibility of a coachload of passengers.

'Why should I mind?' said Mike. 'I'm pleased it's going well for you, old chum. No further trouble from Olga?'

'No, thank goodness! I suppose I was rather a heel, dumping her like that, but I thought it was a mutual decision. Anyway, she seems to have got over it and we're speaking to one another again. It would be better, though, if I didn't have to do this tour any more. I would miss it, but I've almost made up my mind to ask about being transferred to the UK tours.'

'You and me both, then,' said Mike. 'I shall ring Sally today and see how things are going with Tracey. She was in a real tizzy the last time I spoke to her, and I know it's time I thought about being nearer home. Like you, I would miss my trips over here, but there'll be plenty of lads waiting to step into our shoes, you can be sure. Are you serious, Bill, about giving this up? Are you and Christine . . . well, is it going to carry on after you get home?'

'I'm hoping so,' said Bill. 'Fingers crossed and all that. It's not gone very far yet, if you know what I mean. Anyway, she's not the sort of girl to rush into anything like that. That's what I like about her. I don't think she trusted me at first, especially when she found out about Olga. But we've been getting on fine these last few days. I'll have to be careful not to blow it, though. I've planned something special for today.'

'Have you, indeed! What have you got in mind? The weather's not too good at the moment.'

'No, but I'm hoping it will clear up because I thought we'd have a run out to Schneider's Vineyard. We can do the wine-tasting bit and have lunch there. It's much nicer to dine outside, but it's comfortable inside if it's still raining.'

'How are you going to get there? Will you borrow Herr Grunder's car?'

'No, it would be a cheek to ask and he's been very good to us. Anyway, we're not supposed to drive at all, are we? I thought we'd take a taxi; it's not all that far.'

'My goodness, you're going mad, aren't you? You must think she's worth it.'

'It's only once in a while. Anyway, I've saved up a fair bit this year, and the crowd this week should be good for a few extra quid, don't you think?'

'I try not to be so mercenary,' said Mike with a grin. But he knew what Bill meant. The drivers were not highly paid, but the tips they received at the end of the holidays – and most of the clients were pretty generous – made quite a difference to their wages.

'We may not do so well back in the UK,' Mike added, 'but there may be advantages. It's swings and roundabouts, I suppose . . . I hope you have a good day. What time are you going?'

'I said I'd meet Christine in the foyer at half past ten. So I'll see you later, Mike.' Bill stood up, ready to make a move. 'Wish me luck, won't you?'

'Oh, I do, as much luck as you deserve!'

'And how much is that? Not a lot, eh?'

'All the luck in the world,' said Mike. 'Yes, I mean it. I hope all goes well for you.'

The name 'Black Forest' brought to mind a region of mountains and dense forests. There were, however, gentler hills where small farms and vineyards were to be found in the valleys. They were mainly family concerns, the vineyards producing comparatively small quantities of wine, red and white, from sweet to dry, which was sold mainly in their own region. Such a vineyard was the one owned by Rudolph Schneider and his wife, Eva, a few miles outside Freiburg.

'We used to visit it on our tour,' Bill told Christine on their way there in the taxi, 'then the itinerary was changed. There isn't enough time in a week to see all the places of interest, but it may well be included again sometime in the future. It's a shame to miss it, though, and I know Herr Schneider will be pleased to see us. I haven't told anyone else about it,' he added with a wink. 'It's just a secret for you and me. We're not likely to meet anyone from the coach there, and that suits me just fine.'

'They're a good crowd, though, aren't they?' asked Christine. 'No one causing any trouble. I'm sure you must have lots of problems sometimes.'

'No, we can't grumble this time. It's all gone smoothly, apart from Mr Johnson's heart attack and the missing suitcase. They're a good crowd as you say, but the best thing is that I've met you.' He turned to smile at her and took hold of her hand.

It took only twenty minutes or so to drive to the vineyard. A rather faded sign at the entrance held the name of the proprietor and the opening times, surrounded by a border of grapes and leaves; then a short drive led up to a long low white building which Bill said was the restaurant.

'I believe they do very well in the evenings,' said Bill. 'The locals dine there, and Eva is a splendid cook, with a very good team of assistants, of course. But if it's fine it's nicer to dine outside, in the daytime, I'm still hoping we might be able to do that.'

The taxi driver drove round to the back and pulled up in the courtyard. Christine noticed a coach parked there, and the sign on it indicated that it was from Lille in France. Bill paid the fare and explained in halting German interspersed with English – that the man seemed to understand – that he would phone him when they were ready to go back.

The proprietor must have been expecting them because he appeared at that moment, a tall thin man with greying hair and a goatee beard, and dark piercing eyes that lit up with an expression of delight at seeing them. He greeted Bill like a long-lost friend.

'Ah, Bill, it is so good or see you again. It has been too long. And your friend . . .?'

'Yes, this is Christine. She's on the tour and I wanted her to see your place.'

'That is very good. We have a party here just now. They are tasting the wines, if you would like to join them?'

Christine looked around curiously. At the rear of the restaurant there was a paved terrace with wooden tables and benches, with flowering plants and small bushes in terracotta pots; a rustic setting where it would be nice to dine if the rain stopped. It was still drizzling, and she was wearing her anorak, the first time she had needed it during the holiday. A veranda stretched over the area though, so it might be possible to sit there later.

Despite the weather it was an idyllic setting. Beyond the huddle of buildings, which included the red-roofed bungalow where she guessed the family lived, a gentle slope rose upwards where the rows of vines were growing, and in the distance a backdrop of wooded hills. The scene was far different from the steep slopes they had seen along the Rhine valley, mile upon mile of vineyards reaching down to the river.

That was the chief wine producing area of the country where vast quantities of somewhat less expensive wines were produced, such as those sold in supermarkets all over the UK. Connoisseurs were inclined to disregard these products as being inferior, only produced to suit the tastes of a largely undiscerning market.

In the Black Forest region the wine was produced on a much smaller scale catering mainly for the local population and not sold abroad in large quantities. It did, however, find its way across the channel in the bags and boxes of tourists who had been on a wine-tasting trip.

'Come along with me, if you please.' Herr Schneider led them into a building where a group of people were sitting at tables with a row of tiny glasses in front of them. Christine assumed that these were the French visitors from the town of Lille. The proprietor spoke to them in French, and they smiled and nodded at the newcomers, inviting them to sit down and join them.

The young man assisting with the distribution of the wine was a younger edition of Herr Schneider. Christine guessed, correctly, that it was his son, Sebastian. The French contingent had already sampled a few of the wines, but Bill's and Christine's glasses were soon filled so that they could catch up.

'It's a good job you're not driving,' she whispered, after drinking the contents of three glasses, albeit minute ones. 'This stuff's pretty potent. Not like your common or garden Liebfrau, is it?'

'I shall be careful, don't you worry,' said Bill. 'I'll have an odd drink at lunchtime, then keep off the booze tonight so that I'll be fit and ready for the journey in the morning.'

Sebastian walked around the tables filling each of the glasses in turn, whilst his father told the visitors, first in French and then in English, about the wine that they were tasting. There were various kinds of whites and reds, ranging from dry to very sweet, with names that Christine had never heard of before. There was a particularly sweet red wine, which seemed to be a contradiction because reds were usually dry, but this was a wine that was favoured by the local populace and not widely sold abroad. There were bottles of this, however, and of all the other wines, for sale in the shop.

As was only to be expected, at the end of the session they were led into the adjoining shop where they were left to browse among the row of laden shelves. There were wines in abundance, of course; they were by no means cheap, but, according to Rudolph Schneider, you were paying for the quality, that extra something that was not to be found in the mass-produced wines.

There was a vast array of eatables and souvenirs as well as the wine. Chutneys and jams; honey and marmalade; packets of biscuits, fudges and chocolates; carved wooden animals, teddy bears, dolls and trinkets, such as they had seen in the shop with the large cuckoo clock, but on a smaller scale.

Christine had already shopped that week at every place they had visited, so there was nothing else she wanted to buy here apart from the wine. She felt obliged to buy a couple of bottles – it seemed that most of the visitors felt the same judging by the items in their baskets – but she wanted to do so, as well, as a souvenir of her holiday. She chose a medium white, similar to a Liebfrau but rather more mellow and fruity, although she was by no means a connoisseur, and a bottle of the rich red which had almost the consistency of a liqueur.

Bill didn't purchase anything, but then she didn't expect him to. He must have been there many times before. Christine waited in a queue to pay for her purchases and when they left the shop the rain had stopped. A break in the clouds gave promise of a sunny afternoon.

'That's good,' said Bill. 'We'll be able to have our meal outside. And it looks as though we might have the place to ourselves.'

It seemed that the French people were paying only a short visit to the vineyard then moving on to somewhere else. Christine and Bill sat down at one of the rough wooden tables on the terrace.

'It's much posher inside the restaurant,' Bill told her, 'but the food is just the same. Is this OK for you?'

'It's fine by me,' she answered. 'It's a lovely place. I'm glad you brought me here.'

There was a superb view beyond the slope of the vineyard to a wooded mountain range in the distance. The clouds were quickly dispersing as the sun shone through the morning mist and rain. As Christine feasted her eyes on the beauty of the landscape a rainbow appeared over the faraway hills. She was reminded, as she always was at the sight of a rainbow, of the story she had heard long ago in Sunday School, of Noah's Ark and God's promise, following the flood, that He would always be there in the midst of trouble. She did not go to church now – well, hardly ever – but the moment seemed to be filled with a special meaning. She was happy that she was there, happy that she had met Bill, and hopeful that there might be something for the two of them in the future.

Bill nudged her. 'You're miles away,' he said with a laugh. 'Are you thinking of the pot of gold at the end of the rainbow?'

'Something like that,' she replied. 'It's a stunning view, isn't it?'

'I must admit that it is,' he said, 'although I'm not one to wax lyrical. I know I'm ready for something to eat.' He handed her the large menu that was held between the paws of an upstanding wooden bear. 'What do you fancy?'

Her eyes scanned the extensive list, then she realized that several of the items were only available in the evening. But there was still a goodly number of hearty snacks for lunchtime.

'I'm spoilt for choice,' she said, scanning the list of pizzas, pastas and salads. 'You choose for me, Bill. I'll have the same as you.'

'We'll have Flammkuchen, then,' he replied. 'It's a sort of flambé tart. It's truly delicious, home-made by Eva Schneider. I know you'll enjoy it.'

He gave their order, plus two glasses of Riesling, to the waitress who was dressed in a dirndl skirt and peasant blouse. There were a few more customers now, seated at the tables, who looked like locals. It was always a good sign when the local people dined there.

'We may have to wait a little while,' said Bill. 'Everything is cooked specially as you order it, but I can assure you it will be worth the wait. So Christine . . . are you looking forward to going home?'

She didn't answer for a moment, then, 'Yes, I suppose I am really,' she replied. 'It's always good to get home again after a holiday. There's no place like home, as they say. But it's been a fabulous trip, far better that imagined. I've really enjoyed it.'

'Good . . . and could there be any special reason for that?' He raised a questioning eyebrow as he smiled at her.

'You're fishing for compliments, aren't you? I've enjoyed your company, Bill. You've made it all very interesting, showing me places and telling me all sorts of things about the area.'

'And have you thought any more about what I said? About us seeing one another when we get back home?'

'I've thought about it,' she replied. 'But it all depends on Monty. I'll have to see what he thinks about it.' She gave a roguish grin.

'Ah yes, of course, Monty, your chocolate Labrador. Do you think he might take a dislike to me? I like dogs, you know. I've never been able to have one of my own, but I know they're very loyal companions. He'll be missing you, won't he?'

'I'm sure he will, but he'll be OK with Mum and Dad . . . No, I don't think he'll take a dislike to you, Bill. I was only teasing. I've never known him to take a dislike to anyone. He's a very friendly dog. Labradors are, you know. That's why they make such good pets; they're so gentle with children. I'm not sure about being a guard dog, though. He hardly ever barks and I don't know how he'd react to a burglar.'

'You still haven't answered my question. Shall we give it a try, Christine? I'm absolutely sure that I want to . . . if you do?'

'Yes . . . yes, I do, Bill,' she answered. 'We've got along well together this week and yes, I'd like to go on seeing you.'

They were interrupted at that stage by the arrival of their lunch. 'That looks good,' said Christine. 'It's enormous, though.'

The tart filled the large round platter. It was a sort of thin pizza, covered with crème fraiche, crisp bacon pieces and golden fried onions. And it turned out to be just as delicious as it looked. The dry white wine was the perfect accompaniment.

'I'm really chuffed that we can go on seeing one another,' said Bill. She knew that he was not one for flowery phrases, and she felt, now, that she was able to trust him. He had assured her that it was definitely all over with Olga. She guessed that there might have been others, plenty of them, but she was ready to give him a chance.

'I shall ring up the boss as soon as we get back to the hotel,' he told her. 'I'll tell him that I'd like to work in the UK for a while, maybe permanently. I know there are several lads who will jump at the chance of working on the Continent. So now . . . well, it all depends on Monty, doesn't it?'

Nineteen

The phone lines from the Gasthaus Grunder to places in England were busy on that Monday afternoon. Bill, as he had promised, rang his boss in Preston as soon as he and Christine arrived back at the hotel.

'What? You as well!' said Charlie Baldwin, the manager of Galaxy Travel when he heard Bill's voice and had listened to his request. 'I've already had Mike on the phone saying the same thing. What's up with the pair of you? I thought you were both OK, and you get on well together, don't you?'

'Yes, like a house on fire,' said Bill. 'We're good mates, but we both have our reasons. I didn't know Mike had spoken to you, I've not seen him since breakfast time.'

Charlie admitted that he did know why Mike wanted to work in the UK. 'Family problems, I gather,' he said, 'and I can understand that. Wives get fed up when their hubbies are working away, and Mike's been doing the Continental tours for about three years now. He's ready for a break. But what's the problem with you, Bill? You're a single bloke, and I thought you liked it over there.'

'So I do,' replied Bill, 'but I'm the same as Mike; I feel that I'm away from home too much.' He didn't want to say that he had a new girlfriend, one that he had met on this tour and that he was hoping to make a go of it. 'I don't have family commitments in the way that Mike has, but I do have a family – parents and a brother and sister, and grandparents who are getting on a bit. And there are things I like to do like go to football matches, and I'm in a darts team – at least I used to be – and, well . . . I just feel so out of things while I'm over here. I know it has its compensations, and I've enjoyed it, but the shorter tours at home would suit me better.' He decided he'd said enough and maybe he was overbuttering the bread, or whatever the saying was.

'Yes, I see . . .' said Charlie. 'You have a free week after you get back, don't you? And then I think we've got you down for one of the French tours, in the Loire Valley . . .' One of the problems with Galaxy was that you never knew where you might be asked to go from one week to the next.

'I'll think about it,' Charlie told him. 'That's the best I can say at the moment. I've more or less told Mike that it'll be OK for him – he did ask first after all – and there's young Steve dying to have a chance to work on the Continent. He's ready for it now, but he'll have to have someone with him the first time to show him the ropes. I'll see what I can do, Bill, but it's a pity, you were starting to get more experienced over there. It's not a job that anyone can do. Leave it with me, and I'll try to rearrange the schedules.'

'Thanks very much Charlie. I'm grateful to you. It's hard to explain but—'

'Say no more, Bill. We always try to oblige if we can. It makes for a happier workforce. See you on Wednesday then? It's been a successful trip, has it? Apart from the couple of problems I've heard about—' that was the suitcase incident and Mr Johnson's heart attack; they had to report back to HQ about everything that happened '—but you and Mike seem to have coped very well. Anyway, bye for now, Bill.'

At the other end of the line Charlie Baldwin reflected that, knowing what he did about Bill, there was probably a lady involved. But they had a fair number of drivers and there were always men waiting to join the firm; women, too, in these days of equal opportunities.

Bill found Mike in their bedroom, lounging on his bed reading a spy thriller.

'So you beat me to it.' said Bill. 'I've just rung Charlie and he said you'd been on the phone. I get the impression that you're home and dry – you did ask first – but he's going to think about my request. So it's fingers crossed.'

'I hope you get what you want then, if you're sure about it. You had a good day with Christine then, did you?'

'Terrific, thanks! We've agreed to give it a try, and I've a week off when we get back, so . . .' Bill winked and made a thumbs up sign.

'All power to your elbow, then,' said Mike. 'Don't go mucking things up if you think you're in with a chance.'

'I'll try not to. How did you go on with Sally? I take it she's still anxious for you to work at home?'

'Absolutely, but she was a lot calmer, not in such a tizzy as she was the last time I rang.'

He had phoned her around lunchtime, just before she started her afternoon shift at the supermarket.

'Hi there, Sal, it's me,' he began. 'How are things with you?'

'Hello, Mike. I guessed it might be you.' At least she sounded much calmer, and he breathed a sigh of relief at not having to hold the phone away from his ear. 'Things are better here, I'm pleased to say. Our Tracey went back to school this morning with her tail between her legs, as you might say. I've never seen her so subdued. She was cocky about it at first – at least she pretended to be – as though it was just a laugh. But she had a real good telling off from me, and she was grounded all weekend, and for this week as well, unless I relent.'

'Good for you, Sal! She's not a bad kid, though, really, is she? We've done our best to bring her up in the right way, although I must admit it's been largely up to you in the last few years. I'm going to have a word with Charlie about working nearer to home. I shall talk to him today instead of waiting till I get back.'

'That's good,' said Sally. 'Thank you, Mike . . . We do miss you, you know. I know you'd probably be away all week, but at least we would have all the weekends together.'

'We'll have to cross our fingers that Charlie agrees, then. I'll put in an earnest plea.'

'Tracey misses you a lot. I hadn't realized how much, but last night she said to me, "I really miss Dad, you know. It's awful that he's away so much." And she even said, "I'm sorry I've been such a nuisance, Mum." That's all she said, but you could have knocked me down with a feather.'

'It's nice to know I'm missed so much.' Mike felt very touched at what Sally had said, and he was more determined than ever not to be such an absentee father. 'Listen, love, I'll have to go now. Goodness knows how much this is costing.

Bye for now, Sal. love you, and love to the kids. Take care
now . . .'

'Will do. See you soon, Mike. Love you too . . .'

Jane phoned her mother when she returned to the hotel in
the mid-afternoon.

She had spent the day with Dave in Freiburg. The low cloud
and grey skies during the early part of the day had not helped
her downcast spirits. But towards midday the sun had appeared,
and by this time she had managed to cast off most of her
gloom.

It seemed that Dave intended to act as though there was
nothing wrong. She realized he was a pretty sanguine sort of
fellow, determined to look on the bright side and not allow
himself to be downhearted. Did that mean that he was unable
to feel things as deeply as she did? She had not really known
him long enough to have found out everything about him.
She knew, though, that men and women often had a different
outlook on problems.

They had had a pleasant enough day, although there was
that constant niggle at the back of her mind all the while that
this might be the last time they would be alone together. In
a couple of days she feared they would have to say goodbye,
and that would be the end of their all too fleeting romance.

They had dined at lunchtime under the veranda of a cafe
in the market square. It was not so busy as it had been on
Saturday, but there was still a good number of tourists around
and they kept meeting other people from the coach. They
had seen Bill and Christine setting off somewhere in a taxi
earlier that morning, looking very happy together. Whilst they
were having their lunch Shirley and Ellen walked past with
the two brothers, Trevor and Malcolm. Jane was not quite
sure which was which, but Shirley was walking with one of
the men, and Ellen with the other, not arm in arm or hand
in hand, but they seemed very relaxed in one another's
company. Ellen gave a shy smile and a little wave to Jane as
they passed.

'Ellen's a lovely person, isn't she?' Dave remarked. 'She seems
to be getting on well with Trevor – at least I think that one

is Trevor. I get the impression that she's dominated by Shirley a lot of the time, so this should do her a world of good.'

'Yes, I hope so, even if it's only a holiday friendship . . .' Jane's voice petered out. She said no more, but she felt that Dave knew what was in her mind. He nodded but made no comment.

They had a last wander around the square when they had finished their lunch, then took a bus back to the village, which was the nearest stop to the hotel.

'I must finish my packing now,' said Jane, halting at her bedroom door. 'I'm taking back far more than I came with.'

'Me too,' said Dave. 'I'll see you at dinner time then? If we go down early we could have a drink at the bar?'

'Yes, maybe . . .' She smiled brightly as she entered her room. 'See you later, Dave.'

A few moments later, after trying to get herself into the right frame of mind, she went down to the foyer to phone her mother.

'Hello, Mother. It's me.' She hoped she was sounding happier than she felt. The carefree attitude she had tried to assume all day was fast disappearing.

'Yes, I guessed it might be you,' said Alice. 'You'll be setting off back tomorrow, won't you?'

'Yes, eight o'clock in the morning. I'm just going to finish my packing.'

'You've had a good time, have you? You feel the holiday has done you good?'

'Yes . . . yes, I'm sure it has. It's all been lovely. Good weather, and lots of interesting places to see, and nice people on the coach.'

'You've made some new friends then?'

'Yes . . . yes, I have. One or two people I shall keep in touch with.' She had a chance then to mention a particular one, but she did not do so. She might have done, had not Dave told her his true circumstances. But Mother would never get her head round that. 'What about you, Mother? I expect you've made some friends at Evergreen, haven't you?'

'Yes, I suppose so. Like you, there's one or two I might keep in touch with. I said I might pop back and see them sometime. I told you about Flora, didn't I? We get on quite well, and there are one or two others. It's been better than I expected, but I'll be glad to get home. There's nothing like your own bed and your own things around you.'

'I'm glad you've enjoyed it. I said you'd be OK there, didn't I?'

'Yes, maybe you did. I said I'd give it a try, and that's what I've done. Now, when are you coming to collect me? You won't be back till late on Wednesday, will you?'

'No, it'll be too late. I'll come on Thursday morning, so make sure you're ready. It'll be nice to get home,' she said, realizing that, in spite of everything, she had missed her mother. 'It's been a great holiday . . . but all good things come to an end.' She felt her voice breaking, and her mother picked on it at once.

'Jane? What is it? There's nothing wrong, is there?'

'No, nothing at all. It's just . . . it's nothing, Mother. I'll see you soon . . .'

She put the phone down quickly, trying to stem the tears that were welling up in her eyes. She hurried back to her room where she made a cup of tea and tried to compose herself.

She dragged her suitcase from the top of the wardrobe, ready to start packing. It was easier packing to go home as one didn't need to be so careful about folding the clothes. She had a large plastic bag in which she put the items that were ready for washing, but some things would only need a quick iron to be ready to wear again.

There was so much more to take home than she had brought with her. As a result of her shopping sprees in Baden Baden and elsewhere her case was bulging and the adaptable straps stretched to their furthest limit. Then there were all the bits and pieces she had bought as souvenirs or for presents. She had been given a sturdy carrier at one the gift shops and that would hold her purchases and fit into the overhead compart-ment above her seat. One bonus with coach travel was that the luggage was taken care of – although, occasionally, maybe not as well as it might have been! – and the passengers did not need to carry their heavy cases around.

By the time her case was packed, with the clothes she had decided to wear for the last day's travel in the UK at the top, she was feeling more composed. She washed, then dressed with care for the final evening in Germany. That morning in Freiburg, egged on by Dave – he had been determined to carry on as though everything was OK – she had bought a pair of flared trousers in a deep coral shade, and a top with pink and blue flowers on a white background. She knew that they suited her – made her look younger – and she decided as she applied her make-up and combed and rearranged her hair, that she must do her utmost to be cheerful and carefree that evening, and put to one side the jumbled thoughts that were whizzing round and round in her head.

She sat and read her book, getting engrossed in other people's joys and sorrows which was a distraction that helped her to focus her mind on something else, if only for a short time. Dave knocked at her door at six thirty, and she greeted his cheerful, 'Ready, Jane?' with a bright smile.

They sat in the bar area enjoying a pre-dinner aperitif along with several other Galaxy travellers. In fact, by the time they were ready to go for their final dinner almost all of the party had congregated in the lounge. They all knew one another by this time, some better than others, of course. There was plenty to talk about and conversation flowed easily. Jane chatted to one, then another, relieved that she did not have to talk exclusively to Dave.

Just before seven o'clock, which was the set time for the evening meal, Herr Grunder appeared in the lounge. 'We have a little extra treat for you this evening, ladies and gentlemen,' he announced. 'After your meal we will have a get-together – that is how you say it, I think? – here in the lounge. You may not know – my wife, Marianne, and I have only just found out – that this may be the last time that our good friends Mike and Bill will be staying here.' There were surprised exclamations from a few people as he went on to say that the two drivers had decided to give up their Continental tours to work in the UK.

'We have known them for quite some time,' he said, 'Mike rather longer than Bill. They have become good friends to us and we will miss them. And so, ladies and gentlemen, there will be a farewell drink for you all after the meal, "on the house" as you say, then a little entertainment. We will dance and sing and have a good time together, yes? You have been excellent guests, all of you very happy, I think, and no complaints. Marianne and I, we thank you very much. And now . . . your last evening meal awaits you. Please enjoy it.'

There was a round of applause before they all trooped into the dining room. There was a festive air to the room with candles burning – safely in glass holders – on each table, and vases holding fresh flowers: roses, Sweet Williams and sweet peas, their fragrance scenting the air.

The meals at Gasthaus Grunder had all been good, some more palatable than others to English taste, but on the whole their plates had been cleaned each time, apart from one or two dumplings that had proved to be rather too filling. The guests all agreed that the meal on the final evening was one of the best that Herr Grunder and his assistants had prepared that week. Onion soup with noodles was followed by the main dish of succulent roast pork served with asparagus tips, broccoli and potato slices in a cheese sauce. The dessert was Sachertorte, as was served in Viennese cafes, a rich chocolate cake with a layer of cherry jam, served with whipped cream.

The party of six – Mavis and Arthur, Dave and Jane, Shirley and Ellen – had got to know one another quite well over the six days they had spent at the guest house, and they talked to first one then another, with ease. Jane, as usual was seated between Dave and Ellen. Ellen looked very attractive that evening. Her grey hair, which at first had had that tight permed look, was now arranged in a softer style. The coral top she was wearing matched the pink lipstick she had applied sparingly and brought a radiance to her rather pale face. Jane commented that her hair looked nice, and Ellen said that Shirley had washed and set it for her. Most of the ladies had done an impromptu styling of their hair as ten days was too long to go without their usual shampoo and set or blow dry.

'And how did you enjoy your day in Freiburg?' asked Jane. She guessed that the glow that was emanating from Ellen was not entirely due to her discreet make-up and her hairstyle.

'You and Trevor looked very contented together. The man you were with – he is Trevor, isn't he?'

'Yes, that's Trevor.' Ellen smiled, a gentle, secretive sort of smile. 'He's two years older than his brother. Malcolm's just turned sixty, and Trevor's sixty-two. They've both retired recently – they worked in local government – but they decided that they'd worked long enough and want to enjoy their retirement. Trevor is seven years older than me,' she added in a whisper, 'but that's not very much, is it?' She looked questioningly at Jane.

'No, not at all,' Jane replied. 'It doesn't matter how old you are, or who is older than who, so long as you get on well together.' She felt that Ellen was dying to confide in her. 'Are you saying that you and Trevor are getting . . . friendly? That you like one another . . . quite a lot?'

Ellen gave a quiet contented sigh. 'Yes, I think so. He wants us to meet when we get back home. He lives not very far away from me, in Stockport. It's only a short journey away from Manchester on the train, although we both drive a car.'

'Do you really?' said Jane. For some reason it surprised her that Ellen could drive.

'Yes, I decided, when I was in my forties, that it was something I must learn to do. It was handy for driving my parents about. My father had never learnt to drive, but he became very much a back-seat driver! They were glad of the convenience of it, though. I don't drive as much now, it can be murder driving in Manchester. I'm near enough to my work to walk there, but I've kept up with my driving licence. It's handy sometimes.'

Still waters run deep, thought Jane. 'And . . . what about Shirley and Malcolm?' she asked. Shirley was not listening. She was talking animatedly to Dave.

'Oh, I think they're getting on OK together,' replied Ellen, 'but for Shirley it's just someone to be friendly with on holiday, and I think Malcolm feels the same about it. Trevor's the quiet one of the brothers – more like me – but Malcolm's much more lively, more like Shirley. I haven't said very much to her. You know what she's like, she'd tease me unmercifully. No, I think that's the last she'll see of Malcolm, after this holiday.

She's had a few men friends, you know, since her divorce, but she doesn't want to get married again.' Then she looked at Jane in some consternation.

'I'm not saying that Trevor and I . . . nothing like that, but I really think he means it when he says he'd like to see me again.'

'I'm sure he does,' said Jane, 'and I'm really happy for you. We must keep in touch, then you can let me know how you're getting on.'

'And you and Dave, as well,' said Ellen. 'You two are very happy together, aren't you?'

'Yes . . .' replied Jane, a little uncertainly. 'I thought so, but things aren't always as simple as they seem. I've got a mother who's getting on in years, and Dave . . . well, there are one or two problems.' She decided not to say exactly what they were. 'He's a farmer, you know, and he has a lot of responsibility. We'll just have to wait and see how things work out.'

When the meal ended they all adjourned to the lounge for coffee and, after a short interval, the festivities of the evening began. An 'on the house' drink of white wine, lager or fruit juice was brought round to all the guests by the waitresses and Marianne, all dressed in what must be their best National dress they wore for special occasions: dirndl skirts in forest green with a fancy red border at the hemline, richly embroidered peasant blouses, white stockings and highly polished black patent leather shoes with silver buckles.

Then Herr Grunder appeared, dressed likewise in National costume – dark green jacket, knickerbockers and bright red socks. Everyone stopped talking as he stood on the dais at the end of the room.

'Ladies and gentlemen,' he began. 'I would like you please, in a moment or two, to raise your glasses and we will drink a toast to our two very good friends, Mike and Bill.' The two drivers were sitting together near the dais and, as Johann Grunder motioned towards them, they stood, each giving a somewhat embarrassed nod to the assembled audience. Then they sat down again as the proprietor went on with his speech.

'Marianne and I have known these two worthy gentlemen for quite some time, Mike for a little longer than Bill. They have come here several times each year bringing you lovely people from the United Kingdom, and we have had some happy times together. Now they have decided that it is time for a change. I know it cannot be easy spending so much time away from their families and friends at home. And so, as I think you may know, they have decided to carry on with their work as drivers in your own country. I confess that Marianne and I have never visited the place you call the UK, but perhaps when we retire – or maybe before – we will pay a visit to your country, to see London and the other places I have heard you talk about: your Lake District, your Yorkshire Dales, and your Scottish Highlands. And your seaside towns, all around the coast of your little island. That is something we do not have in our own Black Forest.

'So, ladies and gentlemen, we thank you for being such pleasant and friendly guests this week and we hope we may see you again, although it will not be with Mike and Bill. So—' he raised his glass of lager – 'good luck, good health, and a happy life to our friends, Mike and Bill.'

'Mike and Bill . . .' they all echoed as they stood and drank the toast to the men who had become more like friends than drivers over the week that they had known them. Then there came the applause and cries of 'Speech, speech . . .'

But Mike and Bill, unusually, could not be persuaded to say very much. It was Mike who answered. 'Thanks, ladies and gents, for your good wishes, and Johann for his kind words. You have been a grand crowd this week, and I hope we may see some of you again on our holidays in the UK. That's all I've got to say except . . . enjoy the rest of your evening.'

There was time then for general chatter amongst the thirty-six members of the coach party who all knew one another well enough now to find something to talk about. They were all present there that evening, the older ones as well as the younger ones, eager to make the most of their last evening in Germany.

Johann and Marianne Grunder proved that they had other talents as well as those involved in being host and hostess to a guest house full of visitors. Johann took to the stage carrying a huge piano accordion which he played competently to accompany Marianne as she sang some traditional German songs in her melodious mezzo-soprano voice. The words were not familiar – nor did any of them know sufficient German to understand the lyrics – but some of the melodies were well known. Soon everyone was humming or lah-lahing, clapping or tapping their feet to the rhythm of the catchy tunes.

After they had finished their recital, to prolonged applause, it was time for the audience to let their hair down, or to sit back and watch and listen, if they preferred. It was obvious that Herr Grunder, over the years, had collected tapes and CDs of music and songs that would appeal to the visitors from the UK. *Songs from the British Isles* included 'Lassie from Lancashire', 'Blaydon Races', 'Maybe it's because I'm a Londoner', 'We'll keep a Welcome', 'Loch Lomond', and 'When Irish Eyes are Smiling.' Everyone joined in all the songs with gusto, although they were all from the north of England or the Midland Counties.

The more energetic amongst them danced along to 'YMCA', the 'Birdie Song' and the 'Hokey Cokey'; then there were tapes dating back to the time of the Twist, when it became the norm to 'do your own thing' and dance with or without a partner. There were tapes or CDs of Dolly Parton, Bob Dylan, the Beatles, the Rolling Stones, Cilla Black, Matt Monro and Andy Williams.

Jane, as usual, sat with Dave. They talked from time to time, they joined in some of the communal dances, they danced together to a waltz or quickstep rhythm. The problems that they had discussed previously were not mentioned, although Jane guessed that they must be present at the back of Dave's mind as they were in hers. She watched with interest the people with whom she had become most friendly over the last week.

Mavis and Arthur, of course, did not take part in the dancing, although she felt sure they would have done so at one time. They sat close together, holding hands from time to time and smiling at one another, clearly so happy that Arthur's illness had been short-lived.

Shirley and Ellen sat with the two brothers, Malcolm and Trevor. A very different Ellen now as she talked and laughed in a way she had not done at the start of the holiday. Not as unreservedly, though, as her friend, Shirley, who was having the time of her life and whose laughter could be heard above the general hubbub of voices. She and Malcolm – possibly two of a kind – seemed to be having a riotous time, whilst Ellen and Trevor sat quietly together. Jane saw him take hold of her hand as he spoke quietly to her. He was still a good-looking man in an unobtrusive sort of way, with greying hair and kindly grey eyes behind rimless spectacles. She looked away, aware that she was being nosy. But she had become fond of Ellen and felt that she deserved some real happiness in her life, just for herself, as she had spent so much time caring for others.

Bill and Christine, the lady he had met this week appeared very happy and relaxed together. Jane guessed that it might be because of Christine that he, as well as Mike, had decided to work in the UK.

But what about herself and Dave? It had all started so unexpectedly, the attraction they had felt for one another, then had gone on so well, until he had dropped the bombshell that had made her think it had all been a hopeless fantasy.

'Penny for them,' said Dave, taking hold of her hand. 'Come along, let's have a dance. It's a waltz, something I can do quite well.' She smiled at him, and they took to the floor to the tune of the once popular song, 'Around the World'.

'For I have found my world in you . . .' she hummed to herself. She had believed it might be so, only to have the wonder and magic of it all snatched away again.

Twenty

By Tuesday morning, two days before she was due to go home Alice had reached a decision. She usually had every confidence in the decisions she made and, in her self-assured way, would ask for advice from nobody. This time, though, she felt that she wanted to talk it over with someone. And who else but the person she had come to know best during the last week, Flora, the woman she was now regarding as a friend. Alice knew that she had made few – if any – new friends lately, and the ones she had had in the past she seldom saw any more.

Breakfast was a meal that Alice had enjoyed very much at Evergreen. There was a choice of menu – not a big fry-up, bacon and sausage being available only at weekends – but there were eggs cooked in various ways, cereals, porridge, toast and fruit, and muesli for those who liked it. Alice had always thought it tasted of sawdust. This morning she had enjoyed tinned grapefruit slices and a poached egg on toast. At home it was usually cornflakes and toast. When Jane was dashing out to work she had little time to prepare anything more, though she sometimes made bacon sandwiches as a treat on a Sunday. Alice was beginning to appreciate more and more all that her daughter had done for her, and, she admitted to herself, for very little thanks.

When breakfast was over they adjourned to the lounge, and Alice drew Flora away to a corner away from the rest of the guests. 'There's something I want to talk over with you,' she said. 'Let's go over there away from the telly and all the chatter.'

They settled themselves on the settee at the far end of the room. Flora smiled at her. 'Fire away,' she said. 'I'm all ears.'

'I'm thinking . . . well, I've already thought,' Alice began, 'and I've decided – well, almost – that I'd like to stay here permanently.'

'Wow!' exclaimed Flora. 'That's a turn-up for the book, isn't it? When I think how set against it you were when you first came here, determined not to like it . . .'

'I know, I know,' said Alice, just a little tetchily. 'You don't need to remind me what I was like, but I've changed my mind. I know I'll have to eat humble pie. I said to Henry the other day that I most definitely would not come and live here.'

Flora laughed. 'I think that Henry, for one, will be very pleased if you decide to stay here. That couldn't be the reason, could it? Henry and you, you're getting on very well, aren't you?' she said with a twinkle in her eye.

'Don't be ridiculous!' scoffed Alice. 'Yes, I get on well enough with him, and I'm determined I'll beat him at chess one of these days. I hope he'll be pleased if I decide to stay.'

'We'll all be pleased,' said Flora. 'Those of us who have got to know you, at any rate. I would really miss you now, Alice. I was feeling quite dejected at the thought of you leaving us on Thursday. We've found that we have quite a lot in common, haven't we?'

'Yes, so we have,' Alice agreed. Apart from our previous life-styles, she thought to herself, but didn't say, and the fact that Flora was loaded whilst she, Alice, would have to consider the financial aspect very carefully because Evergreen was far from cheap. One of the most expensive homes in the area, she guessed, but then you got what you paid for, as with everything in life.

'So, how has all this come about?' asked Flora. 'Why the sudden change of heart. I thought you were looking forward to going home and seeing your daughter again. After she rang you the other day you said she sounded a bit low.'

'So she did,' said Alice. 'And that's one of the things I have to think about carefully. I just wonder how she would feel if I decided to stay here. I really like it here now. I've settled down far better than I ever imagined I would.' She gave a wry smile. 'I've realized what an awkward so-and-so I'd turned into, finding fault with everything and everybody. I was well on the way to becoming a crotchety old woman. It's no wonder people didn't like me, because I didn't try to like them.'

'Oh, come on now,' said Flora. 'Don't be too hard on your-self. 'I think you're a great person, and so do a lot more of us. Yes, you're dogmatic, and you're not afraid of speaking your mind, but that's because you're such a strong character. There's nothing wrong with that. We're all as the good Lord made us.'

'Yes . . . I know,' said Alice. 'But we can all recognize our own faults if we look for them, can't we? And try to change them.' She hesitated for a moment, pondering the issue that was uppermost in her mind.

Flora prompted her. 'You mentioned your daughter. You think she might not be happy about you coming to live here permanently?' She could not help thinking to herself that the young woman might well have been relieved at her mother's decision if Alice was always so difficult and hard to please as she had seemed on first acquaintance.

'I really can't say,' replied Alice. 'I'm sure she must have wished sometimes that I was somewhere else. We did tend to get on one another's nerves living together – just the two of us – for so long. But as I've just said, I know now that I've not been the easiest person to live with.'

'Are any of us?' said Flora, diplomatically. 'We all have to try to get on with the people we live with, but it isn't always easy. It's a question of give and take, isn't it? In marriage and in other relationships as well.'

'Give and take, yes,' repeated Alice thoughtfully. 'Jane has shared her home with me – Jane and Tom at first, of course. And they both assured me it was my home as much as theirs. But I like to think I've pulled my weight, especially since Tom died and Jane was left on her own. I've helped quite a lot financially, and I'm concerned about how she would manage if I wasn't there to help. I know she has a reasonably well-paid job and her widow's pension, but there's still a mortgage on the property, then there are all the bills and the maintenance of the house and the cost of running her car. I don't want to swan off and leave her to manage on her own.'

'People do manage,' said Flora. 'I know it's easy for me to say because money has never been a problem for me, not for many years, at any rate. But, as you say, she has her job and her pension, and – who knows? – she might get married again.'

'She hasn't shown any signs of wanting to so far. She and Tom were so happy together – just right for one another – and I've heard her say that there could never be anyone else. It would be nice for her if she did find someone, but she's a very reserved sort of girl – more so since Tom died – and she keeps herself to herself a lot of the time. She has a few close friends, and she seems content to leave it at that. I was really surprised when she decided to go on that holiday on her own. It must have taken some courage.'

'And she seemed to be enjoying it, didn't she?'

'Yes, everything seemed to be going well. Good weather and good hotels, so she said, and she'd met some nice friendly people. But the other night, like I said, she sounded a bit down. Perhaps because it was coming to an end or . . . well, I just don't know, do I? But I can't very well tell her, as soon as I see her, that I've decided to come and live here . . . can I?'

'You don't need to blurt it out as soon as she arrives, no, of course not. Just play it by ear, as they say. Anyway, have you made enquiries? Do you know if there's a room for you? They keep pretty busy, you know. Sometimes there aren't any vacancies. You might have to wait a little while.'

'That's what I intend to find out today. Then I'll talk it over with Jane. It would be a big step for me, of course. When I went to live with Jane and Tom I had to get rid of a lot of my furniture and bits and pieces. They talk a lot about 'down-sizing' on those house-hunting programmes, don't they? It seems to be one of the 'in' phrases at the moment. Well, I've downsized once, but this time it would be even worse, wouldn't it? There's not a great deal of room here for your own bits and bobs, is there?'

'We manage,' said Flora. 'A few of your own possessions around you, photos and ornaments and books, and it soon comes to feel like home. In fact you're quite at home here already, aren't you?'

Alice nodded. 'And then there's the financial side of it. It costs a pretty penny to live here, doesn't it? I'd have dismissed it out of hand at one time. Good grief! It costs as much as a three-star hotel.'

Flora laughed. 'You can't take it with you, Alice. I don't know how you're fixed with regard to money, but you have your teacher's pension, haven't you? And your widow's and state pensions as well? Those could cover the cost of staying here.'

'They may well do so,' said Alice. 'And I've a bit put by from the sale of my house. I hoped I'd be able to leave it intact for Jane to inherit, but no doubt I'll have to break into it.'

'From what I've heard about your Jane I'm sure she would want what was the best for you.' Flora smiled at her. 'I'm really pleased and honoured that you decided to talk it over with me, Alice, and I hope I've been able to help you. I'd love you to stay, but you must do whatever you and Jane think is best.'

'Yes of course,' said Alice. 'I'll see what Jane is like when she comes to pick me up on Thursday. If I feel she might be quite agreeable to the idea of me staying here, then I'll tell her what I'm considering. But if I think she might not be too happy about it, then I might have to put it on hold for a while. I don't want to upset the lass. Like I was saying, I got the impression that there was something on her mind. I know we've not always got on together as well as we might, but I know her inside-out by now. I should do, she's my only daughter . . .' And one who is very dear to me, she added, silently to herself. 'I'll just have to wait and see. Thank you for listening to me, Flora. You've helped me a lot, but I know it has to be my decision in the end.'

The journey home, across Germany, Belgium and France, all in one day, was quite a marathon for the passengers as well as for the drivers, and there was not the same excited chatter as there had been on the outward journey.

They had set off from the guest house at seven thirty in the morning, following a breakfast during which none of them felt as bright and bushy-tailed as they had on previous mornings. It was early for the staff to be up and about, and the guests had served themselves coffee, left on the table in large flasks, and a more limited choice of breakfast foods.

Johann and Marianne Grunder were both at the coach, however, to wish them goodbye and a safe journey home. They all agreed that they had been a marvellous host and hostess. Mike and Bill were particularly sad at the thought that they would not meet up with them again, although it had been their own decision to finish with the Continental tours.

As the miles – or kilometres – sped by, the passengers dozed, catching up with lost sleep, or tried to read, or just watched the scenery, firstly the hills and woods to which they had become accustomed, then the flatter fields and the nondescript towns of Belgium, viewed in the distance from the motorway as they flashed past the window.

There were stops every few hours, as was obligatory, at service stations, and from time to time, Mike or Bill put on a tape of 'easy listening' music, or one of an Irish comedian – a tape very popular with the coach drivers – whose jokes and witticisms had many of them quietly chuckling. Anything to relieve the inevitable boredom of the long and rather tedious journey.

Mavis was concerned about Arthur. He dozed for much of the time and appeared to be coping very well with everything, considering his recent heart attack. She was watching him continually, though surreptitiously – Arthur hated anyone fussing over him – but she knew she would utter a prayer of thanks when they had finally crossed the Channel and had set foot once again on English soil. It would probably be the last time they would travel abroad, but she hoped they would have several more years together, and there were lots of interesting places to visit nearer to home.

Shirley and Ellen chatted together, although it was Shirley, as usual, doing most of the talking. They had known one another for many years but they were never short of things to say or discuss. Ellen was filled with a quiet happiness that she was keeping very much to herself. She had had a lovely evening with Trevor and, at a time when Shirley and Malcolm were dancing together and the two of them were on their own, they had exchanged addresses and telephone numbers. Trevor had seemed eager that they should arrange to meet when they got back home, and Ellen believed that he was sincere in what he said. She was hugging the secret to herself. She would tell Shirley, of course, in her own good time, but at the moment she did not want her private affairs shouting from the roof tops. The four of them, Shirley and Ellen and the two brothers sat together at the coffee and comfort stops, chatting as a foursome. Trevor seemed to understand how Ellen felt – which boded well for the future – and was careful not to draw attention to their blossoming friendship.

Conversation between Jane and Dave did not flow as easily as it had done on the outward journey when they were getting to know one another and had found lots of things to talk about. Now, of course, although they knew much more about one another, a certain constraint had built up between them. Dave, far more sanguine than Jane, tried to chat unconcernedly, but Jane, although she tried to act as though things were quite normal, was finding it difficult to respond. They did not refer, during the long journey back across the Continent, to the problems that had arisen in their relationship, but Jane knew – and she was sure that Dave knew as well – that something would need to be said before they parted company back in England the following day.

They both read their books, or tried to do so, although Jane found that her mind was wandering. She could not concentrate even on the latest Ruth Rendell offering. She had finished her Maeve Binchy, a nice comfortable read, and maybe she was not in the mood for murder and intrigue, although she kept her eyes glued to the page, making a good pretence at being engrossed in the story.

The motorway cafe in Belgium where they had their lunch stop was very busy and they waited in a long queue to be served with soup and a bread roll, and a slice of apple tart. A situation that might have seemed unique and interesting on the outward journey – the chatter of foreign voices, the pleasant aroma of the various foods being cooked, and the exciting feeling of being abroad – now seemed to have lost its appeal. Jane was only aware of the crowded eating place and of the way they had to hurry with their meal. Because of the length of the journey Mike could allow only forty-five minutes for the lunch break, although it seemed certain that not everyone would be back in time.

As it happened they all managed to return to the coach only a few minutes later than requested. Arthur and Mavis were the last, but nobody minded about that. Arthur had been determined not to 'gobble my dinner and have an attack of indigestion'. Or worse, thought Mavis, who was in total agreement. This journey was proving to be very tedious. How relieved she would be when they arrived at the hotel in Calais and she was able to get her feet up and rest her swollen ankles, a hazard of coach travel that she had found to be worse than ever during this holiday.

It was six o'clock in the evening when they arrived at the Calais hotel, where they had stayed on the outward journey. It was, therefore, familiar to them, and knowing their way around did help somewhat when they were feeling tired and maybe a little irritable. However, a wash and brush up and, in many cases, a drink at the bar did revive everyone's spirits and put them in a better frame of mind for the evening meal.

This time the tables were set for eight. Jane remembered that on the first visit she and Dave had sat with and become friendly with Mavis and Arthur. The four of them sat together now, with two other couples whom they had met up with now and again during the holiday. They all knew one another now, to a certain extent, and conversation was largely about the sights they had seen, what they had enjoyed the most and, inevitably, polite enquiries about Arthur's present state of health. How had he coped with the wearisome journey? He answered their questions with as much patience as he could muster, telling them he was as fit as a fiddle, but he would be glad to sleep in his own bed again, a feeling that they all endorsed.

The meal was pretty much the mixture as before – onion soup, roast chicken and *pommes frites*, followed by fruit and ice cream. Everyone was hungry after a makeshift lunch and there was very little left on any of the plates.

Coffee was served afterwards in the lounge, but by that time it was turned ten o'clock. Mavis and Arthur declined the coffee saying that they would go straight to bed. Jane and Dave sat with a couple they had dined with, for the sake of politeness more than anything. Then they, too, decided it was time to call it a day.

The two of them took the lift to the third floor. As before, their rooms were adjacent. They paused at the doors ready to enter the rooms with their giant keys. Dave leaned towards Jane, taking hold of her shoulders in a gentle grasp.

'Don't worry, my dear,' he said. 'It will all sort out, I feel sure it will.' He kissed her gently on the lips. 'Goodnight now, and God bless. See you in the morning.'

'Yes . . . see you, Dave,' she replied, smiling bravely at him. Tears were threatening as she entered the room and closed the door behind her. She blinked them away, determined not to give in to the negative thoughts that were invading her mind. Could there be a glimmer of light at the end of the tunnel? Dave seemed to think so.

'Don't worry,' he had just said. 'It will all sort out . . .'

Did he really believe that, or was he just trying to cheer her up? Maybe she had been living in a fool's paradise ever since she met him just over a week ago. He did not know her mother like she did; in fact, he did not know Alice at all. If he did then he might have a better idea of what she was up against. She and her mother lived together. Jane had offered to share her home with her, willingly – well, as willingly as she was able, she confessed to herself – and that was that. How could she, now, cast her aside, 'like an old worn-out coat.' She could almost hear her mother saying the words, or something similar.

And that was not the only problem, even if the living arrangements for Alice could be sorted out. Her mother would go ballistic at the idea of Jane consorting with a man who was still married, even if it was only in name.

Stop it! Stop it! Jane scolded herself. Going over and over the problem only made it worse. Resolutely she undressed and washed and got into bed, setting her little clock for six o'clock. Their cases had to be outside their rooms by seven, and after an early breakfast they would depart at eight for the short journey to the docks.

Fortunately her tortuous thoughts stilled when her head touched the pillow. It had been a tiring day. Sitting still for hours on end on a coach could be just as wearying as a ten-mile hike. Despite her worries she slept until the alarm clock woke her the following morning.

Twenty-One

The sky was grey and overcast and there was a chilly wind blowing when they boarded the coach on the Wednesday morning, following a somewhat hurried breakfast. A very different outlook from the sunshine that had greeted them on their arrival in France and had blessed them for almost the whole of the holiday.

The cross-channel ferry was not so crowded as it had been on the outward journey. They were all used to the procedure by now; they knew the whereabouts of the cafes, bars, shops and toilets, and it no longer seemed quite so strange. Once again the coach was parked near to a staircase, so should be easy to locate when the journey of ninety minutes or so was completed.

Jane and Dave were still together. There seemed to be no way they could separate without appearing impolite or difficult. After all, they had not fallen out, but just come face to face with a load of problems.

Jane, however, did go off to the shops on her own when they had enjoyed a cup of strong coffee and a scone. The breakfast had been rather a hit and miss affair with no one feeling particularly hungry.

'Yes, off you go and treat yourself,' said Dave. He grinned at her. 'You don't want me hanging around.' Shopping, especially in gift shops and the like was something that men only did under protest. She recalled that Tom, an ideal husband in many ways, had preferred to leave Jane to shop on her own, and no doubt Dave was of the same inclination.

Jane felt her spirits rise when she entered the shop. There was a fragrant aroma of perfume, and the shelves were full of all manner of tempting goods, many of them less expensive than in the high street shops . . . but still by no means cheap! Radley handbags and purses, silk scarves, watches and exquisite costume jewellery. Jane looked but did not linger. To indulge in a new scarf or earrings, for instance, would be an extravagance.

But she did ponder at length over the various perfumes: Chanel, Dior, Estée Lauder, Givenchy, Lance, Rochas. There were tester bottles available, and she sprayed each wrist and the back of her hands trying to decide which one she preferred. In the end she was quite bewildered as all the scents merged into one.

An attractive girl with an oriental look came to assist her. 'May I help you, madam?' she asked politely.

'Yes, please,' said Jane. 'Something light and flowery, not too musky . . .'

After sampling one or two more she finally decided on 'Dolce Vita' by Dior. Expensive! But cheaper than in it would be in Debenhams, and what did it matter? She had several euros left and it would save the trouble of changing it back into sterling currency.

The adjoining shop sold cigarettes, wines and spirits, none of which was of interest to Jane, but there was a tempting display of confectionery and chocolates. She bought two boxes of marzipan chocolates, one flavoured with strawberry and the other with apricot brandy, for herself and her mother; then a huge bar of Toblerone, which she had loved ever since she was a little girl. Her purchases had taken care of most of her remaining euros. She felt much more light-hearted now. It was amazing what a spot of retail therapy could do, although it was something in which she rarely indulged.

'I thought you'd got lost overboard!' said Dave when she reappeared in the lounge. 'All spent up?'

'Almost,' she said with a smile.

He stood up. 'Just time to pay a visit,' he remarked, 'then it'll be almost time for us to find our way back.'

All the passengers arrived back at the coach with time to spare.

'We were nearly the first,' boasted Mavis. 'Weren't we, Arthur? We didn't keep you waiting this time.'

'Aye, so we were,' said Arthur. 'I was damn glad to get off that boat, rocking and rolling like a switchback.' He looked rather tired and pale, and Jane was sure it would be a great relief to him, and to Mavis as well, when they were safely back home. The sail had, indeed, been slightly choppy, but not unduly so. Ships were far more stable now than they had been

years ago. She remembered her first trip abroad on a school
visit to France. No one had actually been sick, although they
had felt decidedly queasy.

Anyway, here they were, back on English soil, and as the
coach pulled away from the dock area it was raining. Not
pouring down, but a steady drizzle from a grey sky that showed
no sign of a break in the cloud; a day that was typical of many
in an English summer.

'Put your watches back an hour, ladies and gents,' Mike told
them. So it was only ten minutes past nine, although they all
felt that they had been up and about for ages.

The coach sped along the motorways, heading northwards.
Not the most interesting of journeys, but the quickest route
back to the north of England. There was friendly chatter and
laughter along the way as new friends called to one another,
exchanging addresses and promising to keep in touch.

Jane saw that Mavis and Arthur in the seat across the aisle
were holding hands for much of the time. A real Darby and Joan
couple, she reflected. Whatever might happen between herself
and Dave she must not lose touch with these two elderly friends.
Their home town of Blackburn was not very far from Preston.
It would be easy to pay them a visit, and her mother might enjoy
meeting them, too, if she could be persuaded to go.

They stopped mid-morning at one of the huge impersonal
motorway services. Jane left Dave chatting to another couple
and sought out Mavis and Arthur.

'Here's my address and telephone number,' she said to Mavis,
handing her a postcard with a picture of the market square in
Freiburg, 'and could you give me yours, please? You can write
it here at the back of my diary.'

'Of course, my dear,' said Mavis, getting out her biro. 'We
would love to see you again sometime – and quite soon, I
hope – wouldn't we, Arthur?'

'I'll say we would,' he agreed, beaming at Jane, and she could
tell that he meant it. 'It's been lovely meeting you this week,
and your nice gentleman friend as well!'

'How is it going, my dear?' asked Mavis in a confidential
tone. 'Forgive me if I'm being nosy, but I know the two of
you have become . . . quite friendly.'

Jane had not told anyone of the problems that had arisen, only hinted to Ellen that they had encountered one or two snags. Her face dropped a little as she replied.

'We're not too sure. There's my mother to consider, and Dave's farm. It's not all that easy.'

Mavis patted her hand. 'Life is seldom easy,' she said, 'but he's worth fighting for, believe me. One only has to see the pair of you together . . .'

Jane nodded and tried to smile, but she felt incipient tears pricking at her eyes as she remembered that very soon she and Dave would be parting company. And he was still putting on a front of cheerfulness and normality. Or was it just a show of bravado?

'Must go now,' she said. 'It's nearly time to go back to the coach, and I need to visit the ladies' room.'

The lunch stop was at a similar venue further north. All these stopping places were much of a muchness, and at midday were usually crowded with long queues for sandwiches, soup, salads, hot meals, Costa coffee, soft drinks, or 'do it yourself' tea and coffee. Then there was the ubiquitous WH Smith shop where you could while away the remaining minutes before it was time to continue with the journey.

No one had a packed lunch this time, and so were obliged to pay the exorbitant prices charged to a captive audience. Jane opted for a triangular pack of cheese and chutney sandwiches whilst Dave queued for fish and chips. She was not very hungry, and she had learnt from experience that your meal was apt to go cold while you were waiting in a queue to pay for it. Dave, however, seemed quite phlegmatic about the experience, tucking into his battered fish and greasy-looking chips with enjoyment.

Jane left him finishing his meal and went to speak to Ellen and Shirley who were sitting at a nearby table with Trevor and Malcolm. She gave her address, written on souvenir postcards, to the two ladies, as she had done with Mavis, and they, in turn, wrote their addresses in her diary. Ellen was the one with whom she most wanted to keep in touch, and she felt sure that Ellen was of the same mind. She included Shirley for the sake of politeness, knowing that they were not likely to do more than send a token Christmas card, possibly for only the first year.

'It's been a grand holiday, hasn't it?' remarked Trevor. 'Good weather, lovely scenery, good hotels . . . nice company. What more could you want?'

'What indeed?' replied Jane. 'Yes, it has come up to all expectations.' She left them with a surreptitious wink and smile at Ellen, who smiled back coyly.

They boarded the coach once again. For some of the party it would be the last time. The next stop would be in the Midlands at the Galaxy depot where roughly half of the passengers would be leaving the tour. This was where Dave would leave, and Jane knew that something would need to be said before the two of them said goodbye. After they had sat in silence for about half an hour Dave turned to her, lightly taking hold of her hand.

'Don't be despondent, Jane,' he began. 'I've a feeling that things will work out just fine for us. It may take time, but I'm sure we'll be able to sort something out. That is . . . if you still feel the same way about us, about you and me?'

Jane nodded numbly. 'Yes, I do . . . I'm trying to, but I can't see any way ahead at the moment. Mother . . . I can't just abandon her – anyway, she's so set in her ways. She would never approve.'

'Surely she would if she met me,' said Dave, squeezing her hand and giving a quiet chuckle. 'Who could resist my dynamic personality, to say nothing of my handsome looks! I'll have her eating out of my hand, you'll see . . .'

Jane knew he was trying to make light of the situation, even though he might well be as unsure of the outcome as she was. 'Of course,' she said. 'Who could resist you! No, seriously, Dave—'

'Say no more,' he interrupted her. 'There's no point in going over and over it. We'll wait and see what happens. Here are my telephone numbers, my landline and my mobile numbers. We can't lose touch with one another, Jane, when we've had such a lovely time together.' He was speaking gently and earnestly now. 'I've told you how I feel about you, and I'm sure that you feel the same. You know there was an almost instant attraction between us, don't you?'

She nodded again. 'Yes, I believed so . . . but we were

thrown together, weren't we? Sitting next to one another. A holiday friendship; we're both away from home with our problems left behind us for a little while. But we have to return to the real world, and the problems are still there. They won't disappear overnight. I let myself believe, for a short time, that it might be possible for us to continue our friendship. But I know I was kidding myself.'

What was it her mother had said the last time she phoned her? She'd be glad to get home; there was nothing like your own bed and home comforts. She had admitted that Evergreen had not been too bad, but that didn't mean that Jane could go gadding off any time she felt like it. Those were her exact words, 'gadding off'. So how would she feel about her daughter gadding off to meet a man in Shropshire, a man who still had a wife? And it was during the previous telephone conversation that she had been going on about some man or other at the home whose son was carrying on with a woman to whom he was not married. 'Living in sin', Alice had said.

Jane was silent for a few moments as these thoughts ran through her mind.

'Come along, love, never say die,' said Dave, a trifle impatiently. 'We can't give up before we've even tried.' He pressed the paper with the telephone numbers into her hand and she pushed it into the pocket of her trousers. 'I shall be waiting to hear from you. I refuse to believe that we won't see one another again. Now, give me your phone number, please. Just your mobile number if you don't want your mother intercepting calls from a strange man.'

But Jane shook her head. 'No, let's just leave it as it is, Dave. It will only upset me if you keep ringing up and I have to tell you that it's no use. Mother isn't going to disappear. God forbid! I don't want anything to happen to her.'

'No, of course you don't. But who knows what might have happened while you've been away? Your mother might have a gentleman admirer at this place where she's been staying. I've heard of it happening. There was an elderly couple where my mother lives, both well into their eighties, and they became friendly and got married!'

Jane gave a wry laugh. 'Now you're talking nonsense! You

haven't met my mother. No, I'm trying to be sensible, Dave. I promise I will ring you if I can see any light at the end of the tunnel, any hope of us meeting again. That's all I can say. Let's just leave it at that, eh?'

'Very well, if you say so . . .' Dave sighed. He could see there was no point in saying any more. Jane was feeling despondent. Maybe she was given to highs and lows of mood? He didn't know her well enough to have found out everything about her. But it wouldn't matter to him if she was. He had seen a glimpse of a happy, fun-loving Jane, and he felt, against all odds, that he would be with her again, sooner rather than later, he hoped.

The coach sped on along the M6, eating up the miles until, just north of Birmingham, they reached the Galaxy depot in the Midlands. A good number of people would be leaving there, including Bill, the driver. His home was further north, in the Manchester area, but he was based in the Midlands and would be dealing with the directing of passengers to the various minibuses that were waiting to take them home.

Many of the people who were leaving expressed their thanks to the drivers, in the usual way, as they left the coach. Others, including Jane, had thanked them the previous night. Monetary tips were much appreciated to supplement a reasonable, but not over-generous, wage.

Bill gave a cheery wave to the remainder of the group as he departed. 'So long, folks. You've been a grand crowd and I've enjoyed your company. Hope I'll see some of you again if you decide to holiday at home for a change.'

He said a quiet unobtrusive goodbye to Christine on the front seat. Her home, too, was in Manchester, so she was remaining on the coach. No doubt they had already said their goodbyes in private. Jane hoped that things worked out well for them.

It was time now for her to say goodbye to Dave. He took hold of her hand and kissed her gently on the cheek, '*au revoir*, Jane, my dear,' he said quietly. 'It's not goodbye.'

She smiled bravely. 'Yes . . . *Au revoir*, Dave,' she repeated. 'I hope so, anyway.' She knew that '*au revoir*' meant 'until we meet again'.

She watched him alight from the coach and then wait whilst

Mike and Bill sorted out the suitcases. Then he lifted his hand to wave at her, though not all that cheerily, as he walked towards the waiting minibus.

Jane leaned back on her seat and closed her eyes as the coach set off again. She was determined not to give way to tears. She knew that she must put on a brave face when she said goodbye to her other friends who, like herself, were travelling northwards to the depot near Preston. She took the paper that Dave had given her out of her pocket. She glanced at it briefly, then, scarcely aware of what she was doing, she tore it in half, then into quarters, screwed them up, then shoved them into her shoulder bag.

They had an obligatory 'comfort' stop an hour or so later, but there was little time to chat to anyone, and no one really felt like drinking yet another cup of tea or coffee. She had managed to compose herself by mid-afternoon when they arrived back at Preston.

Mike, at the wheel, said his goodbyes on behalf of himself and Galaxy Travel. 'You have been a wonderful crowd,' he told them. Jane wondered if he said the same thing every time. But to give him the benefit of the doubt, she was sure he meant it. 'Thanks to you all for your enjoyable company, and I hope I shall see some of you again. So it's goodbye for now, and God bless.'

The remainder of the passengers, those who lived near and others from a little further afield, alighted at the Preston depot. Jane's home was not far away, and there would be two couples travelling with her in the same minibus. Mavis and Arthur, bound for Blackburn, would be in the bus for mid-Lancashire. There was a third one which would take Shirley and Ellen, Trevor and Malcolm, and the two sisters, Christine and Norah, to the Manchester area. The added bonus with Galaxy Travel was that you were transported, as they advertised, 'from door to door'.

They all milled around as Mike unloaded the cases. Jane said a fond goodbye to Mavis and Arthur, and to Shirley and Ellen. They were all a little emotional, as they had bonded so well over the past ten days, and it felt as though they were bidding farewell to old friends, not ones whom they had, in reality, known for only a short time.

Mavis hugged Jane, holding her close for a moment. 'Thank you for being a good friend to Arthur and me,' she said. 'You've been such a comfort to me, Jane . . . and I hope that all goes well for you and Dave.'

Jane had not told her about the complications that had arisen, but Mavis had obviously become aware that there were problems. 'Don't worry about me,' said Jane, bravely. 'You take care of Arthur, and of yourself; I'll pop over to Blackburn to see you before long, I promise.'

After a speedy goodbye to Shirley and Ellen – the cases were loaded and the drivers were anxious to be on their way – Jane stepped aboard. She had the seat next to the driver, so she could not converse with the others who were sitting at the back.

Her home was the nearest one to the depot, so it was not long before she was getting off again. She waved to the couples in the back as she accompanied the driver, who was carrying her case, up the garden path to her door.

'Cheerio, love. Take care now,' he said, as she put her key in the lock and opened the door.

The house felt strange and empty; everything looked a little unfamiliar as though she had partly forgotten her surroundings. To be alone again, after the constant hubbub and excitement of the last ten days – apart from the night times, of course – was a shock to the system.

A cup of tea first. That was always the priority. Then she would make herself a meal. She had bought a loaf at the last service station, so beans on toast would suffice. It felt odd without her mother there to greet her. How often in the past, she had longed for a bit of peace and quiet, but to have someone to talk to now would take her mind off her problems. She realized she was looking forward to seeing her mother the following day, and maybe, she thought, surprisingly, to having her home again.

Twenty-Two

Jane thought when she arrived at Evergreen the following morning that her mother would be waiting with her bags packed, ready and raring to go. But that was not the case. Jane was shown into the lounge by Mrs Meadows, the supervisor, to find her mother sitting comfortably in an easy chair, with another woman, rather younger than herself, in the opposite seat.

'Here's your daughter, Alice,' said Mrs Meadows. 'I'll go and make some coffee for you, and then you can have a chat.'

Jane was nonplussed. She stooped to kiss her mother's cheek and to give her a quick hug. 'Hello, Mother,' she said. 'You're looking well. I thought you'd be ready to go, but—'

'Oh, there's no hurry,' Alice broke in. 'Sit yourself down and relax for a few minutes. You've had a good holiday, have you? You've caught the sun, but you're looking a bit tired and strained. Is everything alright?'

'Yes, I'm fine, Mother,' she replied. 'It's been a busy ten days, though . . .' She looked enquiringly at the other woman, and smiled at her. 'Aren't you going to introduce me to your friend, Mother?'

'Give me a chance,' snapped Alice. 'Yes, this is Flora. I wanted you to meet her. She helped me to settle down when I was left here, feeling like a fish out of water.' She was never able to resist a sly dig.

Flora, however, winked at Jane as she shook hands with her. 'Hello, Jane,' she said. 'I've heard a lot about you and I'm very pleased to meet you. Take no notice of what your mother says. She's had a whale of a time here, haven't you, Alice?'

'I'm pleased to meet you as well,' said Jane. 'Thank you for looking after Mother. I had guessed that things weren't as bad as she was making out.'

'Well, I must admit it's been alright, all things considered,' replied Alice. 'I reckon it must be one of the best of these old folks' homes.'

'Now, come on, Alice,' said her new friend. 'You've said yourself that it's not like an old folks' home, it's more like a three-star hotel.'

'Did I say that? Oh well, maybe I did.' Alice actually gave a chuckle, and Jane looked at her in amazement.

'Well, I'm glad you've enjoyed yourself, Mother,' she said. 'I told you it would be OK when you got used to it.'

She glanced round the room. They were in a quiet corner, but there were several other men and women sitting near to the large television set, one or two others reading, and another lady happily knitting in a quiet corner.

Mrs Meadows arrived with the coffee in a silver pot, with china cups and saucers on the tray. We're being treated like royalty, thought Jane, still mystified as to why her mother was not anxious to be on her way home. Flora set out the cups and saucers – four of them – on a small table.

'I'll go and ask Henry to join us,' said Alice. She stood up, and with the aid of her stick, hobbled across to the television area. She returned with an elderly man, tall and upright and, to Jane's eyes, still quite handsome.

'This is Henry,' said Alice, a trifle abruptly. 'He's another friend who's helped to make it not so bad for me. This is my daughter, Jane.'

His handshake was firm, and there was a twinkle in his eye. 'Hello, Jane,' he said. 'Good to meet you. Your mother is quite a character, isn't she? Not so bad, though, when you get to know her and take her remarks with a pinch of salt. And I must say she plays a fair game of chess. She might even manage to beat me, one of these days.'

'Oh, that's good,' said Jane, surprised at the revelation. 'Yes, she used to play chess with my dad, but I never managed to learn . . . You didn't tell me, Mother.'

'There hasn't been any chance, has there?' said Alice rather sharply. 'We had to do something to pass the time. You can't sit watching telly all the while, like zombies.'

They drank their coffee and chatted for a while. It was mainly Flora and Henry who enquired about Jane's holiday, appearing genuinely interested. It seemed that Flora had been something of a globetrotter in the past. She must be the one who, according to Alice, had more money than she knew what to do with, thought Jane. Flora remarked that the memories were still very precious. Henry, too, had enjoyed several holidays abroad. Mother hadn't mentioned him during her phone calls, at least not to say that he was a friend. He might, however, be the one whose son was 'living in sin'.

After a little while Henry and Flora left the mother and daughter on their own. 'We'll leave you to have a little talk together,' said Flora. 'Nice meeting you, Jane.'

Jane wondered when her mother would decide it was time to go home. She did not seem at all anxious to make a move.

'You've made some nice friends here, Mother,' she said. 'You'll be sorry to say goodbye to them. But I could bring you back to see them, sometime, if you feel like it. And fancy you taking up chess again! Now that would be a good interest for you if you started playing again. I remember how good you were. You managed to beat Dad sometimes, didn't you?'

'Yes, so I did, but I've got a bit rusty with not playing for so long. I've told Henry that I'll pop back – sometime – and we'll have another game. And Flora . . . she's a nice sort of woman. Had an easy life, though, since she married her second husband; never done a day's work for goodness knows how long . . .'

'She's the one with more money than she knows what to do with, I take it?'

'Yes, she is. But I must admit that she doesn't boast about it, and she's certainly not a snob. She was brought up quite ordinary, like the rest of us, until she married into money.'

'And what about Henry? He seems a very pleasant sort of man. He's certainly no fool. You couldn't pull the wool over his eyes.' And he's got you weighed up, Mother, she thought, but didn't say. She could imagine sparks flying between the two of them.

'Yes, Henry's OK,' said Alice, briefly. 'A bit argumentative, like, and always thinks he's right. But he's not so bad.'

'Is he the one whose son has been married twice, and has a lady friend. You told me about him when I phoned you.'

'Yes . . . yes he is. Actually, I met his son – Barry, he's called – on Sunday afternoon, and his . . . friend. And I must admit she seems a nice sort of woman; homely and friendly and they're obviously very happy together. I'd imagined some tarty, flashy sort of lass, but she's not like that at all.'

Jane smiled to herself. 'You shouldn't jump to conclusions, Mother. Things aren't always just as they seem.'

'No, perhaps not. But I've always had my standards, Jane, you know that. I still think there's too much chopping and changing of partners, these days. In my day marriage was for life, till death do us part. That was what we promised.'

'Circumstances alter cases, sometimes,' said Jane, cautiously. Could it be that there might be a slight glimmer of light at the end of the tunnel? Mother seemed to be a shade more tolerant after her stay here. 'Anyway, we'll get off now, shall we, if you're ready? You've got your case packed, have you?'

'Yes . . . I have. But there's something I want to talk about before we go. And Mrs Meadows said she'd come and have a chat with you. You see, Jane, I've been doing a lot of serious thinking this last week. And – you may not believe this – but I've realized that I might be quite happy if I came to stay here, permanently, I mean.'

Jane could scarcely believe what she was hearing. Her mouth dropped open in shock and bewilderment as she stared at her mother. 'But . . . after all you've said. It's hard to believe . . .'

'Yes, I know what I've said,' retorted Alice sharply. 'And I still haven't changed my mind about old folks' homes, or about sons and daughters who want to get rid of their parents. But this place is different, or else I wouldn't consider it.'

Jane still continued to stare at her mother, too stunned to smile or to begin to think that this could be an answer to her prayers – because she had dared to ask for a little help from above.

'I know there's a lot to consider,' Alice went on, 'and if you don't want me to, then of course I won't do it. I can see you're not too happy about it, and I can understand that. You might not want to live on your own, and I know that the upkeep of a house is getting more expensive every year. But I won't live for ever, and I've got quite a bit put by . . .'

'Stop, Mother, stop!' cried Jane. 'I wouldn't mind at all, of course I wouldn't. I think it's a splendid idea, but—' She suddenly burst into tears, whether of happiness or sadness she didn't know. They were more like tears of frustration; the pent up anxiety that she had felt for the past few days had to have a release.

'Jane, whatever's the matter? I didn't mean to upset you.' Her mother leaned forward and took hold of her hand in a very uncharacteristic gesture. 'Come on now, love. Don't take on so, we'll be able to sort something out.'

Jane blinked back her tears and tried to compose herself. 'You've not upset me. It's just that . . . you see . . . while I was on holiday I met a man. A lovely man called Dave, and we got friendly. I know we've only known one another a short while, but we would like to carry on seeing one another, but I told him it was no use.'

'Now, why ever did you do that?' Her mother was showing an understanding that Jane had hardly ever seen before. 'I like you to have friends, even men friends, but you've never seemed bothered since Tom . . .'

'I know, Mother. I've never been interested. But Dave is . . . different. We got on so well, but there were problems.'

'What sort of problems? Where does he live? Has he been widowed, like you?'

'He lives in Shropshire. He has a small farm that he runs with his son.'

'A farmer, eh? Well, well!'

'And . . . he has been married, of course. I thought he was a widower, then he told me that his wife is still living, but she won't grant him a divorce. She's a Catholic and she thinks it's wrong; but in spite of this she's living with another man. Living in sin, as you might say, Mother.'

'Now, Jane, don't throw my words back in my face. What did you say before? Circumstances alter cases. Well, perhaps they do. I won't stand in your way if you want to go on seeing this man. You know where he lives, don't you? And he knows where you are?'

Jane shook her head. 'I've been a stupid fool,' she said. 'I wouldn't give him my address or phone number. He gave me his, and I said I would ring if I could see any way round the problem.'

'Well then, you can do so now, can't you? Not this minute,

but when we get home. Yes, I am coming home for the time being. The room I had will be in use for the next fortnight – a short-term resident like I've been – but then I can move in permanently. Mrs Meadows will come and talk to you before we go.'

Jane sighed. 'I've done something very very stupid, and I don't know why I did it. I tore up his phone numbers – I was feeling so miserable and confused – and they're all in pieces at the bottom of my bag.'

Alice shook her head. 'Honestly, Jane! Sometimes I despair of you. But there must be a way round it. You know the name of the farm, don't you? And you know where it is? Directory enquiries will help you. Come on now, what's it called?'

Jane wracked her brains. 'It's near Welshpool. He's called David Falconer. Hillside . . .? Woodside . . .? No, I think it's Cragside . . . Yes, I'm sure it is; Cragside Farm, near Welshpool.

'There you are, you see,' said Alice. 'Problem solved. Jane could tell that she wanted it solving for her own sake as well, but it was great, all the same, that she seemed so pleased about the situation.

'And here's Mrs Meadows. She'll tell you anything you want to know, although I think you found out quite a lot when you came to look round, didn't you?'

'Yes, I knew it was a place with a very high standard,' said Jane, 'and now you know that for yourself, don't you, Mother?'

'Alright; don't rub it in!' retorted Alice, in a quiet voice, as Mrs Meadows sat down beside them.

She was a woman in her fifties, the owner of the home and in overall charge. She and her husband lived in a bungalow nearby, and the residents saw little of him. He worked as a joiner in his own business and was very handy for doing odd jobs from time to time. Jane could tell that she was friendly and had a pleasant way of dealing with the residents, never patronizing them or talking down to them, but she would stand no nonsense.

Jane told her how her mother had said that she would like to come and live there permanently and that she, Jane, was very happy, though surprised at her decision.

'Yes, I think she was a little unsure about us at first, weren't you, Alice?' Mrs Meadows smiled at her knowingly.

'Yes . . . happen I was,' agreed Alice, 'but it didn't take me long to change my mind.'

They talked about the necessary details; the weekly terms, the methods of paying, etc. It was agreed that Alice should return for good in two weeks' time. Jane was amazed at the way her mother waved a cheerful goodbye to the folk in the lounge.

'Cheerio for now, but I'll be back before long. Take care now, and behave yourselves!'

Most of them smiled and waved, apart from one or two who were too engrossed in the chat show on the television.

'Come on now, ring this fellow of yours,' said Alice when they arrived home. 'Are you sure you can't read the telephone number?'

But Jane could not decipher the writing on the screwed up bit of paper. It was surprising how quickly the woman at directory enquiries came up with the number she required.

'Go on, what are you waiting for?' said her mother. 'I'll go upstairs and sort out my things.'

Thankfully she left Jane on her own. Her hands trembled a little as she picked up the receiver and dialled the number.

'It was a woman's voice that answered. 'Hello, Cragside Farm. How can I help you?'

'Could I speak to Mr Falconer, please?' asked Jane.

'Yes, of course. Do you want Mr David Falconer, or his son? They're both outside, but they're not far away.'

'Oh, David, please . . .'

'And who shall I say is calling?'

'Just tell him that it's . . . Jane.'

'Oh . . . oh yes, right away.'

Jane waited, her heart beating rapidly and her stomach churning with butterflies. Then she heard a familiar voice. 'Jane . . . Is it really you?'

'Yes . . . yes, it's me, Dave.'

'And . . .?' That was all he said, but it was a loaded question.

'And . . . it's going to be alright, Dave. I can't believe it, and neither will you. My mother's decided she wants to go and live in the home, for good! So we'll be able to meet. Isn't that wonderful?'

'It's incredible! I could hardly believe it when Kathryn said it was Jane on the phone. That was my daughter-in-law . . . to be. You'll be able to meet her soon, and Peter. I've told them about you, and they know I've been waiting and hoping . . . How soon can you come? Tomorrow?'

Jane laughed. 'No . . . I'm afraid not. We'll have to wait a couple of weeks until Mother goes back to the home.'

'Oh dear! So long?'

'Yes, I know you said, once, that I could bring Mother to meet you – and I know she'll be looking forward to that – but it will be better if I come on my own at first, don't you think so?'

'Whatever you say. I'm just so delighted, Jane, my dear. It didn't take you long to change your mind!'

'I never had any doubts about you and me. It was Mother who needed to change her mind, about all sorts of things. And I really believe she has.'

'That's wonderful . . . I shall be counting the days, the hours. It's almost too good to be true . . .'

'It's true, Dave. It really is. I must go now, but I'll see you soon.'

'Yes, not soon enough for me . . . but I understand. Goodbye for now, or as I said before, *au revoir*. And . . . I love you, Jane . . .'

'Yes, *au revoir*, Dave,' she replied. And then, a trifle shyly, 'I love you too . . .'

CPSIA information can be obtained at www.ICGtesting.com
Printed in the USA
BVOW02*0324130815

412278BV00002B/2/P